Cowboy Ranch

Clean & Wholesome Cowboy Romance

Jenna Hendricks

Contents

Books by Jenna Hendricks (Clean & Wholesome Romance)

<u>Triple J Ranch</u> –

Book 0 - Finding Love in Montana (Join my newsletter to get this book for free)

Book 1 - Second Chance Ranch

Book 2 – Cowboy Ranch

Book 3 – Runaway Cowgirl Bride

Book 4 – Faith of a Cowboy

Book 5 – Cowboy Blessings

Book 6 – The Cowboy's Game

<u>Big Sky Christmas</u> –

Book 1 – Her Montana Christmas Cowboy

Book 2 – Her Christmas Rodeo Cowboy

Book 3 – Her Mistletoe Cowboy
Book 4 – Her Sleigh Ride Christmas Cowboy
<u>Crooked Arrow Ranch</u> –
Book 0 - Wounded Hearts Ranch (join my newsletter to get this free)
Book 1 – A Broken Heart Mended
Book 2 – Hope's Healing Love
Book 3 - Love's Healing Balm
Book 4 – A Crooked Arrow Christmas
<u>Standalone Novels</u> –
Christmas Crazy in July

Rebel Hearts Anthology
See these titles and more: https://JennaHendricks.com

Other Books by J.L. Hendricks (my 1st pen name)

<u>Worlds Away Series</u>

Book 0: Worlds Revealed (join my Newsletter to get this exclusive freebie)

Book 1: Worlds Away

Book 2: Worlds Collide

Book 2.5: Worlds Explode

Book 3: Worlds Entwined

<u>A Miss Claus Shifter Christmas Romance Series</u>

Book 0: Santa Meets Mrs. Claus

Book 1: Miss Claus and the Secret Santa

Book 2: Miss Claus under the Mistletoe

Book 3: Miss Claus and the Christmas Wedding

Book 4: Miss Claus and Her Polar Opposite

The FBI Dragon Chronicles

Book 1: A Ritual of Fire

Book 2: A Ritual of Death

Book 3: A Ritual of Conquest

New Orleans Magic Series

Book 1: New Orleans Magic

Book 2: Hurricane of Magic

Book 3: Council of Magic

Island of Misfits

Book 0: Island of Misfits

Book 1: The Vampire Gets His Mate

Chronicles of the Fae Princess –

Trilogy Published by LMBPN Publishing

See these titles and get their links at https://www .jlhendricksauthor.com/

B y signing up for my newsletter, you will get a free copy of the prequel to the Triple J Ranch series, Finding Love in Montana. As well as another free book from J.L. Hendricks.

If you want to make sure you hear about the latest and greatest, sign up for my newsletter at: - . I will only send out a few e-mails a month. I'll do cover reveals, snippets of new books, and giveaways or promos in the newsletter, some of which will only be available to newsletter subscribers.

Chapter 1

"No, no, this can't be happening. Not now." Callie Houston hit the top of her steering wheel with the palm of her hand as her 2012 Hyundai Santa Fe sputtered and slowed to a stop along the side of a dusty, desolate road.

Once she stopped, she tried turning the key, but it did nothing. Without much else to try, she turned the key again. Callie had zero car knowledge except to take it in for service every five to six thousand miles. And oh, it was best to change the windshield wipers every fall before the big rains began.

She sat there on the side of the road feeling as though she had the worst luck in the entire world.

Callie was on her way to a tiny town called Beacon Creek. It was supposed to be her treat for the rotten month she'd just had. All Callie wanted was to forget about her troubles and have some real down-home country fun.

The rodeo and summer carnival was something she'd read about, and could swear she'd seen on a Hallmark movie recently. It was exactly what she needed to put her worries behind her as she headed home.

Instead, she now had to deal with a car not working. She didn't even know how far out of town she was. Would her cell phone even get any service there?

Once she was safely on the side of the road, she looked to her left and right. All she could see were barbed wire fences and brown grasses being nibbled on by cows. In the north, south, and west were the jagged peaks of mountains. The east was mostly plains, from what she remembered on her drive to Seattle.

This little stop wasn't originally planned, but after her failure in Seattle, she wasn't ready to go home to her empty apartment. She thought stopping off for a rodeo would recharge her and help her figure out what she would do next. Her savings account wouldn't last forever, and she needed a job, fast.

She stepped out of her car after looking in front and behind to ensure no cars or trucks were coming and walked to the side of the road before she pulled her cell phone out of her pocket. Callie could have leapt for joy when she discovered she had signal. It was faint, but if it connected her to the roadside assistance service she subscribed to, she'd be happy with two bars.

Callie had always wondered what the small stakes on the sides of roads were for. The numbers never made any sense to her. Now she was grateful the highway authority put them out. Since she had no clue where she was, the towing company would find her thanks to those little numbers on the mile markers.

Once she hung up, she went and leaned against the fence post as she waited for a tow truck to arrive.

It wasn't long, which meant she had to be close to town, right? When the blue-and-white truck with a crane in the bed came into view, she released a sigh.

A tall, lanky cowboy with dirty jeans, dust covering his shirt, and an old cowboy hat stepped out of the truck. "Howdy, ma'am. I heard you needed some help?"

She recoiled, and then remembered herself. The roadside assistance company wouldn't have sent someone dangerous to help her. He was only a dirty cowboy who had probably been in the middle of fixing a car when he got the call to rescue her.

"Yes, thank you. I don't know what happened, but it just stuttered and then rolled to a stop." She pointed back to her sky-blue SUV and sighed. That car had gotten her through so many ups and downs. Her father had bought it used for her when she graduated high school, and then it carried the small belongings she had to her new life in St. Paul, Minnesota. Now it had abandoned her out in the wilds of Montana.

"Let me take a look and see if I can't help ya get back on the road. How's your gas?" The look he gave her caused her to bristle at his insinuation. She had gassed up not one hundred miles back.

"There's still over half a tank of gas, sir."

"Beg'n your pardon, ma'am. I'm Nick Sands." He held out a dirty hand for her to shake.

Gulping down her angry retort, she nodded.

He looked at his hand and dropped it. "Of course, I was working when I got the call. I should have washed up, but thought a young lady shouldn't be left on the side of the road. Please forgive the dirt."

Callie smiled and realized she was being rude. "Of course. Thank you for coming so quickly. I really do appreciate it. I'm Callie Houston." She put her hand back out, and he shook it lightly.

Resisting the urge to wipe her hands on her jeans, she turned back around to her car. "There's plenty of gas, so I don't know what else it could be. The check engine light never came on, and I haven't had any issues other than what you'd expect from an eight-year-old car."

Her father had insisted she take very good care of her car, and it would take good care of her in return. She'd had the oil changed every five thousand miles, done all the factory-suggested maintenance, and kept the car in the garage when not driving it.

She didn't even have that many miles on it for a car of its age.

Nick walked to the front of the Hyundai. "Can you pop the hood?"

"Sure thing." She went to her car and pulled the lever to open the hood. Not wanting to get in his way, she stayed next to the driver's seat and waited.

The tow truck driver's head went under the hood for a few moments, and when he stood up and lowered the hood, she worried about the grave look on his face.

This wasn't going to be an easy fix.

"I can tow you into the garage and have our mechanic look at it." He went to work moving his tow truck in line with her car while she waited on the side of the road. It didn't take him long to hook her Hyundai up to the tow truck.

When she got into the cab of his truck, she turned and looked at him. "How far is town?"

Once he was safely on the road, he looked at the woman sitting in his front seat. "Beacon Creek is about thirty minutes from here."

She furrowed her brow. "But it only took you about fifteen minutes to get to me once I hung up the phone. How'd you get here so fast?"

He chuckled. "I was on my ranch, just down the road."

"You own a ranch and work at a mechanic's shop?" Callie shook her head, confused by the man next to her.

"Oh no, ma'am. My brother owns the shop. I just help out when he's out of town. I'm a rancher, not a mechanic." His speed picked up until he was driving fifty miles an hour down the road. Then he eased up on the gas and settled in for a slow drive in. Towing the SUV behind his truck meant he couldn't do his normal sixty or seventy on the open road.

"Who's going to fix my car?"

"We have someone who can fix your SUV, don't worry. Mikey's just moved here from the city, and he has experience with Hondas." Nick smiled at her.

She shook her head. "No, my car isn't a Honda, it's a Hyundai."

"Honda, Hyundai, foreign jobs are all the same." He shrugged and kept his eyes on the road.

She wiped a hand down her face. "What am I going to do?" She thought for sure her poor car was doomed.

"Don't worry, Mikey can fix anything." He beamed in her direction before turning his eyes back to the road.

They drove the rest of the way in silence while Callie worried about what would happen to her Hyundai if Mikey didn't know what he was doing.

When they arrived, a tall, burly man with messy black hair walked out of the shop, wiping his hands with a rag.

Callie jumped down from the truck and approached him. "Are you Mikey?" she asked without any preamble.

He smiled. "Yes, and I take it you're the little lady who broke down on the road into town?"

She nodded. "Do you have any experience with Hyundais?" If this man didn't know what he was doing, she'd have to call her father and ask him for help. Even though he was all the way down in Louisiana.

"Some. Most of what I've worked on were Hondas, but I've seen my share of Hyundais as well as other makes." He scratched his head and watched Nick lower the SUV to the ground in front of the open bay.

It was late in the afternoon, and Mikey had been closing up the shop before they arrived.

"Do you have a place to stay for the night? I won't be able to look at your car until tomorrow morning." Mikey put the dirty rag in the back pocked of his dark-blue coveralls.

"I was hoping to find a hotel room here in town. Can you point me in the direction of one?" Callie bit the inside of her lip and prayed that the local hotel wouldn't be too expensive. And she didn't even want to think what the repairs might cost. Not yet, at least.

But she knew that with her luck, it would clean her savings out.

He shook his head and tsk'd. "I'm sorry, ma'am, but the hotels are all booked up for the carnival."

Callie's eyes widened and her body froze. "What? Are you sure?"

"Yup, my wife works for the Beacon Creek Inn, and she told me just last night that everyone is full up." He winced and began to wrack his brain for a solution.

"Why?" Callie looked around and noted that there weren't that many people wandering around. Granted, they weren't in the middle of town, but the place didn't look very big. Maybe they only had one tiny hotel with just a few rooms?

"The rodeo, ma'am. It's a pretty big deal round these parts. Our one hotel and two B&Bs are all full. In fact, most of the cowboys who come to town bring their RVs, and even the RV park is full now." He scratched the side of his head.

Nick walked over to them. "What about the Triple J?"

Mikey considered for a moment and nodded. "I'll give Matthew a call and see if they have any room."

"Triple J? Is that a bed and breakfast?" Callie would be happy with a bed and breakfast. It would probably be nicer than a boisterous hotel full of cowboys.

"It's a ranch that's setting up to house a few ladies," Mikey called back over his shoulder as he walked away.

Callie wondered what that meant, and turned to look at Nick. With a questioning look at the rancher, she waited for him to explain. When it became obvious he wasn't going to say anything, she asked, "Why are they preparing to house ladies?"

Nick took his hat off his head and smiled. "Miss Elizabeth has been working with the homeless population in Bozeman. She's set up a program to help rehabilitate women and get them back on their feet. Her family ranch is being renovated a bit to help house as many young ladies as they can."

Callie blinked. She wasn't opposed to helping the homeless, but living with them was another thing. However, if she was lucky, it would only be for one night. Two at most. Then she'd be back on the road, heading home.

When Mikey came out, he was smiling. "Miss Elizabeth will come by shortly to collect you and your things. They'd be happy to help out."

Callie wasn't sure what to say, or do. "Thank you. I do appreciate the help. But how long will it take you to fix my car?"

"I won't know until tomorrow, when I can look at it. If you'll give me your keys, I'll be sure to check it out first thing in the mornin'. Until then, enjoy the Triple J. You won't find a better meal than what Mrs. Manning cooks up, or the barbecue the brothers make." Mikey licked his lips and looked off into the distance.

Nick chuckled. "The Mannings have the best beef in the country. You'll see." He smiled and waved as he walked back to his truck.

Callie looked between the two cowboys. "Where should I wait?"

A beefy finger pointed to the front of the mechanic's shop. "There's a waitin' room in there. But first, you should probably get your luggage out and take it with you."

Both of them walked to her Hyundai, and when she opened the back door, Mikey reached in and pulled her suitcase out. "Is this all you got?"

She nodded. "I wasn't planning on a long trip."

He smiled and walked her to the waiting room. When he set her suitcase down, he pointed to a small refrigerator. "There's soda and bottled water in there. Help yourself. Sorry, but I've already cleaned out the coffee pot."

With a heavy sigh, she waved away his apology. "Don't worry, I typically don't drink coffee this late in the day, anyway. Water will be perfect." She grabbed a cold bottle and sat down to wait for this Miss Elizabeth to arrive.

Chapter 2

The woman behind the counter always got under Luke's skin. They'd been friends for as long as he could remember, but he couldn't remember why they had never been a couple.

Leah was beautiful. She had long, chestnut-colored hair that went down to the middle of her back. Combined with her chocolate-brown eyes, she was a looker. Not too long ago they'd gone on a date, but it went nowhere. He remembered having a good time, but for some reason he'd never asked her out again.

A nigglin' feeling in the back of her head told Leah to look up. She caught Luke staring at her, and felt the hair on her neck stand on end. Since that one date they'd had, she'd always hoped he would ask her out again, but he hadn't. Instead, he just looked at her with an odd expression. It was as though he was trying to figure out who or what she was, and couldn't seem to do it.

Her friend, Harper, had told her that Luke Manning had a crush on her, but he just didn't know it yet. One day, he'd figure it out and the two of them would be the perfect couple. The only problem: Leah wasn't sure she wanted that.

Sure, he was cute. Everyone thought Luke Manning was good looking. How could they not? He was tall, over six feet, and his brown hair had bits of auburn streaking through. His light-brown eyes with flecks of green and gold were mesmerizing. Not to mention his personality. When most people said a guy had a great personality, it usually meant he wasn't very nice to look at. But not Luke. Nope, he was a keeper.

So why didn't Leah's heart leap in her chest whenever he checked her out? Could it be that she spent so much time joking around with him as a kid that she saw him as more of a brother? Or did she just want to guard her heart against his charms? Make no doubt about it, Luke Manning was a charmer.

"Hiya, beautiful. How's yer day?" Luke smiled, and his eyes sparkled when he tipped his hat.

Leah's stomach did a little flip. Nothing a gymnast would be proud of, but still, it was something. Maybe she was attracted to him and just didn't want to be. "It's been busy. This is the first lull I've had all day." Leah returned his smile. "How 'bout you?"

"Same, busy day. Matthew sent me in to pick up his special order. Said Logan called to tell him it arrived?" He put his thumbs behind his large, silver belt buckle, and took a few languid steps toward the counter where Leah stood.

She held back a snort, but just barely. Shaking her head, she said, "Don't mention him."

"Who? My brother?" Luke asked.

Leah chuckled. "No silly, my brother. Logan took off at lunch to go over weddin' plans with Elizabeth, and he hasn't returned yet. He was supposed to cover me for lunch when he was done, and I'm starvin'." With the thought of food, Leah's stomach gurgled. Then she wondered if those butterflies a moment ago had been from hunger and not from the cute cowboy standing in front of her.

With raised eyebrows, Luke whistled. "Sounds like someone's gettin' a bit hangry. Want I should head over to Rosie's and get you somethin'?"

She shook her head. "Nah, I've been snackin' on these here new protein bars Logan had us stock last month." Leah pointed to a small box on the counter that only had two bars left.

"Whoa, little filly. How many of those bars did ya eat?" He chuckled.

She tilted her head and pursed her lips. "I didn't eat them all. I only had two. The rest have already been sold. In fact, we've gone through all the boxes Logan bought. This here is all we've got left." She pointed to the two lonely bars in the box.

"Hm, maybe I should buy them." He picked one up and read the ingredients and then put it back down. "Nah, that's one of those healthy bars for people with food allergies." A shiver ran down Luke's spine just thinking about how gross the bars must be.

Leah's laugh had him smiling. "Silly cowboy. They're actually really good. Some people are a bit addicted to them."

"But they don't even have real sugar in them. Coconut sugar crystals? Really?" He stuck his tongue out.

Leah pulled one bar out and opened the package. "Here, try it. On me."

The cowboy scratched the afternoon stubble on his jaw and pulled back.

"Oh, come on now. Don't be a baby. It's not like it's going to hurt you or anything." She giggled.

"Hmph. Alright, but if it makes me sick, then you have to make me an entire batch of your beef jerky." He put his hand out for the healthy food bar.

Leah nodded. "Deal." She handed him the opened package.

He took a little nibble. "Hm." He furrowed his brows and took a little bit bigger bite. "Not bad." Without even thinking about it, he took a full bite and chewed the nuts covered in dark chocolate and a hint of mint. "It's actually kinda good." He chuckled at his joke. "See what I did there? It's a Kind bar." He laughed before taking a bite a quarter size of the bar.

Leah shook her head. "Boys."

While he continued to chew his overly-large bite, he took the last bar out of the box and handed some cash to Leah to cover both.

She handed him back half the money. "I told you the first bar was on me."

He shook his head. "Nuh-uh. I can't let a little lady pay for something that good." When he swallowed the last of his bite, he asked, "Speaking of great food, when are you going to make up another batch of your famous jerky?"

Leah's head tilted down, and she looked up through her lashes. "You like my jerky?"

He nodded as he filled his mouth with the last of the Kind bar.

"Well, I guess it all depends on when you give me more tri-tip." She smirked, knowing that would get him to give her an entire side of beef if she promised him some of her beef jerky.

It took her three days to marinate the jerky, and then another two days to dehydrate it enough for the Manning family. But if they supplied the beef, she'd be happy to spend a week making jerky.

The Triple J Ranch, owned and operated by the Manning family, had the best beef in the country. Maybe even the world. At least, that's what all the residents of Beacon Creek thought. Ranchers came from far and wide to learn how the Mannings raised such tender beef. And grocery stores all got in line to get their beef when the cattle went to slaughter.

Luke stood up taller and cleared his throat. "Really? You're ready to make more?"

She nodded. "Sure, why not? It's been a while."

He thought about their supply of tri-tip and said he'd get her thirty pounds by next week.

When she agreed, he smiled and asked, "Great. How about that special order?"

"Right." Leah had forgotten why the middle Manning son had come into her family's general store to begin with. "Be right back."

Leah walked to the back room, and Luke looked around the store, checking to see if there was anything new that he had to have.

His mind wandered to the pretty salesgirl, and he wondered if asking her out for dinner would be weird. They were going to be in-laws of some sort soon. Was she going to be his sister-in-law? He wasn't sure how it all worked, but once his sister married Leah's brother, they'd be family. Maybe not by blood, but still.

Or would it even matter? Leah was a couple years older than he was, which he thought was hot. But would she want to date a man two years her junior? Ten years ago, that would have been just gross to his barely teen mind. But ten years from now, the age difference wouldn't mean anything.

Something on a shelf caught his attention, and he decided to shelve the idea of asking Leah out. At least until he could talk to Matthew. His oldest brother would know what to do.

Just as he went to pick up a black Stetson, his cell phone rang. Shaking his head, he reached for the phone instead. "Yup, this is Luke."

"Oh good, I caught you," Elizabeth Manning, Luke's older sister, said.

"What can I do for ya, sis?"

"I'm supposed to head over to the Grease Monkey and pick up a woman whose car broke down on her way into town, but I can't get away from the wedding planner. Can you pick her up and take her home? She's going to be staying at the ranch until her car's fixed." His sister sounded exasperated. In the background, he could hear Logan groaning and complaining about another issue with their wedding plans.

Luke didn't know why they didn't just have the weddin' at their ranch. They had a big enough back patio that if they brought in a large tent, they could handle the guest list. But Elizabeth and their ma wanted a larger wedding that wouldn't fit in the backyard.

"Sure, I'm at the general store now. When I'm done here, I'll head over. What's her name?" Luke wasn't sure he was ready to leave the store yet. He was still debating asking Leah out for dinner. Maybe he could come back into town the next day when he finally made up his mind.

"Thank you! You're a life saver. Her name's Callie Houston."

"Sure thing, but you owe me one," Luke joked.

"If memory serves, you owe me at least a million by now," Elizabeth teased.

The Manning family never kept track of favors owed, but they liked to joke about it.

"Oh," Luke added, "Leah said that Logan was supposed to be back a while ago to break her for lunch. You might want to send him back here soon." He looked up when he heard footsteps coming toward him.

"Oh, nuts. That's right. It was only supposed to take a short time over lunch. What time is it?" Elizabeth squeaked when she looked down at her watch. "I gotta go, I'll see you later." She hung up before Luke could even say his goodbyes.

"Geez, sis. Nice chatting with you, too." He shook his head and chuckled as he put his phone away.

"Was that Elizabeth? Did she say anything about my wayward brother?" Leah asked when she set a package on the counter.

"Yes ma'am, that was her. She and your brother are stuck at the wedding planner's office. It sounded like there was some issue going on. I told her to send her fiancé back here. I don't think they realized the time." He shrugged. "I don't get the whole weddin' plannin' thing. Why can't we just have a big barbecue in the backyard after the ceremony in the church?"

Leah laughed. "Are you serious?"

"Yeah, why?" The area between his eyes creased.

She sighed. "For one thing, our church isn't large enough to seat everyone invited. Plus, your backyard isn't exactly conducive to a sit-down dinner." She threw her hands in the air. "And never suggest a barbecue for a wedding dinner. The bride would never get the sauce out of her white dress."

"Dress? What self-respectin' cowgirl wears a dress? No, all brides should wear jeans and a cowgirl shirt. That way, they don't have to worry about getting dirty." He wiped his hands. "Easy peasy."

"I can't wait to see how your future bride takes your ideas for her weddin' day." Leah chuckled and handed him the package.

"I wouldn't marry anyone who didn't love barbecue as much as I do."

"Okay, we'll see," Leah responded, knowing that one day he'd be in for a rude awakening, and she hoped she'd be around to see it. If nothing more than to get a giant laugh. She'd have to make sure she remembered to bring popcorn when he approached his future bride about the wedding he envisioned.

"We shall." Luke waved as he walked out of the store.

His mind shifted to the task ahead. "What kind of woman wants to stay at our ranch? The ladies' dorms aren't even ready yet." He shook his head and made his way to his truck and the woman he had to pick up.

Chapter 3

Callie paced the little waiting room. She thought Elizabeth was going to be right there, but it had been thirty minutes since she arrived. Mikey was nice, but it did seem like he was ready to go home to his wife, and she hated that he had to wait.

"Honestly, I can just wait outside until Elizabeth arrives. It's no big deal. Go home to your wife. She's probably holding your dinner for you." Callie knew that cowboys went to bed early and ate dinner early, but did mechanics do the same?

"No, ma'am. It would be rude of me to leave you sittin' here outside my shop. I'm sure Miss Elizabeth will be here any minute. She's the town veterinarian, and her office is only a few blocks away. I'll bet someone came in with a pet needin' her help. But don't worry, she'll be here shortly." Mikey smiled and tried his best to make the little lady comfortable.

He really didn't mind waiting with her. His wife would tan his hide if he left her here all alone. It wasn't that Beacon Creek was dangerous—just the opposite, in fact. But with all the people here in town for the carnival and rodeo, you just didn't know. He'd never forgive himself if something went wrong because he left her there all alone.

The sound of tires screeching outside caught Mikey's attention. Callie's head also turned toward the sound of the stopping vehicle.

When a cowboy got out of the truck, Callie's shoulders drooped. It wasn't her ride. She checked her phone again for an Uber in Beacon Creek, but there wasn't one. One would think with an event as large as the Beacon Creek Summer Carnival, some-one would have thought to sign up to be an Uber driver. They'd make a killing here. Surely cowboys loved their beer, especially after a rodeo.

Maybe she'd have to check into setting up a Lyft account? If Elizabeth took much longer, she'd ask Mikey about taxi services in town.

Mikey opened the door and shook hands with the tall cowboy entering the business. He was young, but nice looking. She couldn't help but check out the auburn hair, hazel eyes that sparkled when he looked her way, and those long legs. The man also had a nice, broad chest. He definitely worked hard, but was dressed in clean clothes. His boots, however, needed some polishing.

"Luke, whatcha doing here? Where's your sister?" Mikey asked.

"She's stuck at the weddin' planner's office. She sent me instead." He took off his cowboy hat and smiled at Callie.

Her stomach did a somersault. She'd never seen such a beautiful smile on a man before. His teeth were strikingly white, and his eyes crinkled, making Callie think he smiled a lot.

"Ma'am, I'm Luke Manning, your taxi driver today." He nodded in her direction, and she wanted to curtsy after his formal greeting.

"Nice to meet you, Luke. I'm Callie Houston." She put her hand out for him, and instead of shaking it, he turned her hand so he could kiss the back of it. Before he lifted his head, he winked at her, and her heart beat double time. She'd have to watch out for this cowboy—he was a flirt.

Luke couldn't believe how he was acting. He'd seen some actor do that in a movie his sisters loved to watch, and for some reason his body acted without thought. Thankfully, Callie didn't slap him. Instead, her cheeks turned a beautiful shade of pink.

Mikey looked between the two and chuckled. "Well, Miss Houston, I'll call you in the mornin' once I've looked over your Hyundai. Luke will take good care of you. Have a good night."

She smiled at the mechanic. "Thank you, Mikey. I really appreciate it."

He ushered everyone out of the shop so he could lock the front door and get home to his wife's beef stew. The thought of her yeast rolls had his stomach growling with anticipation. They did eat supper early, but only because they both started their day before the sun rose.

Luke took the suitcase out of Callie's hands. "Let me." Then he led her to his truck. He put her bag in the bed of the truck and opened the passenger door for her.

Once they were on the road to the Triple J, he asked her, "So, where ya from?"

"St. Paul, Minnesota. But I was on the way back home from Seattle when I thought I'd stop in for your summer carnival. I've always wanted to check out a real western rodeo." The blabbering caused her cheeks to heat up, and she almost put a hand over her mouth to shut herself up. She always said too much when she was nervous. And she was. The man sitting next to her was the embodiment of a hunky cowboy.

'What about you? You live here all your life?" Callie wanted the conversation to move to him and away from her. After her last few days, she just wasn't in the mood to even think about her life and where she was heading.

"Yes, ma'am. Born and raised on the Triple J Ranch. In fact, it was started by my own family a few generations back. Always been a Manning running the place." He smiled, but kept his eyes on the road in front of him.

They'd have at least a twenty-minute drive, so he got comfortable in his seat and thought about what he'd ask her next.

"A generational ranch? That's got to be pretty cool. I've heard of them, but this will be my first time seeing one. Well, one that isn't on the Hallmark channel, that is." Her light giggle sounded wonderful to Luke's ears.

He chuckled. "My sisters love that channel. What is it with women and Hallmark movies? I don't get it." He shook his head.

He couldn't remember a time recently when his mother and sisters didn't have that channel on. After Sunday suppers, the guys would all head into the living room to watch sports, and the girls would go into the front room—or front parlor, as his mother called it—and they'd have the Hallmark channel on. All that mushy romance stuff usually made him sick.

One time, he watched a movie with his mother when everyone else was out of the house. He swore to himself that he'd never sit through one of those ridiculous shows again. Those men weren't real. Neither were the women. It was all fantasy.

The last girl he dated wanted to sit at home one night and watch a western. He thought she meant *The Good, The Bad, and The Ugly*, or maybe even something more recent like *The Magnificent Seven*. He'd never even once thought she meant a romance set on a ranch. When they sat down to watch it, he got right up and suggested they go out instead. They didn't last long.

"I think women today want a man who will respect her, even if they start out as enemies. The idea of those men treating women like ladies just gets to us. In here." She tapped her chest, over her heart.

"But women today are so independent. They get mad when we try to open doors for them and pay for everything, or try to take care of them in any other way. Why would you watch movies where men do that sort of thing and say you wish for it, when in real life you push it away?" That same girl he dated who wanted to watch that western romance also rebuffed his every move to open doors for her. And she never let him pay. Well, she did on the first date, but then it was always dutch after that.

"Women," he mused.

Callie giggled and put a hand over her mouth. "Yeah, I guess it's a fine line. We do love it when the *right* man takes care of us. But the right man also knows to give us a certain amount of independence and respect that we can take care of ourselves."

"That makes no sense. Either you can take care of yourselves, or you need our help. Which is it?" He rubbed the stubble on his chin as he stared out the window.

She took a moment and thought about it. "I think...when the couple are right for each other, they take care of one another. A woman doesn't need a man in this day and age to care for her needs, but men today still need to feel needed. One way a woman can show respect for the man is to let him open doors, pay for dates, that sort of thing. Show him she respects his needs, as long as he can respect hers." She shrugged.

Callie wasn't sure what she'd said was correct, but it did feel right in her bones. She hadn't met the right man, yet. But she also enjoyed it when men opened doors for her. She could totally do it herself, but when a man, even if he was a stranger, did that for her, she felt like he saw her. Really saw her, and was showing respect in a tiny way.

Her last boyfriend never opened doors and always expected them to split checks. Not that she *needed* him to do anything for her. She was a modern woman and felt that men and women were equal. But she was starting to see that men were created differently than women.

She'd read that book, *Men are From Mars and Women are From Venus*, and had to agree that the sexes were wired very differently. If women expected men to treat them as equals, then women needed to realize that men had different needs than women.

Not all women wanted a man to open a door for them, she knew that. But since it was something she liked, Callie knew her Mr. Right would open doors for her. He'd put his hand on the small of her back and lead her through, just like in the movies.

They both stared out the window and wondered about the differences between men and women.

Callie also wondered how in the world they had gotten onto this topic. She'd just met the man not thirty minutes ago and she was already sharing deep feelings and talking about relationships. For all she knew, this cowboy had a girlfriend, or was engaged. She shouldn't be discussing a topic so private with a total stranger.

The feeling in the cab of the truck was a bit too uncomfortable for Luke. He had no clue how they had begun talking about romance and relationships. Definitely not his favorite topic. If his brothers knew what they had discussed, he'd never hear the end of it.

Matthew would probably plaster his bedroom walls with romance movie posters. Mark would probably put all his mother's romance DVDs in his room. And he didn't even want to think about what John would do. That brother could be cruel in his practical jokes.

Wanting to change the subject, Callie asked, "So, Triple J? Why three Js in the name of the ranch? Your family name is Manning, with an M."

A feeling of relief flooded his body, knowing she wanted to change the subject just as much as he did, and it helped Luke to relax his shoulders just a bit. "My great-grandfather, Josiah Manning, started the ranch with his brothers, Jacob and Joel. The brothers were named after Biblical men whose names all started with J."

The custom had stuck with the Manning family, and everyone born into the family had a Biblical name—well, except for Chloe. Her mother wanted one child named something different. And when she had twin girls, she saw her chance.

She nodded. "So, you were named after the doctor in the New Testament? What about your other siblings?"

His wide smile reached his eyes, and Callie couldn't help but smile in return. It was contagious. "My parents weren't too unique. They named all of us boys after books of the Bible."

"Let me guess, one of your brothers is named Hebrews? Is another Ezra? Or Nehemiah?" She laughed and hoped his brothers had better names, like Peter or Timothy.

"Good one." He laughed. "Nope, we were named in order of the New Testament books. My oldest brother is Matthew, then Mark." He pointed to himself. "Me, then John, and the last boy is Roman."

"Your sister is named Elizabeth. That's not a book of the Bible, as least not as far as I remember." Callie thought hard, but couldn't remember if a book of the Bible was titled Elizabeth. The only women's names she remembered were Ruth and Esther. Both pretty names, but not very current.

"Elizabeth is the cousin of Mary, the mother of Jesus. She was also the mother of the Prophet John. The name fits my sister quite well."

"I see. Any other siblings? That's a huge family." She looked at his profile while he kept his face straight ahead.

He smiled. "Elizabeth is a twin. Chloe is my other sister."

Callie furrowed her brow. "I may not be up on all the Bible names, but that one isn't from the Bible."

"Nope, my mom got to name one kid something different. We used to tease Chloe about it." He wondered if that was why she always wanted to leave town. Did they make her feel like an outcast? He really hoped not. Luke loved his sister and missed her a lot. He'd have to have a conversation with her next time he saw her and make sure she understood their teasing was just that of stupid brothers.

Callie raised a brow. "Poor girl. Will she be at the ranch, too?"

He shook his head. "No, she moved last year to Frenchtown. We see her every few months." He considered for a moment before going on, "She might be coming to town this weekend for the carnival. Last I heard, she was going to try and come for at least the day. If you're still here, you might even get to meet her."

"Well, I'm not sure how long I'll be here. I need to get back home as soon as I can. My plan was to spend one night here and check out the carnival and go home the next day." She hoped her car would be ready tomorrow, but even if it was ready by the end of the day, she wasn't sure if she should leave and try to find another place to stay along the way, or just enjoy a second night of the rodeo and carnival.

"It doesn't start until Thursday night. So you'll have to stay a few nights if you want to see anything," Luke informed her.

"But all the hotels are already booked up. People are here, aren't they?" She had thought it started today, Wednesday, but maybe everyone came in beforehand to get an early start on Thursday? But if it didn't start until Thursday night, why would people already be here?

"Today is more of a setup day. The performers come in early to get their horses or other animals accustomed to the area and do a few test rides. So there might be some practice sessions to watch, but not a lot of the booths will be open until tomorrow." Luke took the turn to his ranch, and all talk ceased as Callie opened her eyes wide and her mouth dropped open a little bit.

"This is your ranch?" She was in awe. It was just like she imagined. The entrance was a wrought-iron gate displaying their logo in the middle of each side: the words *Triple J Ranch* above a cowboy riding a horse. There were two wooden posts with a large beam between them at least twenty feet in the air, and another logo hung from the center of the crossbeam.

On each side of the gate was a wooden fence exactly like she expected. There wasn't any wire; it was all wooden posts with three lengths of wood between each post. She could imagine Luke leaning against the top rail of fence with his booted foot relaxing on the bottom rail. He would have his cowboy hat on, and a piece of straw hanging from his mouth with that tantalizing smile of his that would send any woman swooning.

She shook herself and looked past the entrance. A long road led up to the house in the distance. It was still too far to get a good look, but she could tell it was a single-story ranch home. It had to be quite large, with seven children and their parents all living there.

Anticipation drove her to want to get to the house faster. If this ranch and its over-sized house were any indication, she thought those cheesy romance shows she watched on TV might not be so cheesy after all. Maybe, just maybe, there would even be a large selection of hunky, single cowboys at the rodeo, just like in the movies.

After all, the inspiration for those books and movies had to come from something in real life, right?

And if the sexy cowboy on the seat next to her was any indication, she was going to enjoy her stay here. Luke was probably too young for her—he seemed like he might only be twenty-one or twenty-two—but he had older brothers. Maybe one of them would be right for her?

What was she thinking? She didn't live anywhere near here. A little flirtation might be nice to get her mind off her problems, but anything more than that wouldn't happen. Not in just two days.

Chapter 4

They rode up the dirt driveway, and as she got closer to the house, she noticed how large the dwelling was. The middle of the house had a front porch with a nice overhang and several chairs along with two porch swings. It all looked cozy, like a place she'd want to spend spring or autumn evenings sipping tea with her family.

As she continued to evaluate the house, it appeared to have been built in stages. The middle was most likely the oldest part of the house, maybe even the original homestead house.

There was a long wing off to the right with wood siding that was different from the front of the house, which was what made her think it was added on sometime later. The left also looked a bit different. It wasn't that it was a mismatched house, but each wing was distinct enough to tell anyone who looked closely that they were not built at the same time. Not that it mattered; it actually gave the house its own character and told a story of the progression of the family.

"Home sweet home," Luke said when he opened her door for her.

She stepped out and looked around. "I love it. How many stay here?" She hadn't asked about the lodging service that Mikey told her about, so she wasn't sure how it all worked, but if the family lived in one wing, then maybe the other was where the rental rooms were located? Or maybe they had a hotel of sorts in a different building out back?

Before Luke could answer, a motherly woman with a sprinkling of gray hair and a huge smile came bounding down the porch steps. "Hello, and welcome to Triple J. I'm Judith Manning." She held out her hand.

Callie stepped forward and shook it. "I'm Callie Houston. Thank you so much for allowing me to rent a room here. How many rentals do you have?"

Mrs. Manning put a hand on her Wrangler clad hips and looked to her middle son. She was the epitome of a country mother. Even her red and white checkered button up blouse was what Callie had pictured a ranch mother wearing. "Didn't you warn her?"

Callie's eyes widened, and she looked to Luke. "Warn me about what?"

He took his hat off and ran a hand through his thick, wavy auburn hair. "Well, we aren't exactly set up like a hotel."

"Then your place is a B&B?" Callie asked.

"No, ma'am." He winced and wondered how he could say it in a nicer manner.

Mrs. Manning beat him to the punch. "We're more of a halfway house. We take in homeless women who need help getting back on their feet, and then when they're ready, they move on."

"Oh." Callie wasn't sure what to say. Mikey had said something about them helping homeless women, but she didn't think it was as bad as a halfway house. Weren't those for people trying to get off drugs or coming out of prison? She hoped she'd be safe here, and then reconsidered how long she might actually want to stay.

Mrs. Manning held up a hand. "Don't worry. It's perfectly safe here. We actually don't have any residents at the moment. Our last one, Ana, just left last week to go back home to her family."

The woman teared up, and Callie wondered if she missed Ana or if the girl had caused problems. She hoped it was the former.

Mrs. Manning was tall, but not as tall as her son. She had a sweet look about her, just like what you'd expect from a ranch mother. Or maybe what Callie expected after watching so many western romance movies. This ranch mother wore jeans, a red-and-white checked, button-up shirt, and a white shirt underneath. Her hair was pulled back into a chignon, and she had no makeup on, but her skin was flawless.

The wrinkles around her eyes and mouth told Callie that this woman laughed a lot. Luke had the same look. Which meant it was a happy home, like hers. Instantly, she felt a sense of longing to see her parents again.

Not knowing what to say, Callie just nodded. "Your ranch is beautiful." She looked back to Luke and noticed he had her suitcase in hand and was heading inside.

He motioned with his head for her to follow.

"Dear me, where are my manners? Please come in. Would you like some tea? Or perhaps coffee?" Mrs. Manning followed Callie inside.

"Tea would be great, thank you. How does this work, then? I'm not a homeless woman needing help. I just need a room for a night or two, until my car is fixed." Callie shrugged. She felt a bit uncomfortable staying somewhere that wasn't any sort of public lodging.

They took in strays here, and she wasn't a stray. Or at least, she didn't think she was. Maybe she was and just didn't realize it yet. If things didn't turn around for her soon, she could become homeless.

Well, that wasn't entirely true. If she couldn't get a job soon, she'd always be welcome back home with her parents.

"We aren't set up to take payments of any sort, but if you want to help out around the ranch, we won't say no." Mrs. Manning led Callie into the kitchen while Luke turned left down the first corridor.

When she looked back for Luke, Mrs. Manning said, "Don't worry, he's just putting your bag in your room. I'll set you up in Anna's old room. It's the closest to the main part of the house and already set up for guests."

Callie bit her lower lip. "I don't want to put you out or anything."

"Oh, it's no trouble at all." Mrs. Manning waved a hand. "In fact, I'm looking forward to having another woman in the house. Both of my daughters moved out a while ago, and with Anna gone, I'm all alone with six burly men." She laughed as she pulled out the glasses from the cabinet and then pulled the jar of sun tea out of the fridge.

"Do you like sugar in your tea?" Mrs. Manning asked as she poured the cold beverage into ice-filled glasses.

"Yes, please." Callie had always loved sweet tea. Her grandma had gotten her into the habit when she was a little girl visiting her in Mobile, Alabama.

When they had fixed their tea the way they both liked it, Luke entered and poured himself a tall glass of tea and then joined them at the table. "Ma, Mikey will call tomorrow morning with the prognosis on Callie's car. But I think she'll need to stay for a couple days."

Mrs. Manning's eyes lit up. "Do you like carnivals and rodeos? Oh, what am I saying, of course you do. Who doesn't? You should stay through the weekend and join us at the Summer Carnival."

Callie was already starting to relax, and she knew she was going to like Mrs. Manning. "Thank you, but I don't want to put any of you out. I do want to go over tomorrow and check it all out, if anyone's going." Since she didn't have a car, she wasn't going to be able to do anything without one of the Mannings ferrying her around. She was too far out of town to walk in, and since they didn't have Uber, she was stuck.

"And I'll be happy to help out here on the ranch, wherever you can use me." She wasn't sure what she could do other than cook and clean, but she'd always wanted to try a dude ranch, so maybe she could learn how to feed cattle and muck out a stall?

On second thought, mucking out a stall didn't sound the least bit interesting, only dirty and stinky. But still, there had to be other things she could do to help around the place.

"Have you ever worked a ranch or farm before?" Mrs. Manning asked.

She gave a half-smile. "No, but I learn fast. And I don't have a problem with hard work." She'd never had a manual labor job, but she was sure she could do whatever they asked of her. Or at least she'd give it her all.

Luke put his empty glass on the table. "I could show you how to feed the horses. Have you ridden a horse?"

Callie shook her head. "No, but I've always wanted to ride."

"Did you bring jeans and boots?" Mrs. Manning looked at Callie's nice slacks and blouse and raised an eyebrow. "If all you brought are nice clothes, you might not be able to do any work on the ranch."

Callie looked down. She had brought one pair of jeans and a t-shirt. That should do fine for working around the ranch. After her disaster of an interview at eight that morning, she'd gone straight back to her hotel and packed up her bag and then checked out and got right on the road home. There was no sense in waiting around, and she didn't even think about changing into something more comfortable for the drive. If she had, she'd be in yoga pants and an oversized t-shirt instead of her interview clothes.

"I do have a pair of jeans, but no boots. Will tennis shoes work?" If she had to, she could probably charge a pair of boots and another pair of jeans, if they had a discount cowgirl clothing store in town. She didn't even know what she'd need, or how much they would cost. But since she was staying rent-free for the next few days, she could afford a trip to the store, maybe.

"Boots are more than a fashion accessory on a ranch—they're for safety as well. What size do you wear? Maybe one of the girls left a pair here you could wear." When Mrs. Manning looked down at Callie's feet, she felt a bit uncomfortable. She hated how big her feet were.

She wasn't a giant, but she was taller than most of her friends back home. The size nine shoe she wore was larger than any of her friends. Margie told her that her feet were too large for her five feet seven inches. The fact that she'd never been able to borrow shoes from her friends, who all wore a size seven or eight, had always bothered her.

"Elizabeth wears a size nine, and Chloe a size nine-and-a-half. Would either of those work for you?"

Callie thought the two Manning girls must be giants if they wore those sizes. "Actually, I wear a nine." She couldn't look at Luke. Callie didn't know if he understood women's shoe sizes, but she'd always been a bit embarrassed at her shoe size and didn't want to see the judgment in his eyes if he did understand she had giant, ogre-sized feet.

Mrs. Manning stood up. "Perfect. Come with me and we'll see if there's a pair you can wear."

An hour later, after Callie had tried on two very worn pair of boots and changed her clothes, she was back in the kitchen helping Mrs. Manning set the table. While she was in her room getting things together, the rancher's wife had made dinner for everyone.

There were so many cowboys to meet, and no women sitting next to any of them, and no rings, either. Well, Mr. Manning wore a wedding band. But the rest had no jewelry on at all.

It was just Mrs. Manning and Callie along with six cowboys. All tall, and with huge appetites. She couldn't believe how much meat was on each man's plate. And then the potatoes and vegetables. They must have worked up an appetite out on the ranch all day. There was no way she could eat that much in one day, let alone in one meal.

As she was introduced to each brother, they all smiled and checked her out. Even Roman, the youngest Manning boy who was preparing to go off to his first year of college in the fall, seemed to be looking her over. It wasn't in a leering way, but it did seem these boys appreciated her looks.

Callie felt her cheeks warm and hoped she wasn't blushing. Even though she had been checking them out, she hadn't thought they'd all want to check her out as well. If she was honest with herself, it was all a bit overwhelming, and exciting.

"So, Callie," Matthew started, "will you be attending the rodeo tomorrow night?"

She put her fork down and swallowed the steak in her mouth before taking a drink of sweet tea. "I was hoping I could catch a ride, if any of you are going tomorrow night."

"I'd be happy to take you in and show you the town and our little carnival. I'm sure it's nothing like what you'd see in St. Paul, but I think we do a nice job of it here in Beacon Creek," Mark answered before anyone else could ask her out.

She looked down at her plate, trying to hide the smile and blush she felt creeping up her cheeks. The Mannings sure knew how to make a girl feel welcome. "Thank you, I'd like that."

Callie hoped it wouldn't be just the two of them. Even though Mark was a handsome cowboy, she didn't want to start something she couldn't see through. And forget about long-distance relationships—they never worked.

She should know, she tried when she left for college. Her high school sweetheart said he'd wait for her, but he didn't. She wasn't gone two months before he broke her heart. A year later, he married the girl he'd cheated on her with. It took her a long time to get over that, and she still wasn't sure she could trust a man with her heart.

Oh, she'd dated her fair share of men over the years, but nothing ever lasted. Trust was something that none of them engendered. Callie's friend, Sabrina, said she had trust issues and until she gave it up to God, she'd never trust a man enough to give him her heart. It was probably true.

But that didn't mean she couldn't have fun flirting with the Manning brothers. Well, as long as they didn't take it too far. A little bit of attention never hurt a girl's ego.

Mark smiled and puffed his chest out like he had just won the blue ribbon in his 4-H club. Callie wasn't sure if she should be offended or excited. She looked around at the downcast faces of the other brothers and thought maybe it was a good thing. Then again, maybe it was just a contest amongst the brothers to see who could get her on a date first?

She had to remind herself that it didn't matter, she'd be gone in two days if all went well. If she was really lucky, her SUV would be ready before the rodeo began, and Mark would in essence just be taking her into town to get her Hyundai before the evening festivities began.

After dinner, Callie helped Mrs. Manning clean the table and do the dishes. The boys all went into the living room and turned on the news. It sounded like they were getting sports scores, so she tuned out their conversation and instead focused on her hostess.

"Callie, I can't tell you how nice it is to have another woman in the house again. Those boys of mine"—she tilted her head toward the living room—"are all about sports and running the ranch. I can't get a single one of them to see a movie with me, or talk about a book I might have read." She laughed and shook her head as she rinsed the dishes and put them in the dishwasher.

Callie was scraping plates into the trash and handing them to Mrs. Manning. "Yeah, I guess it could get lonely on a ranch. Especially when it's so far into town. How often do your daughters visit?"

"Well," Judith Manning began, "I only have one daughter in town. Did Luke tell you about Chloe?"

Callie remembered the sister with a non-Biblical name. "Yes, she's in Frenchtown, right?"

"Right. But Elizabeth is here. She's just really busy with her veterinary practice and wedding plans. Other than Sunday suppers, she hasn't been out here to see me in weeks." Judith sighed and looked out the window overlooking the stables behind the house.

The sun was setting, painting the sky in oranges and reds with white wisps running throughout the canvas.

Callie looked out the window and smiled. "It's such a beautiful sunset. We don't get many like this in a big city."

"Have you ever considered moving to the country?" Judith looked over her shoulder at her young guest and thought she might make for a nice daughter-in-law, if only she lived closer to their tiny part of the country.

Taking a moment to consider, Callie pursed her lips and looked back out the window. The air was clear—well, other than the smells of a working ranch. The sounds of the horses whinnying in the distance was soothing. A feeling of peace she hadn't felt since leaving her small part of New Orleans all those years ago to attend college in St. Paul, Minnesota, began to permeate her entire being.

"I hadn't really thought of it. It's not like my job would be in high demand in a small town."

"What do you do?" Judith asked.

"I'm a contracts associate." She looked at Judith and realized the woman was confused. It wasn't uncommon. Not too many people knew what a contracts manager—or purchasing manager—was, let alone an associate.

With a light chuckle, Callie explained, "I work in corporate procurement. Large companies need to buy a lot of goods and services in order to keep their company going. If they're in manufacturing, they have to buy raw goods needed in order to make their finished products. All companies buy services such as consulting or marketing."

Judith nodded and focused on Callie.

"I come in and write up and negotiate the contracts between the two companies to ensure both sides understand what they're responsible for, and what will happen should someone not live up to the expectations of the deal. I also help negotiate pricing for my employer, or the sales price when we're the one selling something. But most of the time I'm on the buying side."

It wasn't that Callie loved what she did, but she was good at it. She'd even recently received an award from her company for negotiating large cost savings. However, that didn't prevent her from losing her job when they downsized.

But it was dry work. She'd done it from the time she left college, and she wasn't sure she should even try finding something new. Callie seriously doubted there would be any need for her particular skills anywhere in Montana, let alone a small town like Beacon Creek.

"Sounds like something all ranchers do for themselves. We have to negotiate rates on our beef when we sell it, and again when we buy more cattle. Then there's also the feed when we can buy it in bulk. And the worst part—water rights." Judith shuddered. Water was always a source of contention amongst the ranchers.

"Water rights? What's that?" Callie had never had to worry about water. She paid her water bill and used as much as she wanted. It wasn't like she wasted water; she tried to be a good steward of the natural resource, since it wasn't something that they had an unlimited supply of, but she never considered how ranchers got their water. Didn't they have wells on their land?

"Even though we own our own land and any minerals in the soil, we don't own any of the water that may run through our property. The state of Montana owns it all, including well water. Since the Triple J Ranch was created before 1973, we have a large right to water. But there's always someone trying to challenge how much water we can legally use to water our crops or feed our cattle." Judith tried to stay out of any conversation that had to do with water rights. Ranchers were always fighting over it, especially during droughts. And non-ranchers were always trying to take away their rights.

"It sounds confusing. Do you have an attorney or organization who works on your behalf?" Callie wasn't an attorney, but she knew enough about the law to wonder how they could have issues with water rights if they had a legal right to certain amounts of water each year. How could there be an issue with rights if they'd already been established?

Judith nodded and went back to loading the dishwasher again. It was almost full, and once it was full, she'd have to finish up the dirty dishes by hand before turning on the dishwasher.

"We do, and there's a great collective who works tirelessly to make sure ranchers aren't taken advantage of, but it's still something we have to deal with regularly. Especially after a drought. When there isn't enough water to meet everyone's needs, the state has to ration the amount of water we all get. Since I've been here, we've been on water rations four times."

"What, do you take your dirty dishwater and put it in the toilets?" Callie was only joking, but it was something she'd heard of.

The wry smile on Judith's face caused Callie to stop.

"Really? You've had to do that?" She couldn't imagine it ever getting that bad.

"Among other things, yes. We buy bottled water by the pallet and drink that, and always have at least one pallet in stock just in case. When we know a drought is near, we up our stock to two pallets. There was one year we didn't have enough water to grow our own hay, and we had to buy the hay from the open market to feed our stock. Thankfully, our local feed store has a reciprocal agreement with another store two states away. It helps when feed and grain production are low in our own state." There were so many other issues ranchers had to deal with, but Judith figured this was enough and wanted to talk about something nicer.

Before Callie could ask any more questions on the topic, Judith brought up the rodeo and carnival. "Luke said you were on your way here for the rodeo and carnival when your car broke down outside of town. How'd you hear about us?" The dishwasher was now full, so Judith added the powder and set the timer so it would run on its own in two hours.

Callie chortled and shook her head. "Don't laugh, but it's kinda weird how I heard about this place."

Judith frowned. "How so?"

"I saw a movie on Hallmark, and it was about a rodeo star who married his sweetheart. She was a barrel rider, and they married after he won a rodeo in a small Montana town." She shrugged.

"Oh, I just love that one!" Judith smiled at Callie. "You know it's a true story, right? They didn't film it here, but this is where Chuck and Lilly were married. They come back each year and he still competes in the rodeo. He won last year as well. We get tons of press coverage from it. Which is why our hotels are all booked up the moment they open up each year."

"I looked it up. I was curious about where they filmed it, since the town was so cute, and discovered it was based on a true story here. I've wanted to come and visit ever since I learned about it, but just haven't had the chance." She shrugged. "I was driving home from Seattle and thought I had the time and I deserved a treat." Callie put a hand on her heart. "So I came at the last minute, not even thinking about the need to reserve a room." She waved her hand around the kitchen. "But I think I might have ended up with a much better place to stay than a loud hotel."

Both women laughed when the boys in the next room burst out into cheers.

"Okay, so maybe it's not as quiet here as I thought it would be." Callie giggled and looked in the direction of the excited sounds.

"I think their baseball team must have won." Judith plugged the sink and began to fill it with sudsy water.

"Does that mean they aren't always this loud?" Callie asked.

"Well, they aren't in the house all day long, only at night after dinner." Judith kept her eyes on the dishes in front of her.

"Uh-huh. So what you're saying is that it's quiet during the day, but not after dinner?" Callie laughed and picked up a pan to dry and set on the dinner table. Judith had told her to just put the dry dishes there, and she'd put them away when they were done.

"Well"—Judith stretched out the word before continuing—"it's not that loud every night. Most nights they're all in bed asleep before nine o'clock."

"Got it, they work sunup to sundown and get to sleep early. But in between, it's a free for all?"

The rancher's wife nodded and continued washing the dishes.

"Alright, tell me about the rodeo. Is it just like in the movie?" Callie asked.

"Pretty close. We don't get too many men getting hurt, but sometimes the bulls do get a bit too rambunctious and someone will be injured, but then again, sometimes the bulls do nothing. Same with the broncs. There are times when they come out of the gate and don't do their part. But most of the time it's a very enjoyable show. The worst injuries are usually rope burns."

"Sounds like fun. I can't wait to see it all. Is the carnival big, too?" Callie had been to carnivals in Minnesota and back home in Louisiana. They varied in size and what rides and booths were available. Sometimes the same carnival could vary from year to year, but she always enjoyed the Ferris wheel and the fun house with mirrors.

"Ah, yes. The carnival. That's actually my favorite part of the whole event. Did you know that my Caleb proposed to me at the top of the Ferris wheel?" Judith looked to her ring finger and sighed.

"Sounds very romantic." Callie looked at the small diamond ring set in gold on Judith's finger.

"It was. Every year we ride it together, and at the top he kisses me just like he did back then and tells me how much he loves me."

Callie had to wipe a tear from her cheek. It wasn't that she was sad, it just was the opposite. To have a man love her so much to do something so sweet year after year would be a blessing.

"Your husband sounds wonderful. I hope to find a man who loves me that much one day." She also hoped he would be as romantic as Mr. Manning.

Chapter 5

The next morning, Callie woke to the scent of coffee, bacon, and some sort of pastry. She quickly dressed and went out to the kitchen, and the only person still there was Judith.

"Is everyone already out on the ranch?" Last night before heading to bed, Callie had asked to join the guys in the morning so she could see what they did on the ranch.

"Yes, they just left." Judith poured a cup of coffee and brought it to the table for Callie. "Cream and sugar?"

"Yes, please. And thank you." She looked at her watch and saw that it was only six-thirty in the morning. "It's so early, I thought I'd be right on time. Normally I'm still sleeping at this time. Why didn't anyone wake me?"

"Don't worry, we understand city slickers don't get up as early as we do. The boys will be close to the house for a while this morning. Why don't you eat a good, hearty breakfast before joining them? You'll need the energy." Judith set to making a plate full of bacon, hash browns, and chocolate chip pancakes.

"Wow, this is incredible." Callie took a bite of pancake with warm syrup and thought she must have died and gone to heaven. "If you eat like this every day, how do you stay so slim? Is it genetics?"

Judith laughed. "Oh mercy, no. We work hard here on the ranch. Everyone burns so many calories on a normal day that they have to take in more just to keep on their feet than the regular person who works behind a desk."

If she was going to eat this entire plate before her—and she wanted to—Callie knew she'd have to work harder than she'd ever done before in her life to keep these calories off her hips.

"Thank you, Mrs. Manning. That was the best breakfast I've had in years. Have you ever considered turning this place into a dude ranch? You'd get people coming from all over just to eat your food." Dinner the night before had been better than any restaurant Callie had been to in years. And now with this breakfast, she wasn't sure she wanted to leave.

Laughing, Mrs. Manning waved a hand. "Oh, be off with you. The men are waiting at the barn." She motioned to the back where the barn stood. "Do you know how to get there?"

Callie laughed. "Alright, but seriously, you could open a restaurant with your cooking. And thank you again for your hospitality. I don't know what I would have done last night if I didn't have a place to go."

Her hostess's cheeks turned pink with the praise, and she waved the compliments away. "It's my pleasure. Just don't let those boys work you too hard. You need to have some energy left for tonight. Keep that in mind."

Judith waggled a finger at Callie, and she nodded. "Yes, ma'am."

Walking out to the barn, Callie felt butterflies begin to awaken in her stomach. She'd never ridden a horse, and today she was going to learn how to, as well as who knew what else. She only hoped mucking out stalls was one of the things she wouldn't have to learn.

"Miss Callie, good of you to join us." Luke strode out to her before she could get inside the barn. "Did you sleep well?"

Normally, Callie didn't sleep well the first night in a new place. "Surprisingly well. Thank you. I don't know what it is about your ranch, but I don't remember waking at all during the night. In fact, I don't believe I even moved. Once I was out, that was it until I smelled the coffee this morning."

"Good to hear it. My ma makes the best breakfast and coffee in the world." Luke beamed.

"Really, where all have you traveled?"

"Huh?" Luke rubbed his clean-shaven chin.

Callie took a closer look at the cowboy's face and realized she really liked his features. He had pronounced cheekbones, a sleek nose, and his hazel eyes matched his auburn hair quite nicely. Those pesky butterflies had woken, and she wished they'd go back to sleep.

"What are you comparing your mom's coffee to? Not that I'm complaining—I loved breakfast and dinner." She smirked when she noticed his chagrined look.

"Ah, it's an expression. Although, everywhere I've been in the US usually has me wishing I was back home with Ma's cooking and coffee." Luke turned and walked back into the barn with Callie on his heels.

She felt kinda bad. Was it rude of her to insinuate that his mom's cooking or coffee may not be the best? She wasn't sure, but she grew up just outside New Orleans. No coffee tasted as good as Café du Monde's. And she'd just come back from Seattle, where coffee shops were on every corner. Some even had two or three on one corner.

It was sweet that he thought so highly of his mother's cooking. She couldn't think of anyone she'd met before who swore their mom was the best cook they knew. He deserved a break. Besides, he was still a bit young.

"Sorry, I didn't mean anything by it. I was really curious if you've traveled anywhere outside of Montana before." If he had, she'd be surprised.

"Hey, I've been to Washington State, Oregon, Idaho, California, Arizona, and quite a few more states. Not to mention many trips across the border to Canada. I've done my fair share of traveling." He winked at her, and a shiver went down her spine.

"All for fun, or business?" Callie wasn't sure why a cowboy from Montana would go to so many states for business, but she figured it was most likely for pleasure.

He stopped in front of a horse's stall and put his hand out for the tall, black horse to sniff the palm of his hand. "Both, I guess. I've traveled around on ranch business, but I've also gone to see friends compete in rodeos. Vegas hosts the rodeo finals every year, and I try to go when I can."

The horse whinnied when Luke ran a hand down the front of its head between the horse's eyes.

"Do horses like to be pet there?" She pointed to the area directly between the horse's eyes.

Luke took her hand and held it under the horse's mouth. "Let her sniff you."

The squeal that came out of her mouth shocked even her. She'd never touched a horse before, and to have one put its mouth on her hand surprised her. She wasn't freaked out—nope, not her. Not at all.

"Hey, hey. What are ya doin' to my date for tonight?" Mark sauntered in with a couple carrots in his hand.

If the heat in her face was any indication, that pesky blush was coming up again. What was with her and blushing in front of these men? She had to get a handle on her nerves. They were just cowboys. *Cute* cowboys, but still men she wouldn't see again once she left town. Nothing to trip over.

Oh lordy, she thought. That was all she needed. If she fell flat on her face in this barn in front of these two hunky cowboys, she'd never be able to look them in the eyes again.

Mark winked at her as he handed her a carrot with the green shoots still hanging off it. "Here ya go. Put this on your hand, and Whiskers will be your friend forever."

"Whiskers? Is that her name?" She looked between Luke and Mark when she took the carrot.

Mark punched his brother's shoulder. "What's wrong with you, man? You didn't even introduce the little lady to the horse you planned to saddle up for her?" He tsk'd and shook his head.

"Hey, I would have. You interrupted us." Luke smacked his brother's shoulder.

These brothers were crazy. She didn't know if she wanted to be around when they decided to actually fight. Since she didn't have a brother, she wasn't used to watching siblings hit each other.

Callie took a few steps back while still holding the carrot in her hand.

Matthew stepped up and got between his two younger brothers. "All right, break it up. No fighting in front of guests, you know the rules." He looked at

Callie and quirked a brow. "Are you alright? You look a little piqued."

A laugh bubbled out of her. "Is it always so rough around here?"

Matthew chuckled. "Pretty much. We love each other, but we do enjoy a good fight now and then. Just ignore them. I usually do."

Mark and Luke both said, "Hey, now!"

Luke took a step toward Callie. "I'm sorry. I shouldn't have been rough with my brother in front of you. You don't know us well enough to understand that's just us messin' around." He gave her a small smile.

"Thanks. It's all just a bit weird for me since I don't have a brother." She shook the image of them horsing around out of her mind and looked back at Whiskers. "So, what do I do to feed the carrot to her?"

Luke chuckled and said, "Follow my lead." He walked over to the horse next to Whiskers. "This is Pippi Longstocking. Pippi, meet Callie." He rubbed his hand down her neck.

The horse's coat was a reddish chestnut with what looked like freckles. She looked just like her namesake.

"Hi, Pippi. Nice to meet you." Callie petted her mane like Luke had.

Luke put his hand with the carrot palm up in front of Pippi's mouth, and the horse snuffled it up rather quickly.

"Okay, your turn. Put the carrot on your palm and your hand under Whiskers' mouth." He gave her a reassuring smile. "Don't worry, she won't hurt you. She just wants the carrot."

With a deep breath to steady herself, she walked over to Whiskers' stall. The black horse with cat whiskers had her head over the door, waiting. It was as though she knew Callie was going to be giving her a carrot, and she patiently waited her turn. Callie couldn't help but smile and relax her shoulders.

When she put her hand under the horse's mouth, she felt the scratchy whiskers and the horse's rough tongue lap the carrot off her palm. "Eww, that was gross. But kinda cool." She giggled and wiped her wet palm on her jeans.

"We'll make a cowgirl out of you yet," Mark said, and winked.

Luke gave his brother a hard stare. Then he softened his expression and looked back at Callie. "Are you ready to learn how to saddle and ride a horse?"

Anticipation flowed through her veins. This was something she'd always wanted to do, she just hadn't ever had a chance. Maybe breaking down on the road was a good thing. Lady luck just might be smiling on her.

With two guys basically fighting over her, and now a chance to ride a horse, and then later heading to a rodeo, she was having a pretty great day.

Luke helped her to saddle Whiskers before he saddled his horse, Midnight—a black stallion that was taller than anything she wanted to ride.

When Luke took Whiskers over to a tall box with two steps, she furrowed her brow and asked, "What's this?"

"It's a mountin' block. Greenhorns use it to get on horses. Later, when you've practiced enough, you'll be able to use the stirrup and mount your horse on your own. But for today, I want you focused on ridin', not mountin'. So we'll use this to help you get on the horse." Luke tied Whiskers to the stall door next to the mount and put his hand out for Callie.

With her hand in his, she stepped up on the wooden block and looked at the horse. Her nerves fired up, and she felt the little hairs on her arms stand on end. While she wasn't afraid, there was a bit of trepidation coursing through her veins. The last thing she wanted was to make a fool of herself and not be able to mount the horse. Or worse, fall off on the other side.

"Hold on to the saddle horn, here." Luke pointed out the horn and grabbed it with his right hand to demonstrate. "In your left hand, take hold of the reins." He handed her the reins. "Then raise your right leg over the saddle and take your seat."

After taking in a shaky breath, she did just as he said. "I did it!" She beamed at him and straightened herself in the saddle.

The horse beneath her began to get restless, and she moved around a little bit.

"Whoa, it's alright, Whiskers. Give the little lady a break. This is her first time." Luke rubbed the horse's neck as he calmed her down.

"What's wrong?" Callie's excitement began to turn to fear. Had she done something wrong? Did she hurt the horse in some way?

"Don't worry, Whiskers is fine. She's just excited to have a rider. She belongs to Chloe, and she hasn't been ridden by a lady in a while. My brothers and I take turns riding her every now and then, but it's not the same for Whiskers." He patted the horse's neck and walked her over to where Midnight stood waiting for him.

Luke mounted his horse using just the stirrups, and Chloe was impressed. Midnight was a very tall horse. Even though Luke was tall—she guessed him close to six feet—that still wasn't tall enough to easily get into that saddle.

"Luke, how tall is your horse?"

He grinned at Callie. "Midnight's seventeen hands."

"Um, I don't know that form of measurement." Her nose scrunched.

When Callie scrunched her nose, Luke's heart beat triple time. It was the cutest thing he'd ever seen. "One hand equals about four inches. So Midnight is sixty-eight inches high."

Callie's eyes widened. "No wonder I don't want to ride him. That's taller than I am." She laughed nervously and looked down to the ground. "Whiskers isn't that tall. What's her height?"

"The horse you're on is fifteen and a half hands, about sixty-one inches."

"So, she's five feet, one inch tall." Callie nodded. "I can handle that."

Luke chuckled. "Just watch, in a few days you'll be wantin' to ride Midnight!"

She shook her head. "Not on your life."

Luke took the lead and looked back over his head. "Hold the reins in both hands and squeeze your knees against Whiskers lightly. That'll get her going."

Callie followed his instructions, and was surprised at how smooth the gait was on the horse beneath her. They followed Luke and Midnight out of the barn and into the yard.

"We'll take it nice and slow, just keep pace with me. If Whiskers goes too fast for you, pull back on the reins. But whatever you do, don't squeeze your knees against her unless you want to go faster." Luke led them toward a trail that passed down to their small lake.

"Okay, I got it. I think." Callie focused on the horse and her reins as Whiskers walked next to Midnight. She wanted to look out at the scenery around her, but she also wanted to make sure that she kept her eyes on the road, so to speak.

"You know, you can look around. It's not like driving a car." He chuckled and pointed to a copse of trees off to their left.

Her gaze followed his hand, and she smiled. Tension she didn't realize she held began to ease out of her body, and she sighed. "This is so beautiful. I can see why you love it here."

The sun was already making its climb high into the sky, even though it was still early morning. Callie had checked the forecast the night before, and it was supposed to be clear skies and a high of eighty-three. Even though the morning was a bit nippy, she knew it was going to be hot when you factored in the humidity and the direct sunlight.

A sound behind them caught Luke's attention. He turned in his saddle and scowled.

Callie noticed and turned around, too. "What's wrong?"

"Nothin', just my brothers not playing fair."

Behind them Matthew, Mark, and John were riding their horses and catching up quickly.

"I thought we agreed I'd take Callie out for a ride this mornin'?" Luke's harsh tone caused Callie to raise her brows.

"We did." Matthew said. "But we have to check the fences on this side of the property, so we thought we'd join you for part of the ride. Didn't we, fellas?"

All three cowboys wore cheese-eating grins. They all looked very pleased with themselves, like they were getting one over on Luke, which they probably were.

Mark sidled up on Callie's other side. "How do you like Whiskers?"

She returned his smile. "She's fantastic."

"Good. Maybe tomorrow morning you'll ride out with me?" The sun glinted off the lenses of Mark's sunglasses.

It wasn't that she didn't want to spend more time with Mark, or Luke. It was just that she needed to get home and start searching for another job. Plus, she knew how her heart worked, and there was no way she going to tempt it to stay behind in Montana. The sooner she left, the better for her health.

"Sorry, but I'm planning on leaving tomorrow morning." She still hadn't heard anything from Mikey, but it was pretty early yet. The hope was that by lunchtime, Mikey would be calling to say it was something he could fix and it would be done by the end of the day.

"And what if your car isn't ready today?" Mark asked without looking in her direction. He had prayed she'd be stuck with them for several days, and then maybe he could talk her into staying longer.

A small smile lifted the corners of her mouth. "I have a feeling it'll be done today. If not, then I'm sure it'll be fixed tomorrow."

"So that's a yes?" He quirked a brow.

"To what?"

"To riding with me in the morning." He turned his full gaze on her and waited expectantly.

Matthew interrupted. "I think Miss Callie might enjoy a ride tomorrow morning with all of us. We'll have to ride out to the back forty for the day, and I thought we might bring a lunch and all of us can show her what it's like to work on a ranch."

Callie wasn't sure what was going on. Having two brothers fight over her was more than enough attention. If Matthew was going to start flirting, too, she'd have to hang out in the kitchen with Mrs. Manning. She hoped and prayed that the rest of the Manning boys didn't start flirting with her.

Her face must have conveyed her concern, because Matthew continued, "We really do need to mend those fences before the cattle get loose." He nodded at Callie with a look that wasn't flirtation. She wasn't sure what he was trying to convey, but she was starting to think that maybe he was just trying to save her from his own brothers.

She nodded in reply. It would actually be nice to see what a normal workday was like for a rancher. And mending fences sounded much better than mucking out stalls. Callie had promised to help around the ranch in exchange for room and board. Staying with the group of them just might be better than being alone with one of the brothers who was interested in her. Not that she feared them, but she did fear what her heart was doing when Mark or Luke looked at her.

The ride this morning was a sort of date with Luke, and later in the evening she'd be out with Mark on a date. Maybe Matthew was giving her a chance to keep it all friendly and comfortable.

"I'd like that. Thank you, Matthew." She smiled at him.

He nodded in reply.

Nothing in his countenance screamed flirtation, or interest. Roman and John were quiet. So maybe the three of them had made a pact to keep Luke and Mark from getting too close? They probably didn't approve of her as a romantic option for their brothers, anyway. She did live a long ways away.

No, she'd keep things on friendly terms. As a city girl, she wouldn't mesh well with cowboys. And the last thing she needed was to cause a family feud. Having all the brothers around would keep things simpler. Even if she was tempted to flirt with Luke and Mark, she couldn't.

For the next few minutes they all rode in silence, taking in the beauty of the morning. The tense feelings that had arrived with the other brothers dissipated, and Callie let herself enjoy the ride.

Sounds to her left brought her out of her own head. She looked and saw several cows running past them. When she looked behind her, there were a lot more gaining on them.

Fear took hold, and she grasped the reins in her hand too tightly and Whiskers came to a stop. But she wasn't happy; her hooves scraped the ground in front of her, and she tossed her head.

"Sorry, girl. I didn't mean to do that." Callie loosened the grip on her reins and Whiskers moved again. But this time she went faster. They began to gallop, and Callie didn't know what to do. She could hear the cattle coming up behind her, getting close, and when she passed Luke, she screamed out, "Help!"

"H'ya!" Luke screamed, and kicked his horse to move faster. "Hold on, Callie. I'm coming." His horse caught up in no time, and he herded Whiskers and Callie off to the right, out of the path of the stampeding herd.

Behind them, his brothers were trying to get the herd to move away and slow down.

Something had spooked the cattle, but there didn't seem to be anything—or anyone else—around.

Matthew called out, "Keep Callie safe. When you can, take her back to the barn. We'll take care of the herd."

Luke agreed, and he continued to use Midnight to herd Callie off to the right. Once they were far enough away, he reached over and pulled on Whiskers' reins.

Both horses slowed down together, but Callie's heart hadn't received the memo. The rushing sound running through her head kept her from hearing anything Luke had said. She looked at him and saw his mouth moving, but couldn't hear him.

"Are you alright?" Luke asked again.

She shook her head.

Once the horses came to a standstill, he jumped off Midnight and stood next to Callie. He put his left hand with Midnight's reins on Whiskers' neck, trying to calm the horse while his right hand rubbed Callie's back. "It's alright. We're safe now. Do you want to get down?" He removed his right hand from her back and took the reins out of her clenched fists.

"What happened? Why did those cows come at us like that?" Callie's eyes were still wide, but the rushing in her ears had subsided, and she flexed her hands once the reins were taken from her.

"Come on, let's tie up the horses and walk around a bit." Luke led both horses to a nearby tree and tied them both to low-hanging branches. Then he pulled Callie out of her saddle and held her up until she got her legs under her.

Callie's hands instinctively went to the cowboy's chest, and she rested her forehead against him.

Luke wrapped his arms around the girl and rubbed her back. She felt good in his arms, and he wondered what it would be like to date her—*really* date her. Then he remembered she was leaving the next day, and he stomped down those thoughts.

He and his brother Mark may have been fighting over her attention, but it was just a fun flirtation. It had been a while since a new girl came to town.

They were both just having a little fun before she left. Nothing would happen between them. It was harmless.

Then why did his heart beat so fast, and why was his stomach tied up in knots? It must have been because he had seen how frightened Callie was when the herd stampeded.

A stampede was dangerous. More than just cattle could get hurt if they weren't careful. And someone who had never even ridden a horse before would have a difficult time getting out of the way on her own.

It just must have been his instincts kicking in, and the need to protect her. That's all those strange feelings were about. His parents did raise him to be a gentleman. Part of that meant always keeping women safe, no matter who they were.

She took a few deep breaths before stepping back out of his arms.

Callie was embarrassed and nervous all at once. Having Luke wrap his arms around her felt good and right. She reminded herself that this was a dangerous situation, and not just because of the stampeding herd. If she wasn't careful, her heart would be trampled upon.

She had to get control of herself. It was stupid to enjoy his arms around her. Surely it was just because of the dangerous situation. The cowboy in front of her was too young for her, anyway.

Mark was the right age for her.

It was probably a good thing that Mark wasn't the one who got her out of the way. She might have kissed Mark if he were the one holding her instead of his younger brother, Luke.

She couldn't remember the last time she had been kissed. Not because it was all that long ago, even thought it had been a while. It just wasn't a memorable kiss.

Maybe that was what this was all about? Her subconscious mind wanted a memorable kiss to keep in its data banks. Especially if she wasn't going to be dating anyone any time soon.

Chapter 6

"I'm so sorry about that. I don't know what happened, but my brothers will get to the bottom of it." Luke put a reassuring hand on Callie's arm.

She nodded and drew in a few more deep breaths.

"What do you say we take a short walk, away from the action?" He chuckled. "It might help you clear your head."

"That sounds nice. But are you sure we're safe here?" Callie wasn't ready to get back on the horse yet, but she also didn't want to take a chance she'd be run over by the herd.

He looked around them and then back down at Callie. "Yes, I'm certain. They went in the opposite direction of us, and I can't even hear them anymore. We're safe. But don't worry, we won't walk far."

They began to walk in circles around the thicket of trees they were in. But they stayed relatively close to the horses.

After about five minutes of walking without talking, Luke asked, "How are you feeling? Ready to get back on the horse?" He chuckled when he realized what he'd said.

Callie wasn't quite ready to laugh, but she did give him a smirk. "Almost. Talk to me. Tell me about life on a ranch."

He rubbed his chin and thought about some of the stories he could tell her. There was no way he'd talk about the fights he and his brothers got into, or the practical jokes they played on their sisters. He needed to come up with something fun and soothing.

"One summer when all of us were still living here on the ranch, we picnicked at the lake. It was a very warm day, and we all wore suits under our clothes so we could go swimming." He paused and looked as though he was remembering the event with fondness.

"Elizabeth and Chloe had their inner tubes tied off to a tree. My brothers and I were joined by Logan, Elizabeth's fiancé now, and we quietly untied their rafts." He chuckled and shook his head. "The lake was moving along nicely, it had been a snowy winter and there was still some runoff coming from the mountains. I don't know if they had fallen asleep or what, but they didn't even seem to notice that they were floating down the lake toward the mouth of the creek."

"What? That sounds dangerous." Callie couldn't believe these boys.

Luke put up his hands. "No, no. It wasn't dangerous. Even though the lake was full enough to move them, the creek was still relatively small. They could have just stood up and walked out once they were in the creek. I doubt their rubber donuts would have taken them very far before a rock or branch stopped them."

She shook her head and wished she'd had a brother or two growing up to play jokes on. Or at the very least to play with on a lazy, sunny day. Her sister was nine years older than her, and they didn't really play much as kids. Sheila was more apt to babysit her than play with her.

"So what happened?" Callie wrapped a strand of hair around her finger and watched intently as Luke reminisced.

"Huh? Oh, yeah. Sorry." He chuckled. "That was a great summer. Elizabeth and Logan hadn't yet realized they were in love. They were still just great friends, and he enjoyed teasing her along with us. But he's always been very protective of her."

Callie furrowed her brow. She knew Elizabeth was marrying a man named Logan, but didn't realize they'd grown up together. Her own high school sweetheart had messed everything up for her. It must be nice to know that some couples could make it through and eventually marry.

If Elizabeth was older than Luke, and a veterinarian, she had to be in her late twenties. So why did they wait so long to marry? Did they break up when she left for college and just recently get back together?

She motioned for him to continue.

"When it looked like they still had no clue what was going on, Logan jumped into the water yelling out, 'Lizzie! Lizzie, wake up!' He swam as fast as he could toward her and Chloe, and right before he got there, he splashed enough water that the girls woke with a start." Luke chuckled and leaned over to pick up a stray shoot of wheat and put the stalk in his mouth.

"Was the water very cold?"

"Oh, you have no idea. It's runoff from the nearby mountains, so yeah, it's cold. Later in the summer it's much warmer, but early summer I wouldn't suggest swimming in the lake unless you're a member of the polar bear club." He grinned at her.

Laughter bubbled up and forced its way out of her. She could only imagine waking up in the middle of a lake being splashed by cold water. "Thanks for the heads up. I'll keep that in mind."

"How're ya feelin'? Ready to ride back?" He had guided them back toward their horses, and Luke figured it was safe to ride home. He really wanted to know what happened to cause the stampede, but answers weren't going to drop from the sky any time soon.

With a huge sigh, she nodded. "But how will I get back on Whiskers?" She eyed the height of the horse and knew she couldn't just put her foot in the stirrups and get herself up. Not yet.

"Don't worry, I can help you." Luke walked over to Whiskers' left side and knelt on one knee. He cupped his hands and waited for Callie to get the picture.

"Is this how men in the Victorian era helped women to get on their horses?" Callie loved reading Regency and Victorian books, and always wondered how the heroines got back on their horses when there wasn't a mounting block nearby.

He chuckled. "Yes, ma'am. Cowboys and gentlemen have always enjoyed helpin' little ladies get back on their mounts." He winked.

She shook her head and sighed. "I guess there's worse ways of getting back to the house."

"We could walk." The deadpan expression on Luke's face sent chills down Callie's spine. They had to be at least three or four miles from the ranch house. While she could walk that far, she had no desire to do so. Not when there was a capable horse next to her.

Now she understood the phrase, *gird your loins*. She did just that and put her left foot into Luke's hand while throwing her right leg over the back of the horse when he pushed her up.

"Thank you, Luke. I don't know if I told you that yet, but I really appreciate you taking such great care of me." She realized that this was one situation where her independent nature wouldn't have helped her at all. Since she had zero experience with horses or cattle, she really did need him to swoop in and save her.

He tipped his hat. "You're mighty welcome, my fair lady." Then he turned and undid the reins holding the horses to the trees.

Once he had given Callie her reins, he mounted Midnight and led them home.

The entire household was in the paddock waiting for them when they returned to the barn.

"Oh, thank the good Lord!" Mr. Manning exclaimed. "I was worried you might have been injured." He came over to Callie's side, and Mark went to the other side.

She chose to let Mr. Manning help her down. "I'm fine. A little rattled, but fine. Luke took good care of me."

Mr. Manning beamed at his middle child. "That's my boy." Once Callie was standing firm on the ground, he walked over and patted his son on the shoulder.

"Pops, what happened? Why did the herd stampede like that right behind us?" Luke took his hat off and ran a hand through his sweat-dampened hair.

Mr. Manning frowned and looked at the scowls covering his other children's faces. "Mr. Johnson's bull got through our fence and thought he'd see to his business."

"You've got to be kidding me. That old bull has been nothing but trouble for the past five years. When's he going to fix the beast?" Luke ran a rough hand over his face and sent an apologetic look in Callie's direction.

She didn't know what that all meant, but it didn't sound good.

Mrs. Manning interrupted. "Every time a fence post breaks, that bull finds his way here on our property. I can't tell you how many times we've had to mend the fence between our lands." She shook her head. "The bull has a thing for a few of our heifers. They don't like him messing with them, so they always run when he comes near."

Mark spoke up. "But this is the first time it resulted in a stampede."

"That we know of," John added.

"True, there could have been several out in the back parts of our land that intersect with the Johnson property." Matthew rubbed his chin. "We got the bull back on his side of the fence and did a temporary fix. But we'll have to go back out there now and make sure he can't break it down again."

"Wow, it's crazy all the dangers of living on a ranch." Callie shook her head, and she hoped that raging bull wouldn't cross over to the Triple J again.

"Come on, I could use some help in the kitchen getting lunch ready." Mrs. Manning waved for Callie to follow her.

"Don't I have to do something to Whiskers first?" She didn't know what was needed, but the phrase *ridden hard and put away wet* came to mind. She most likely had to brush the horse down or clean her, or some other such thing.

Luke put a hand on her shoulder. "Don't worry, I'll rub Whiskers down and give her some extra grain for all the excitement this morning." He nodded toward the house.

"Okay. Thanks, Luke." Instinctively, she leaned over and gave him a hug. With her nerves calming down, she was starting to see a bond developing between them after this scare. If Luke turned out to be a good friend, she'd call this a win.

Chapter 7

Matthew, Mark, and Luke all rode out to fix the fence, and they missed lunch with everyone. But Mrs. Manning put aside some food for them for their return.

While Callie was washing dishes and putting the kitchen back to rights, the three older Manning brothers returned with grins on their faces.

Mr. Manning eyed his three eldest. "What? Those grins usually mean you're up to no good."

"Let's just say that Mr. Johnson's bull won't be an issue for a little while. We'll have enough time to fix all the fence lining our property with him." Matthew high-fived Mark.

Mr. Manning cleared this throat and narrowed his eyes at his oldest child. "Do I want to know?"

"Uh, probably not." Mark held up his hands. "But don't worry, we didn't do anything to hurt anyone."

"And what about the bull?" Mr. Manning crossed his arms over his chest.

Callie watched, and was excited to hear what mischief these men had gotten up to. From the little she'd seen and heard, these guys were great at practical jokes. They might go a bit overboard, but she doubted they'd do anything to actually hurt the bull.

"Don't worry, he's very happy right now." Luke grinned.

Mrs. Manning threw her arms in the air. "Oh, please don't tell me you put that feisty old bull in the field with Mr. Johnson's heifers."

All three cowboys burst out laughing.

"You should have seen the old bull. I could have sworn he was five years younger, the way he chased after the girls." Mark slapped his thigh and kept laughing.

Luke was bent over laughing, and Matthew held his stomach he was laughing so hard.

Mr. Manning chuckled. "Well, it looks like the Johnson ranch is going to have a large group of calves next spring."

Callie's cheeks went hot. Immediately. She'd had no idea what they were talking about until now. She'd never even thought about how cows reproduced. All she cared about was that the milk was at the grocer's and the meat was in the butcher's inventory when she wanted it.

"Alright, now let's get our conversation under control. We have a lady in our presence." Mrs. Manning was a lady, but she was also a rancher's wife and mother of five boys. None of this conversation was new to her. When a woman grew up on a ranch, this was just daily life.

Callie bit her lips and stayed quiet. She had no idea what to say in this situation.

"Here." Mrs. Manning pulled out the lunch she had put aside for the three boys. "I think you need to eat. Have you washed your hands?"

All three of them groaned like pre-teen boys being told to wash behind their ears when bathing. "Yes, Ma. We know better than to come into your kitchen without first washing our hands." Luke sat down at the table and piled two thick slices of roast beef between two pieces of bread.

His brothers joined him, and they all began making their pot roast sandwiches.

"Is this a normal day on your ranch?" Callie asked Mrs. Manning.

The older woman thought for a moment, then nodded. "Yep, pretty much."

"I'd hate to see an exciting day on the ranch." Callie rolled her eyes when Matthew snorted and tea blew out his nose.

"Manners," Mrs. Manning chided.

Matthew put his napkin over his mouth and gave a contrite nod.

The two ladies took their tea and went into the living room to give the boys some space. Their father stayed in the kitchen with them.

While Callie and Mrs. Manning chatted about nothing of consequence, they could hear the occasional bout of laughter coming from the kitchen.

"Boys." Callie shook her head.

"They're probably going over how they steered the bull toward the cows and heifers on Mr. Johnson's land." Mrs. Manning paused. "While I don't condone their behavior, I do think it might be what was needed to keep that old bull off our land."

"Is it so bad if the bull mates with your cows?" Mating practices weren't exactly something she wanted to discuss, but since she'd never even thought about it before, she saw this as a learning moment.

Tilting her head to the right, Mrs. Manning considered the question. "Normally it wouldn't be a big deal. But with you here, I don't want that mean ol' bull wandering around. There is an element of danger. Since you aren't an experienced rider, I think it's best he stay out of our fields."

"Normally I'd take offense at people trying to protect me, but I think in this case I'll agree." She held up her hands. "I have no experience, or even knowledge, dealing with raging bulls."

They spent the next few minutes discussing the carnival. That is, until Callie's cell phone rang. She had been itching to call Mikey and see if he had any news for her, but if he was working on her car, she didn't want to disturb him.

"Hi, this is Callie." When she didn't recognize the caller ID, she just assumed it was the grease monkey.

"Hiya Miss Callie. I have some news." Mikey's voice sounded hesitant. But since she didn't know him well, she couldn't tell if that was just his regular phone voice, or if something was wrong.

She chose to believe nothing was wrong. No use worrying about something that hadn't happened yet. Her Granny used to say, *No use crying over tomorrow's spilt milk today*. That platitude had gotten her through quite a bit of stress in college as well as the last few years of working in corporate America.

"Okay, is my car fixed?" The hope in her voice was clear on the line.

"Well, I've got good news and bad. Which do you want first?" He still sounded hesitant.

Since he was offering up both good and bad, Callie chose to believe it wasn't going to be too bad.

"Um, let's start with the bad. Then the good will sound even better." Her hand clenched the phone a bit too hard, and she forced herself to relax her hand before she broke her phone. That was the last thing she needed—another important item broken. Her checking account couldn't handle buying a new phone right now.

Mikey hesitated. He cleared his throat. "Your car's transmission is shot. In fact, you're lucky nothing bad happened. There's a recall out on your vehicle due to some pretty nasty accidents. Did anyone from Hyundai contact you?"

She tried to remember if she'd had any calls from the dealership, but didn't think so. "No, but I can't be sure. Sometimes I ignore calls if I don't recognize the caller ID."

Mikey chuckled. "Well, I suggest you start answering your phone."

"So what does this mean? I need a new transmission?" There was no way she could afford that.

Callie was going to have to call her father and ask for a loan. She hated to do it, but what else could she do? She was stuck in a strange town far from home. Her roadside assistance company wouldn't tow her all the way home to St. Paul. That had to be over a thousand miles.

"Yes, but that's not the worst part," Mikey said.

All she could think was that it was going to cost an arm and a leg. Could she sell enough blood and plasma to pay for it? Better than selling her appendages.

When a long silence came from the other side, Callie prompted, "And? What does this mean? Just tell it to me straight."

"Right. Well, the reason you probably haven't heard from the dealer yet is because they're short on parts. There ended up being a lot more need than they had supply for." He took another break.

Callie was going to wring his neck if he didn't just come out with it. She growled, "And?"

"And it's going to take at least two weeks to get a new transmission from the dealer." Instead of taking a break, he kept going. "But the good news is that the entire cost will be borne by Hyundai. Since it's a recall issue, you won't have to pay anything for it."

She sat there in stunned silence, staring out the window of the Manning parlor. Two weeks. "Two weeks?" she mumbled, and hadn't heard anything he said after he dealt her the harshest blow she'd had to deal with lately.

Mrs. Manning must have seen the desperation on her face, or heard it in her voice. She put a hand on Callie's. "Don't worry, dear. You are more than welcome to stay here as long as you need. In fact, I'd love to have you stay longer. Maybe we can even find you a job in the area."

The last sentence came out chipper, and caused Callie to look into the face of her hostess.

"Miss, did you hear me? It won't cost anything," Mikey repeated.

She refocused on the call. "What? Sorry, I didn't hear anything after 'two weeks.'"

"Because it's a recall issue, you won't pay a dime for the fix. Hyundai will send me the part free, and I'll just bill them for my labor." Mikey sounded much happier than when he'd first called.

"That's something. But what am I supposed to do for the next two weeks? I have to get home and find a job." Maybe she could work on her resume some more and apply for jobs online while she was stuck here.

But she hated to take advantage of the Mannings' hospitality. She wouldn't have a car to use at all. Basically, she'd be stuck on the ranch unless any of them took pity on her and brought them into town whenever they went.

Then there was church. It wasn't like she was all that regular in attending, but she had started going more regularly the past six months and really enjoyed the series her pastor was working on at the moment. Did the Mannings attend church? If they did, what kind was it?

"Miss Callie, I'm sorry it's going to take so long. But at least we have the carnival right now. You can attend with the Manning family every day and enjoy it." His chipper voice was starting to grate on Callie's nerves.

"Right. If there's any way you can get the part faster, will you let me know?" Callie wasn't sure what to do. Could she source it herself? Did her dad know somewhere to get one faster than two weeks?

She'd spend the next few days trying to find it herself. But for now, she needed to hang up and get ready for her date with Mark. It seemed she was going to have time to get to know both Mark and Luke better, after all.

Chapter 8

"Wow, you look fantastic," Mark exclaimed when he met Callie in the living room.

Callie had borrowed boots from Elizabeth, and she paired them with her jeans and another borrowed shirt from Chloe's closet. She felt awkward using shoes and clothes from women she hadn't even met yet, but Mrs. Manning assured her the Elizabeth and Chloe would insist upon it if they were there.

She hoped their mother was right.

"Thank you. So do you." Callie appreciated the black cowboy hat on the tall man with brown hair. She wasn't sure if it was the black hat or the navy shirt that helped bring out the blue in his eyes, but they were so vibrant she couldn't stop staring.

The cocky smile on his face brought her back to earth, and she chuckled. "Right, time to go?"

He put an arm out for her, and she wrapped her hand around his bicep. Silly as it was, she squeezed just a bit and felt him flex his muscle for her. Callie pursed her lips to keep her laugh inside. He knew she was checking out his arm, and instead of being embarrassed, he was going to help her along.

What she wanted to do was ask him to flex both arms and do a superhero pose for her, but of course she never would. Not in a million years.

The gentleman opened the truck door for her, and she hopped inside the Ford F-150 pickup. While Mark walked around to the driver's side, Callie looked around and noticed that it was very clean. He must have washed it inside and out right before their date. There was no way a truck on a ranch could be that spotless unless it was just washed. She couldn't help but appreciate the effort he went through for her.

Once he was inside and had the truck started, he looked her way. "I'm sorry it's goin' ta take so long for your SUV to get fixed, but I'm also not."

She furrowed her brows. "What?"

His million-watt smile sent the butterflies in her stomach into overdrive. "This means we'll get to spend more time together before you leave. I must say, I'm looking forward to getting to know you better." He put the car in drive and drove out of the ranch, toward town.

"Yeah, well, I have a lot I need to get home for. While I love your ranch, this really puts a kink in my plans." Her elbow rested on the door just below the window, and she put her chin in her hand.

"Do you have a job to get back to?" Mark hadn't heard anything about her work situation. He had no idea what she even did for a living.

A sigh escaped her lips. "No. I don't. But that's why I need to get home. I have to start looking for a job."

She knew she wasn't going to get the job in Seattle, and even if it was offered to her, she wouldn't take it. The manager who interviewed her was skeevy, and she had no desire to work for a man like that. Or at a company that employed someone who blatantly checked out the women he interviewed.

His eyes on her chest would have made more sense if she was scantily dressed, but she'd worn a button-up blouse with only the top button undone. There was nothing to cause him to look there.

"Hmm, how about looking for a job here? I mean, I don't know what you do, but surely there are places in Bozeman that are hiring."

She chuckled. "What I do is kinda off the beaten path. I seriously doubt any company in the state of Montana would have need of my skills."

He took a quick peek at the woman sitting next to him. "What do you do?"

She told him about her past job and her skillset, and how few small companies ever needed a contracts specialist.

"I mean, you're young. You could still change careers, couldn't you? What's your degree?" He slowed down when he saw something near the road up ahead.

She looked forward when she noticed he had slowed down. "What's that?"

He shook his head. Pieces of a fence had been torn away and littered the highway. Mark pulled over and took out his phone. "Dad, I'm out on the highway leading from our ranch, about mile marker sixty-four. Someone has destroyed part of our fence."

Mark listened as his dad relayed the message to someone else in the room.

"Is Callie with you?" Mr. Manning asked.

"Yeah, we were on our way to the rodeo," Mark responded.

"Alright, go on ahead. We'll come and fix it before joining you." Mr. Manning hung up before Mark could ask him what was going on.

"Why would someone want to tear apart your fence? That doesn't make any sense." Callie looked around to see if she could see anyone. The area was clear of people and animals.

"Yesterday we had several hundred head of cattle in this pasture. They were moved late in the day to the section next to it. Someone must have wanted to steal our cattle, or make sure they all got out. Either way, this is sabotage." He rubbed a hand down his face and blew out a breath.

They didn't need any more issues. For the last few weeks there had been small problems, but nothing like this. Nothing to make them think someone was doing it all on purpose. They would have to be extra vigilant and check fence lines on a daily basis. The sheriff would also have to be notified, but his pops had told him to go on to the rodeo.

If there was anyone still around, it wouldn't be safe for Callie to be here. As much as he wanted to investigate, he wasn't about to put the city girl in danger. He had his suspicions as to who was doing this, and if he was right, it was dangerous. No, he needed to get going and let his family deal with it.

Starting the next day he was going to be armed, and make sure his entire family never went any- where without a shotgun. And maybe even wearing pistols. They all had them, and had grown up prac- ticing with all forms of firearms. He could even sink a bullseye with his recurve bow from one hundred yards.

Her eyebrows shot up. "Really? Who have you ticked off enough to want to hurt your cattle?" The Manning family was nice and very generous. They helped homeless women get back on their feet, and even took in stray city girls. Who could want to hurt them?

"You'd be surprised at how many enemies ranch- ers can have," he practically growled out.

She knew this was a serious situation, but she won- dered if it had anything to do with women. The Manning boys were flirts, and very good looking. She could see women fighting over them. "Do I need to watch my back tonight? Will there be scorned women out for my hide?"

He snorted and gave her a half-smile. "I wish it were that simple. But no, none of us have any scorned exes. This is something else." He really didn't want to talk about it. Not tonight.

"Is there anything I can do to help?" She wasn't sure what she could do, but she wasn't a shrinking violet. Callie was a city girl who knew how to take care of herself and help others when the situation called for it.

While keeping his eyes on the road in front of him, he continued to scan the fence line as they drove closer and closer toward the Johnson ranch. So far, that one spot was the only one. As he neared the Johnson place, he wondered if the bull getting into their pasture earlier wasn't an accident.

He had been out to the spot in the fence line where the bull got through. It was a weak part of the fence. They had that section on a list to repair. Either the bull forced his way through on his own, or someone helped him. The posts were felled from the Johnson side of the property, as though the bull had charged and knocked it down.

When they inspected the fence, it didn't look like someone had messed with it. But, could it be possible someone lured the bull there and prompted the bull to ram the weak fence line? Now that he thought of it, the other issues that seemed like bad luck or just accidents may have actually been sabotage.

"Mark? Did you hear me?" Callie had waited patiently for his response, but when he stayed quiet, she wasn't sure he'd heard her.

"Hm?" He looked over at the pretty girl in his front seat. "Sorry." He turned his eyes back to the road. "I was thinking about what's been going on lately. What did you ask?"

"I know I'm not a rancher, but is there anything I can do to help?" Fixing fences wasn't her thing, but she'd give it a try if it would help. She could also use her investigative skills, if needed.

She wasn't a cop or anything, but she did have some experience in this arena.

Mark knew there was nothing she could do, but he had to lighten the situation. He had let himself get maudlin, and that wouldn't do for a first date. Especially not when he was competing with his brother for her attentions. "Not unless you're a detective." He smirked.

Her nose twitched, and a small smile escaped her lips. "Well"—she paused and kept her eyes forward, watching for any signs of someone out there messing with the rancher's fence lines—"my father is."

"What?" Mark spluttered.

"Yeah, he's kinda tough. And he's worked some pretty crazy cases in his time. I've even helped out a little when I lived at home." She hadn't been deputized, but her father did bring his work home sometimes, and since he had no boys, he had used some of his cases to teach her how to investigate.

"Why aren't you a cop?" He eyed her curiously.

She shrugged. "I guess I've seen too much evil and didn't want to be a part of it."

Mark rubbed his chin. "Why business?"

She sighed. "It seemed like the safest thing. You gotta understand, I'm from New Orleans originally. With all the voodoo and criminals, things could get really...odd. Some of the cases my father worked on were more than just scary. They had demonic undertones, at times."

"Is that why you live in St. Paul?"

"Yup. I left for college and never moved back. I mean, I go home all the time to visit, but living in an area where I can actually feel the demonic presence..." She shivered. "It's just too much."

He watched her out of the corner of his eye. "Are you a Christian? Or Catholic?"

"Christian. And you?" She was curious. If he didn't believe in Jesus, then she wouldn't let this date go anywhere past casual friendship.

"My entire family is Christian. We attend a local Baptist church and are very involved. Since you'll be here for a couple weeks, you should join us this Sunday."

"Hm, that sounds good. Thank you." If they were all Christians, she wondered if God's hand hadn't been in this breakdown.

She doubted God caused her car to break down. There was an issue, even if she didn't know about it until today. But she could have broken down anywhere, including back home in St. Paul. Why did she break down in Beacon Creek, Montana?

"If you want to tell me what's going on, I'd be happy to help out wherever I can. Even if it's only fixing fences." Calluses would be in her future if she helped fix fences. She had seen them on Mark's hand when he opened the door for her. While her hands weren't used to manual labor, she'd still help. It was the least she could do if they really were going to put her up for the next two weeks and not accept any payment for her room and board.

"I'll let my father know about your offer. Thank you." He wasn't about to start telling her all their issues. Besides, he wanted to change the subject. Talking about sabotage and danger wouldn't make for a nice date.

"So, tell me about this rodeo and carnival." Callie had picked up on how uncomfortable he seemed when she brought their conversation back to the saboteurs.

She didn't want him worried. What she wanted was to have a good night. This was her chance to live out a Hallmark movie. Ending up with the cowboy wasn't going to happen, but she was going to enjoy her time in this setting and see what it was like to be a cowgirl in a romantic story.

Chapter 9

When they drove into the parking lot for the city festival grounds, Callie looked out the window in awe. There had to be hundreds of cars and trucks in the lot. She knew it was going to be an exciting night, and couldn't wait to get out of the truck.

A huge smile covered her face, and Mark couldn't help but feel her enthusiasm for the event. Her joy helped him to put the thoughts about the saboteurs out of his mind, if only for the evening.

The sounds of the excited cowboys and cowgirls swallowed them up, and she had to yell to be heard. "I can't believe all these people!" Callie hollered.

He nodded and smiled at her before taking her hand in his. "I don't want to lose you to the crowds."

She laughed and squeezed his hand.

When they got up to the gate, she headed toward the box office, but Mark pulled her back to the entrance line. "We already have tickets." He held up paper tickets in his hand.

"Alright, cowboy. How'd you get them already? Weren't you busy all day today on the ranch?" She hadn't seen anyone leave the grounds, but that didn't mean someone hadn't driven in and bought tickets early.

"A cowboy has to have some secrets." He grinned at her, and they inched their way forward.

Once they got to the front of the line, the ticket taker looked at their tickets and smiled. "Mr. Manning, thank you for joining us tonight. Please put these bands on to get your VIP access." The worker gave them blue bands and ushered them inside.

"VIP access?" Callie's brows raised in anticipation of how this had happened.

He chuckled. "Alright, I guess it's no secret. My family sponsors this event." He held up a hand. "We aren't the only ones. But we get VIP access and tickets for the entire three days." Mark shrugged.

"I should have known." She licked her lips and looked around for VIP signs. "So, where do we go?"

He pointed up. There was a large boxed area above the stadium seats. "Up there."

She whistled. "Sweet."

Once they had their bands on, he led her up to their seats.

"Wow, what a great view of the arena." She looked through the glass enclosure out over the dirt arena and could easily see the entire place without anything getting in the way of her view.

Her head tilted down, and she noticed the grandstands were already filling up. So far, in their boxed room which sat at least twenty chairs, they were the only ones there. "Are there going to be others in here with us?"

"Yes, my family will join us as well as a few other sponsors. There's other boxes next to us on either side that also seat twenty in each. All sixty seats will be full each night." Mark looked around. "My guess is everyone's in the banquet room."

He led her back out the door and then through another one behind them. It led to a large room on the back side of the stadium that overlooked what she had to describe as backstage. There were multiple trailers, trucks, and all sorts of metal fencing set up like a maze with animals all over the place. She could see cowboys with chaps and numbers on the backs of their safety vests.

There were also women dressed up in fancy cowgirl costumes next to their horses with matching saddles. She pointed to them. "Are they the barrel riders?"

Mark looked down and smiled. "Nope, they're entertainment. The barrel rider girls look like normal cowgirls. They'll be in wranglers and have numbers pinned to the backs of their shirts." He pointed to one on the outer edge. "There."

If Mark hadn't pointed her out, she would have thought the girl to just be a cowgirl sitting on a horse. She wasn't what Callie expected. The girl was pretty, with curly blond hair and a nice turquoise, button-up shirt, but she thought barrel riders were splashier.

Her attention was brought back to the room when she noticed a banquet table on one side with about ten people milling around it. She hadn't seen any of them before.

A pretty cowgirl with auburn hair walked toward them with a smile on her face and a handsome cowboy at her side. "Mark, where's everyone else?" Elizabeth hugged her brother.

Logan shook hands with his future brother-in-law. "Hey Mark."

"Elizabeth, Logan, I'd like to introduce you to Callie Houston. She's the one stayin' with us for a bit." He gestured to Callie.

"It's so nice to meet you. Mom told me all about you. Is it true you're stuck here for two weeks?" Elizabeth's smile calmed Callie, and she instantly liked the Manning girl.

"Thank you, it's nice to meet you as well. And I have to thank you for letting me use your boots. I don't think my tennis shoes would have survived one day here." Callie laughed.

"I'm just glad someone's getting some use out of them. Feel free to use anything in my closet. I doubt I'll need any of those clothes anymore."

"Lizzie, the rest of the family will most likely be a little late. We had an issue with a fence fallin' apart." Mark didn't want to announce to everyone in the room they were dealing with sabotage. At least not until they could talk to the sheriff.

Gossipmongers in this town were worse than teenaged rich girls with nothing better to do. The Diner Divas didn't even get the gossip right most of the time. Mark knew those ladies had nothing better to do than talk about everyone else's lives, but he hoped Elizabeth's new initiative would keep them too busy to spread other people's issues about town.

Elizabeth's brows furrowed, and Logan was about to ask when his father walked up the small group.

"Mark, it's good to see you. Since I've semi-retired I don't get to see you as much as I once did. You'd think that now that we're going to be family, we'd be spending more time together, but it seems to be the opposite." Mr. Hayes shook Mark's hand.

"Mr. Hayes..." Mark began.

"Mark, how many times do I have to tell you? It's Hank," he chided. Mr. Hayes turned toward Callie. "I don't think we've met yet, have we?"

"Pops, this is Callie Houston. She's staying at the Triple J while her car is being fixed. She's the one everyone's talking about." Mirth-filled eyes looked at Callie.

"People are talking about me?" Callie asked.

"Sadly, the Diner Divas heard about your car dying. Now it seems that you crashed into a fence and let a herd of cattle loose on the highway." Lizzie laughed and shook her head. "But don't worry, we're all working to set any rumor right."

"Wait, what? I never crashed. And I didn't get anywhere near a fence." She looked between Mark and his sister.

Elizabeth sighed. "One thing you need to learn about this town is that we have a *gossip girl* problem."

Callie couldn't keep her laughter from bubbling up. "What? You have a group of rich academy kids living here?"

Logan shook his head. "Worse. Four retired women with nothing better to do than sit around the diner and talk about everyone else. They don't mean to hurt anyone, they're just bored."

"Cindy Macon retired way too soon," Mr. Hayes said. "In fact, all of them should still be working. They aren't old enough to lounge the day away. That's why they gossip so horribly. And why most of what they spread around town isn't even accurate."

Callie rolled her eyes and realized gossip was the same no matter where you were. "Well, my car died on the way into town. There wasn't anything exciting about it. When the engine died, the car rolled to a stop." She shrugged. If that was exciting, then she was really worried about how she'd spend her time until the car was fixed.

"Is anyone saying anything about her staying with us?" Mark asked.

Elizabeth shook her head. "Thankfully, no one thinks anything about us helping out a stranger."

"How long will you be stuck in Beacon Creek?" Mr. Hayes asked.

Callie proceeded to explain the situation, and they all commiserated with her.

"Well, at least you'll get the best barbecue in the country while you're here," Logan joked.

"I heard it was the best in the world." Callie winked at Mark.

"She's not wrong," a new voice said as a tall cowboy walked up and joined their little group.

Everyone agreed.

"Calvin, this is Callie." Mark introduced Callie to one of the area ranchers.

"Nice to meet ya, little lady." He tipped his hat. "Where's your pa, Mark?"

"He's running late. But he'll be here." Mark turned to Callie. "Calvin's another sponsor, and he usually shares our box with us."

Calvin smiled. "Have you had a chance to check out tonight's dinner? My ranch supplied the pork for the pulled pork sandwiches." He stood taller and stuck out his chest. "We've got the world's best pork."

Everyone laughed good-heartedly.

"That sounds wonderful." Callie looked from Mark to the banquet table, and he nodded.

"Go ahead, I'll join you in just a moment."

Elizabeth and Logan went with her to sample the dinner supplied by the sponsors.

"Mark, I wanted to ask your father about some disturbing things we've had happen lately on our ranch." Calvin paused. "Are you having any trouble?"

Mark looked around and whispered, "Yes, we are. I suggest you come over tomorrow and talk with my dad about the issues. I don't think this is the best place to discuss them."

Calvin looked around and nodded. "Agreed. I'll ask the sheriff to join me."

"Let's make it a barbecue. I'm sure my parents will be happy to have you all over for lunch." Mark noticed Mr. Johnson eyeing him cautiously, so he smiled and acted as though he was just offering up a lunch to a friend.

Callie stopped in front of the tables of food and gawked. "There's so many options here. It's not just pulled pork sandwiches." She looked at the various plates of pork dishes.

When she pointed to the simmering pot with beans and barbecue sauce, Elizabeth said, "You have to try Calvin's baked beans. They're the best in the world."

The three of them laughed, and Callie had to stop herself from snorting. If everything they saw was going to be *the best in the world*, she'd end up needing new clothes to fit her expanding waistline.

"But seriously," Elizabeth continued, "everything made with bacon is pretty darn good."

Callie nodded. "True. Do you have bacon-wrapped chocolate?"

Logan shook his head and sighed. "Sadly, we don't. We only have chocolate-dipped bacon."

Callie giggled and looked for the treat. She liked these people. They had a great sense of humor, and she felt instantly comfortable with them. If she lived close by, she knew they would all become fast friends.

"Well, I haven't had chocolate-dipped bacon, so I won't have anything to compare it to, but I'll give it a try." With a serious face, she began filling up a plate with the various pork options, and even added some green beans that looked to have little bits of crumbled bacon on them to her plate. Once it was full, she went to the dessert table and added three pieces of the chocolatey bacon to the top of her plate.

Mark walked up and gave her a questioning glance.

"What? There's so much to eat here, I thought I'd start with dessert and make my way backward." Callie grinned at the cowboys next to her.

Another man she hadn't met yet picked up two of the chocolate-dipped pieces of bacon and added them to his plate. "That's a mighty fine idea, miss." He nodded at her and then joined his group of friends on the other side of the room sitting at a round table for eight.

She pointed to the man's back as he walked away. "See, I'm not the only who thinks it's a good idea to have dessert first."

Mark shook his head. "Alright, you've convinced me." He put four pieces of the chocolatey pork on his plate and took a bite of one before putting anything else on his plate. "Mmm, you're right. Dessert first is perfect." He put the last bite of the dessert into his mouth and gave her a closed-mouth grin.

Once everyone had their plates of food, they went to an empty table and sat down to eat. No one mentioned the troubles again. They all chatted about the rodeo and who was performing. Some of the men made silly bets about who would win.

If Mark lost, he'd have to wear his sister's dress into the general store. But if Logan lost, he'd have to spend a day working in place of Mark on the ranch. Callie thought it was a good bet. She hoped they both lost so she could see each of them making good on their silly wagers.

Everyone was in the box waiting for the first event to begin. It was for the little kids, though Callie had never heard of "mutton bustin'."

Kids aged five through seven who weighed under fifty-five pounds could come out of a stall riding a sheep. Mark said it was the kids' equivalent of riding a bull. The sheep bounced around; a couple even bucked a bit to rid their backs of their riders. The kids wore protective gear, including helmets, and several adults were close by each one.

As the event came to a close, everyone in the box stood up and began to mingle while they waited for the arena to be changed out for the next event.

The one that stood out in her mind the most was of a little girl with long, blonde pigtails. Her sheep—or mutton—flew out of the chute with her white-knuckling the strap around the animal with one hand, and the other in the air just like a bull rider.

The sheep ran one way and then another around the arena. On the opposite side inside the fence were all the other sheep who had already performed, just milling about.

When the little girl's sheep got near the bunch, her sheep bucked, but she stayed on its back. The rest of the sheep bayed and moved away from them. Then all of a sudden, the sheep just fell over and lay on the ground. At first Callie thought something was wrong with the poor animal, until the audience went wild.

The little girl had lasted longer than eight seconds, the minimum requirement.

They both lay there motionless for a few seconds. But before the animal could hurt her, she jumped up and waved her hands in the air. Then the sheep stood up and rambled away. It was as though they were both momentarily stunned, or the sheep thought it could get away with playing possum. Callie wasn't sure which.

It didn't matter; the little girl won first place, and the entire arena cheered her on. Even Callie got on her feet and roared with the crowd.

The rest of the Manning family didn't show up until after the first event. She was still laughing at some of the images that stayed in her mind of those little tykes riding sheep.

When Mr. Manning entered, Mark walked over to meet his family. Then he pulled his dad to the back corner. Callie couldn't hear what they were saying, which was probably a good thing. If she couldn't hear, then neither could anyone else. She didn't want the Mannings to have to deal with gossip. Not after everything that had happened in the past twelve hours.

She didn't even know what else had been going on, just that there were other instances of issues. If she wanted to help, she'd have to wait until they were back at the ranch and could talk without prying ears overhearing.

Luke sat down in Mark's seat and put his arm around the back of her chair. "Well hello there, little lady."

When he smiled, she couldn't help but laugh. "Luke, you know I'm here with Mark tonight, right?"

He nodded. "But it seems to me he left you all alone." He put a hand to his chest. "I wouldn't leave you alone if you were my date."

"Hey Luke, you had your time with her this mornin'. Tonight's my time." Mark pulled his brother by his shirt collar.

Luke put his hands in the air. "I'm goin', I'm goin'." Once he was standing, he looked his brother in the eye. "You might want to rethink leavin' such a pretty date all alone." He winked and walked away.

She was afraid that if she let this go on much longer, the two brothers might get into a real fight. While it definitely bolstered her ego, she wasn't about to get in between brothers.

Mark was right about one thing: Luke had his date with her earlier, and now it was Mark's turn. Callie needed to give him his time and her attention. When the night was over, she'd have to tell them both she only wanted to be friends. No matter how bright their smiles were, she couldn't want more.

If there was a chance it could become a real romance, she might consider choosing one of them, but since it would only be a two-week flirtation, she didn't want to cause a rift between the brothers. It wasn't worth it, no matter how gorgeous they both were.

Mark took his seat and frowned. "I'm sorry. My brother can be so immature sometimes."

Callie bit her lip. Both cowboys were being immature. Fighting over a girl was childish. And Mark had done his share of trying to hone in on her date that morning with Luke. Instead of arguing the point, she focused on the rodeo. "What's up next?"

He looked down at the arena and smiled. "Ladies' barrel racing is up next. Then there's some entertainment with the trick riders. And after that is the first round of bull riding."

"I've seen barrel racing on TV before. It looks really fun." Callie had never thought she would ride a horse, let alone compete on the back of one, but if she was being honest with herself, she may have had a fantasy or two about barrel racing. But after her experience earlier in the day, she wasn't sure that would ever happen.

The rest of the evening went by so fast, Callie couldn't believe it was all over. The carnival was still open, but the rodeo was done for the night. All the horses and animals were led out to their stalls or pens.

"Well, do you think you'll want to come back tomorrow night?" Mark looked hopeful.

She wasn't sure if he was asking her on another date or suggesting she join him and his family as a friend. She was going to have to tell him soon what she had decided.

"What about the carnival? As much as I want to see more of the rodeo, I don't want to miss out on the carnival, either." She looked to Elizabeth and waved her over.

"I hear you helped to plan the carnival each year. Will you be over there tomorrow? Do you need any help?" Callie figured if she could hang out with Elizabeth, then she wouldn't have to worry about the guys trying to pin her down for a date.

Elizabeth looked between Callie and Mark, then over to Luke. The smirk on the sister's face was enough to convince Callie that she understood. "Actually, I'm going to enjoy the evening with a few of my friends. But you're totally welcome to join us."

Callie shook her head. "Oh, I don't want to intrude, especially if it's a date night for you and Logan." She motioned between the engaged couple.

Logan held up a hand. "Not at all. I'll be over here watching the rodeo with the guys." He looked at his Lizzie. "But when it's over, you promised me a ride on the Ferris wheel."

Elizabeth wrapped her arms around Logan. "Of course." She kissed his cheek.

Matthew said, "Oh, not again. Come on guys. I know your weddin' is just around the corner, but can you cut out the PDA? Please?"

Mr. and Mrs. Manning laughed, and Caleb leaned down and kissed his wife on the lips. "Oh, I don't know. I think it's a great idea. What do you say? Wanna head to the Ferris wheel now?" His eyebrows rose up and down suggestively.

Mrs. Manning giggled like a school girl whose crush had finally noticed her.

"Ugh, of course you would. You and Ma are totally, madly in love." Mark shook his head.

He looked at Callie. "Sorry, my family can be a bit touchy-feely sometimes. Not very cowboy of our men to act this way."

"I think it's sweet." Callie sighed. She wasn't into public displays of affection, but to see a couple who had been married as long as the Mannings was romantic.

Mark raised his eyebrows. "Really?"

When he took two steps closer to her, Callie pushed back and laughed. "Only for married couples."

He stepped back and chuckled. "Okay, I see how it is."

"Do you?" She narrowed her eyes at him.

Mark blinked and tilted his head. "Hm, did you want to go home now? Or..."

Luke interrupted. "Mark, we have to be up early tomorrow if we want to fix that line of fence."

"I think I'm getting tired. It's been a long day." Callie agreed it was time to head back. Not that she didn't like being with Mark, but she didn't want to give him the wrong idea.

Before they left the group, Elizabeth called out, "Callie, I'll call you tomorrow and we can set up a time for tomorrow night. It's going to be a lot of fun. You're going to love my friends."

"Yeah, that sounds great. Thank you." Callie smiled and realized she really was looking forward to spending the evening with Elizabeth and her friends. If she was going to be here for two weeks, it would be nice to have some girlfriends.

On the way back to the ranch, Callie decided that was probably the best time to broach the subject. When they got inside, she doubted they'd have any time alone to talk.

A nervous flutter rolled around her belly, and she wondered why she was nervous. This was something she needed and wanted to do. So why did something seem off?

Chapter 10

Callie wanted to just blurt out that she wasn't interested, but she knew that would hurt his feelings. Plus, it was just plain rude. She'd have to find a way to let him down lightly.

"Mark, I had a really great time tonight with you and your *family*." If she stressed the word *family* a little bit, she hoped it wouldn't offend him while still getting the point across.

He smiled and kept his eyes on the road. "Yeah, they're pretty cool. I got lucky."

She thought about that. He *was* lucky. His family was great. They made her feel so welcome that she felt comfortable being with them, and she'd only met them last night. Had it only been yesterday since she met them? Callie shook her head.

If she wasn't careful, she'd have a tough time leaving them in only two weeks.

"You really did. My family's great, but I only have an older sister. And we're so far apart in age we aren't close."

"Are you close with your parents?" Mark asked.

She nodded, then realized the dark cab was barely highlighted by the lights on the dashboard. He couldn't have seen her gesture. "Yeah, we are."

Callie looked outside and noticed the blanket of stars. Even with the lights from the truck, the sky was full of stars. When a shooting star passed by, she closed her eyes and made a wish.

"Whoa! Hold on." Mark put and arm in front of her when he slammed on his breaks.

Her eyes flew open, and she looked around expecting to see cattle on the road, or some other animal. But when the road was totally clear, she turned confused eyes on the driver. "What happened?"

The truck slowly moved backward. Mark looked over his shoulder out the back window. "I saw someone on the side of the road."

Callie turned in her seat to see if she could spot anyone back there. She couldn't. But what she did see caused her heart to jump. "I thought your family fixed the fence. And wasn't it closer to the house than this spot?"

He nodded. "Yup, this is new. Stink!" He pounded the steering wheel. "Stay here and lock the doors. I have to check this out." He grabbed a flashlight from under his seat.

"Wait," Callie called, but Mark didn't stop.

He jumped out his door and closed it.

She hit the door lock button and took off her seatbelt so she could watch him. He strode with purpose, and the beam from his flashlight moved back and forth as he walked toward the hole in the fence.

On the other side were several heads of cattle lying in the tall grasses.

Callie sent up a prayer of thanks that the cattle hadn't left the pasture yet. Maybe they could get help and fix this before any of the herd got out. "Lord, what's going on here? Why is someone purposely breaking their fences?"

She pulled her cell phone out of her purse and was grateful Mrs. Manning had given her all their numbers. Mr. and Mrs. Manning had a romantic ride on the Ferris wheel planned, so she called Matthew.

"Hello?" The voice on the other end of the phone sounded confused. He most likely didn't know it was Callie calling him.

"Matthew? It's Callie. Are you on your way home?" She continued to scan the area for anyone who might jump out and try to hurt Mark.

"Just leaving. What's wrong?" His voice got husky.

"We stopped on the side of the road just past the Johnson ranch, where your fence begins. Someone ran it in again. There's cattle on the other side, and Mark got out to investigate."

"Shoot. Are you safe?" A Toby Keith song sounded in the background before Matthew turned it off.

"I'm locked in the cab of the truck. It's Mark I'm worried about. He's outside with nothing more than a flashlight. Hurry." She didn't like the pleading sound in her voice, but it couldn't be helped.

If Mark had seen a person on the side of the road messing with the fence when they first passed it, then where was that person? And did he have a weapon?

"Alright, I'm only about ten minutes from the Johnson ranch. I'm going to hang up and call the sheriff. Luke left before me, so he might see you soon. He'll stop if he sees a truck on the side of the road. I'll call you back after I reach the sheriff." Matthew's voice sounded calmer, like a manager detailing what needed to be done on the job.

"Okay, I'll keep an eye out for Luke. Thanks." She hung up and scanned the area for anyone out there besides Mark. She couldn't see anything in the dark. If only it was a full moon, then there'd be more light.

She got an idea, but wasn't sure if it was smart. Callie scooted over into the driver's seat and put the truck in gear. She did a three-point turn and directed the truck's lights to where Mark was. Doing this made her position on the road such that she was blocking the other side, but she figured if anyone was coming the other way, they'd see her with plenty of time to stop.

Mark gave her a thumbs-up, and she sighed with relief. She had done the right thing. And she could

see him plainly. But that didn't stop her from looking around for anyone else.

A distant sound grabbed her attention, and she
looked in the direction of town. Headlights coming
toward her slowed, and the vehicle pulled up next
to her passenger window. Since it was a truck, she
hoped it was Luke, or someone else heading out to
the Triple J Ranch.

She pushed the button to lower the window.

The other window lowered, and she saw a scowl on
Luke's face. "What's wrong? Where's my brother?"

Callie pointed to where she had last seen Mark.
"He was right there. Did Matthew call you?"

He nodded and put his truck in gear before turning off his engine. Then he got out and came to her
side of the truck. "I don't see him."

She lowered her driver's side window.

"Luke!" Mark yelled out.

"Go!" Callie pushed Luke's shoulder to run toward
his brother's voice.

Without a backward glance, he took off toward the
voice.

Callie wasn't sure what she should do. If she had
a weapon she could join them, but if someone else
came along the road, she needed to be there to
tell them what was going on. Indecision tore at
her until she heard rustling and another scream. It
didn't sound like Mark, but she didn't know him
well enough to know his scream. It could have been
Luke's, for all she knew.

"Screw this." Callie rolled up both windows, turned off the truck, and got out. She left the lights on and hoped they would stay on and not automatically turn off after a minute like so many of the newer vehicles did.

"Mark! Luke!" she called out when she stepped off the paved road and onto the soft dirt. She heard rustling just ahead of her and wished she had turned the vehicle a little more to the left so she could have seen what was happening.

As she got closer, she saw three people wrestling on the ground. They had all lost their hats somewhere, but she was able to make out which of the men were Mannings. To her right was Mark's flashlight. She ran to it and picked it up.

The guys were rolling around, and now that she had the flashlight shining on them, she could see that the stranger was a mess. He was all dirty and wearing grimy clothes. He looked as though he hadn't bathed or changed clothes in weeks.

Mark and Luke each worked together to pin the stranger down on the ground.

"Let me go!" the man on the ground screamed. "You don't know who you're messing with. He's going to get you, just you wait and see!"

The man was a lunatic. He had to be. Callie watched as the crazy man screamed and tried to get out of Mark and Luke's control.

"Who is he? Do you know him?" Callie asked. She kept the strong flashlight off to the side so as not to blind anyone, but enough of the high beam shone on all three men that she was able to see everything going on.

In the distance she heard the scream of a siren coming closer, and when she turned her head she could also see the flashing red and blue lights of the sheriff's vehicle.

"He's the one who just destroyed our fence line," Mark said.

"And probably the same one who broke the fence earlier today," Luke added through gritted teeth.

The man on the ground kept trying to move about enough to get out of their grip, but the boys were practically lying on the man to keep him down.

"How does he have so much strength? I don't get it," Callie said.

Mark and Luke were both strong men; she'd seen some of the work they did on the ranch, and even felt Mark's bicep earlier. There was no way a scrawny man like the one on the ground could weasel out of their hands, let alone a full-body pin down. But if it weren't for Luke joining Mark, he probably would have gotten away.

"Probably on some sort of drug. His eyes are crazed, and he's wicked strong," Luke added.

A screeching sound behind her brought her attention back to the sheriff's truck, which stopped right in front of Mark's truck. The headlights from the police vehicle shone brightly on everyone, and she had to put a hand in front of her face to protect her eyes.

"What's goin' on here?" a deep male voice boomed from behind Callie.

Another man walked next to who she assumed was the sheriff. Both were in the brown-and-green uniforms of the sheriff's office.

Mark looked up quickly and then back down to his captive. "I caught this man breaking our fence tonight. Someone broke another one earlier. If I hadn't stopped tonight, we would have lost several hundred head of cattle."

"I heard about some of the events happenin' on the Triple J." The sheriff nodded to his deputy.

The deputy walked over to the three men. "Get him up on his feet and we'll bring him in."

"Hey, I didn't do this. You don't have any proof." The criminal spewed a few vulgar words that had Callie's ears burning.

"We don't take too kindly to men speaking like that in front of ladies. You'll shut your mouth if you know what's good for you," the deputy said.

"You'll let me go if you know what's good for you!" The criminal still on the ground tried to spit, but the saliva ended up back on his own face. He wiggled around and caused Mark to almost lose his grip, but the cowboy lay flat on the man.

"He thinks he's someone important and that if we don't let him go, we'll bring the wrath of God down on us, or some sort of nonsense." Luke chuckled and tightened his grip on the man.

"Just what we need, another tweaker. What drugs are you on?" The sheriff leaned over, and his nose scrunched when he got a whiff of the man. "And when was the last time you bathed?"

"You might want to hose him off before you put 'm in a cell," Mark quipped.

"And we'll need to hose out the truck after we take him in, too," the deputy joked.

"You joke, but that's going to be your duty tomorrow, Deputy." The sheriff flicked the underside of his hat's brim and grinned.

Callie watched in horror as it took three grown, large men to get the criminal up off the ground. The man got his hand loose and tried to punch Luke, but he blocked it, and the deputy grabbed the man's loose hand.

It took all three of them to get the guy up to the sheriff's truck and get him handcuffed. Then it took the deputy and the sheriff both to force the man into the back seat.

The deputy was reading the man his rights while the sheriff spoke to Mark and Luke.

Once they gave him their version of events, the sheriff came over to Callie. "Howdy, ma'am. I'll need your statement as well."

"I didn't see much. I stayed in the truck when Mark got out until I heard screaming." She continued to tell him her story and he wrote down some notes, but also recorded their conversation on his smart phone.

"Alright, I'll have more questions tomorrow, but why don't y'all get home and get some rest? Come by the station tomorrow later in the morning." The sheriff put his phone and notepad in his pockets and turned back to his truck.

"We can't leave the fence line like this," Matthew said. He had arrived while everyone was giving their statements and stood off to the side, waiting until they were done.

"Agreed," Luke and Mark both said.

"I'll head home and get some wire to temporarily fix it. Then we'll have to come back out here at first light and properly mend it," Mark said. "And I can take Callie home at the same time."

Everyone agreed. Matthew and Luke stayed by the fence to keep the cattle from leaving while Mark and Callie headed home.

"Is it always so crazy around here?" Callie didn't think this was normal for the country, but what did she know? She was a self-proclaimed city girl.

Mark shook his head. "No, but we do hear stories of cattle rustlers once in a while. Ranchers who regularly check their fence lines tend to avoid gettin' hit, but it can happen."

"Do you think that's what this is about?" Callie chewed her lower lip.

He thought about it for a moment. "No, I think it's about somethin' else." His country drawl was coming through strongly, but the anger in his voice from earlier had settled, and now he only seemed frustrated.

"What?" Callie turned her gaze to the man behind the wheel.

He scratched the scruff growing on his chin. "We've made a few enemies in Bozeman recently, trying to help the women on the streets get cleaned up." He pointed behind him. "That man, I think he's a homeless man working for Big Bart."

Callie snickered. "Big Bart? Really?"

"Yeah, it's a lame name. But he's big and controls most of the homeless population in Bozeman through intimidation and, at times, beatin's." Mark winced when he thought about Ana and how many times Bart and his goons had hurt her.

"I'll admit, I don't know much about the homeless. But aren't most of them there because they don't want to work?" Callie hoped she wasn't being callous, but she really didn't know anything other than what she saw on the news. Sure, she'd seen some in St. Paul, but she mostly ignored them. Except for when it was women with small children. Then she gave them money.

She also volunteered once a year for an organization that put together care packages for the homeless. She never interacted with the homeless people who used the services, she just put food and clothing items into a box or bag that was later distributed to those who needed it. The woman who ran the agency did tell her that sometimes they gave their boxes or bags of food and clothing essentials to very low-income families who needed a little extra help. So she wasn't always helping just the homeless.

Mark tilted his head and thought. "Sure, that's the case for some. But most are on the street because they either had no one to help them, and for some strange reason didn't qualify for help from any agencies. Then there's those who have serious mental issues. If our government identified them, they'd be in a mental institution."

"Wouldn't that be better for them?" Callie asked.

"I don't know. I think for some it would be the best place. Especially those who are criminally insane. But for a lot, they just need counseling and maybe some medication. Locking them up in a padded room won't always help." Mark had been looking into what some of those he met in Bozeman needed.

While there were some services out there, they didn't help all homeless people. The veterans could get help from the VA, but they had to ask. Most VA centers didn't send people out to scour the streets for homeless vets. He wasn't sure that was what was needed, either. He did know that the Kalispell VA center had a large number of vets they were helping. Some lived there, and some just came in once or twice a month for help.

He didn't know what everyone needed, but he did know that they *didn't* need Bart.

Callie winced. "I guess the situation is more complicated than I ever realized, isn't it?" Callie knew there were services out there for those who needed a little helping hand to keep them from having to live on the streets. Maybe not all cities had such organizations?

And maybe she just didn't know as much as she thought she did.

Chapter 11

Cock-a-doodle-doo was *not* what came out of real roosters.

Callie lay in bed the next morning, holding a pillow over her head to keep the sound of the stupid rooster outside her window from her ears.

"Move along. I don't need your help to wake up," she mumbled into the pillow.

Where was a good boot and an open window when you needed one?

The rooster wasn't going to stop any time soon, if cartoons were any indication. The sun wasn't even up yet. Or at least, she didn't think it was. The curtains in her room were drawn, and she couldn't see any sunlight peeking around the edges yet.

Yesterday she'd slept in—if you called six am sleeping in—and didn't hear the annoying fowl outside her window. Maybe this was unusual? How did farmers and ranchers deal with roosters who went off *before* the sun rose?

"Earplugs? Is that the solution?" She knew she was basically talking to herself, but she didn't care. It was o'dark-thirty in the morning, and after being up so late the night before and then taking forever to calm her brain enough to fall asleep, she must have only had three or four hours of sleep.

Thank goodness for audiobooks. She would listen to something entertaining when she couldn't get to sleep. It helped her focus on something else, and eventually she would go to sleep.

Her app had a timer she could set, and it would turn off on its own, hopefully right as she was falling asleep. However, last night, she continued to turn it back on for a couple hours. That was the longest it had ever taken her to get to sleep.

The rooster kept crowing its high-pitched, grating noise into her window. It had to be sitting right under the ledge outside her room. It was so loud, she probably couldn't even drown it with a radio turned up full blast.

"Ugh, he's never going to shut up, is he?" she asked the empty room.

The rooster responded in the affirmative. Or at least, that was what it sounded like to her.

"Fine, I get it." She sighed and threw her covers off.

After taking a long, hot shower, she got ready and went out into the kitchen. She had been right: the rooster jumped the gun and had been crowing before the sun was up.

The kitchen was full of Manning men all eating breakfast and drinking coffee.

"Mornin'," the room said in unison.

"How do you all sleep through the racket of your rooster?" Callie went to the counter to get herself a cup of coffee. "Hmm." She breathed in the pungent aroma and began to feel herself waking up.

Everyone chuckled.

"Ol' Red was outside your window this morning?" Matthew chuckled. "Welcome to the family."

Mrs. Manning put a plate of scrambled eggs, bacon, and hash browns in front of her. "Eat up, honey." She patted Callie's back.

Callie bowed her head and prayed for God to bless her breakfast and to help the Manning family deal with their saboteur. And she may have even prayed that the stupid rooster would stay away from her window. But she'd never admit that to anyone but God.

"Does he do that to everyone?" Callie asked between bites of heavenly bacon.

"Pretty much. Ol' Red has taken it as his duty to ensure everyone is up in time for chores," Luke chimed in.

"But he was outside my window before the sun even came up," Callie complained.

Mark chuckled. "Callie, what time do you think it is?"

She hadn't bothered to look at the clock. In fact, her vision was pretty blurry until she began drinking her coffee. Callie pulled her phone out of her pocket and her eyes widened in shock. It was already after seven am.

Callie's eyes squeezed shut and opened a few times, and she looked again. "How is it so late? And why are all of you still here?"

Mr. Manning answered, "We were all up before dawn and out to fix the fence properly. Judith held breakfast for us until we got back."

Callie slumped back in her chair. "I guess the curtains in my room really work to keep the sun out, huh?"

Everyone chuckled. "Yup."

"Aren't you all tired?" Callie looked around, but didn't see any bags under anyone's eyes. She had no clue how they could have functioned on only a few hours of sleep.

"Sure, but we're used to getting up so early," Roman responded.

John added, "Plus, we took a thermos of coffee with us. I think we're on the third pot of coffee already this morning."

Callie nodded. "Yes, more coffee, please." She tipped her cup back and finished it off before getting up to refill her mug.

"So, other than being woken up by the world's loudest and most annoying rooster, how'd ya sleep?" Mark asked.

She shrugged as she finished her bite of eggs. "Not bad, once I got to sleep."

Mrs. Manning gave her a sympathetic look. "You could take a nap today, if you like."

"I don't normally nap, but I might have to if I'm going out with Elizabeth tonight." Callie dug into her food and realized it had helped to wake her up and given her the energy she needed.

An uncomfortable feeling stole over the room. Callie lifted her head from her plate. "What?"

Mr. Manning cleared his throat. "Girls' night has been cancelled."

At first, Callie was confused. Then realization dawned. "Because of this Big Bart character?"

"Yes. Logan doesn't want Elizabeth out of his sight. Especially at the carnival. With so many strangers in town, it would be difficult to recognize danger before it was too late." Mr. Manning got up to refill his mug. "Anyone else want a top-off?"

Three mugs went in the air, and Mr. Manning chuckled. "I would have thought you'd all have had enough coffee by now." But he went ahead and filled them all.

When he was done, the pot was empty, so he began to make a fresh one.

"Is everyone going to the rodeo tonight? Or the carnival?" Callie asked. It wasn't that she minded staying back at the ranch, but if anyone else was going, she wanted to tag along.

"We're gonna split up in groups. Half will stay close to the ranch tonight, and the other half will go to the rodeo and carnival. But no one is to be out alone," Matthew said.

Mr. Manning added, "And I would prefer it if you stayed close to at least two of us while you're here. I don't want to take a chance at Bart and his gang seeing you as a way to get to us."

"This Bart character is pretty dangerous, huh?" Callie furrowed her brows. She'd dealt with bullies before. The best method was to stand up for yourself. Bullies were looking for the weak ones who didn't stand up for themselves. Her experience taught her that after she stood up to them once or twice, they left her alone.

Mark scowled. "Very. We've seen the evidence of his temper. He enjoys beatin' up women who don't do what he says."

"So he's more than just a bully—he's a true criminal?" Callie knew how to defend herself, but she doubted the Mannings would be comfortable giving her a gun. And she doubted they had a stun gun.

Back home in Louisiana, her father had taught her how to use a Taser. And she was even licensed to carry one. Before she left on her trip, she decided to leave it in her St. Paul apartment. Now she wished she would have traveled with it.

While she could have easily bought a gun, she didn't want to take the chance she would use a real gun in self-defense and kill someone. Instead, she decided that a stun gun would work just fine to defend herself from a home invasion. Guns were all fine and everything, but it wasn't something she wanted to carry.

A Taser was much more to her liking. Even though it wouldn't work long distance, it would keep her personally safe if someone tried to attack her. The only reason she left it at home was because some cities still had issues with them. While driving across various states, she didn't want to have to check each city ordinance on the road to make sure she wasn't breaking a law.

Now she wished she did.

"Last night, I saw a lot of people carrying guns in holsters. Isn't that illegal? Or is it easy to get permits?" Callie knew most states didn't require a permit for shotguns, but for a handgun there were different laws based on different states.

"No, ma'am. You're in Big Sky Country now. We proudly bear arms here," Roman stated.

"Well, you have to have a permit to carry a concealed weapon, but that's fairly simple to get as long as you're a law-abidin' citizen," Matthew added.

"I guess that makes sense. So, what? You'll all be carrying tonight?" Callie wasn't sure if she was comfortable with them all having guns, only because she didn't know them well.

"We'll be carryin' handguns and shotguns from here on out." Mr. Manning paused. "Well, until the criminals are caught and it's safe once again to roam the land without a weapon to defend ourselves with."

"Back home, I have a Taser I keep in my apartment," Callie admitted.

"Really?" Mrs. Manning's eyes brightened, and she looked at Callie, waiting for more.

"My dad's a police detective. I was raised on the gun range, but I feel more comfortable with a Taser." She didn't want to explain her reasoning; they probably wouldn't understand. Her parents didn't get it. They thought she'd be better off with a small handgun like a .22 in her purse. But she never wanted to carry.

All the men sat up straighter.

Luke smiled. "Really? How about we go out to our range and you show me what you got?"

Callie took a deep breath. "I guess I could. What sort of handguns do you have?"

They all spent the next few minutes discussing the merits of each type of gun the Mannings possessed.

After breakfast, Matthew, Mark, Luke, and Callie all went into town to see the sheriff and give more detailed versions of what happened the day before. It didn't take long, since none of them really knew much. Mark and Luke had the most to say, thanks to their skirmish with the drugged-up saboteur.

They all made it back in plenty of time for lunch.

After lunch, Luke met Callie out back with his horse and Whiskers all saddled. Both horses wore several long bags over their sides. Luke's saddle also held a shotgun holster with a weapon in it.

She raised her brows. "Expecting trouble on the way to your range?"

He shrugged. "Pops said we all have to carry now, no matter how close we are to the house. Even Ma has a handgun she's wearing when she leaves the house."

Callie wondered if she should call her dad and ask him for a ticket home while her car was being fixed. Things were escalating pretty quickly around here. Not that she was chicken and wanted to run away, but this wasn't her fight.

Luke helped her into her saddle, and they took off toward a part of their property they had fenced off for their firing range.

Both of them enjoyed a casual ride with small talk. Neither wanted to discuss the problems with Bart, or whoever it was targeting them. Instead, Luke regaled her with tales of his younger brother, John. He had spent two years on the rodeo circuit before deciding he would never be a championship bull rider and decided to come home before he was seriously injured.

John seemed like a quiet guy, and Callie couldn't imagine him doing one of the most dangerous careers out there. No wonder the entire family was so into rodeo that they sponsored the local event. John had probably gotten his start at the Beacon Creek Rodeo when he was younger. Maybe he was even one of those cute kids who tried their hands at mutton bustin'.

Once they arrived, Luke began the process of unfolding and preparing the various weapons he'd brought with him. "I thought you might want to try a recurve bow, since you seem to like unconventional weapons."

The fact that Luke had paid attention to what she said about her preference for a Taser spoke volumes about the kind of man he was. Callie had never used a bow, but had wanted to try her hand after watching a certain series of movies where the heroine preferred a bow and arrow.

"Thank you, Luke. That was very thoughtful. Now, how do I use this thing?" Callie dismounted the horse on her own and walked to where Luke stood holding the bow.

He showed her how it worked, and they spent the next hour practicing with it, until Callie hit a few arrows close to the bulls-eye.

"Very nice. You have a natural gift for the bow. With a little more practice, you could be an expert." Luke smiled and began to put the bow and arrows away in his saddle. "Now, how about showing me your talent with firearms?"

Chapter 12

That night Callie found herself back in the box at the rodeo with the Manning family. Well, half of the Manning family. Mr. and Mrs. Manning stayed home with Mark and Roman.

Matthew, Luke, John, and Callie all rode together in Matthew's midnight-blue Ford F-250 quad cab truck. All three cowboys had insisted she sit up front with Matthew while Luke and John sat in the back. She was grateful they were such gentlemen. The last thing she wanted was for Luke to think this was another date.

Earlier in the day when they were out on the range, he didn't act like that was any sort of date, to her relief. With the craziness of the night before, she hadn't had a chance yet to tell the guys she only wanted to be friends.

Now that they were in the same boxed seating as the night before, Luke took the chair next to her. Matthew and John sat on her other side. She could take that as them protecting her. She knew Matthew wasn't into her. And she and John had barely spoken to each other, so it only made sense Luke would sit next to her and John on the other side of Matthew.

The moment they entered the rodeo, John seemed like a completely different cowboy. He was talking about the different men who'd be riding that night, and who he wanted to see win. Both Matthew and Luke knew exactly who he was talking about.

These cowboys talked about rodeo like most men in the city talked about football or basketball. They had their heroes and those they didn't care for. In one sense, it was comforting to hear them talk about sports, but since she didn't know much about rodeo, she couldn't really participate in their discussions.

Instead, she looked out the window and watched as the arena was set up for the kids' roping competition. This was the event she most wanted to see that night. Young kids, eight to twelve years old, would ride out on their horses and try to rope a calf their own. Most of the contestants were boys, but there were a few girls who did it as well.

Once the evening got going, the Manning cowboys sat back and watched. It was so entertaining that it didn't take long before Callie was on her feet, rooting for each and every kid who participated. It didn't matter to her who won—all that mattered was each kid gave his or her best in this sport.

Maybe if she knew them she'd be more interested in who won, like the rest of the people in the room with her.

Next weekend, John was going to get his truck washed by Matthew thanks to a little side bet they'd placed with each other on who would win. Tommy, the little eleven-year-old boy who won, was the nephew of one of John's rodeo friends. John told everyone that Tommy's dad was a championship team roper, but Matthew wanted to see a different kid win.

Callie felt the stress of the day work its way out of her tight muscles, and she laughed and cheered the night away as each event came through. She even allowed herself to enjoy the bull riding. That was the one sport no one bet against John on. He told them who he thought would move forward to the finals the next night, and he was right.

When the rodeo was over, they all agreed a quick trip through the carnival was in order. Elizabeth and Logan had joined them, and they all headed to the Ferris wheel.

Callie thought she'd have a permanent smile plastered on her face for the rest of the night. Everything was going so well. Luke wasn't acting like it was a date, and no one mentioned Big Bart or any of his men. Everyone was joking and laughing, and they ate some of the best food she'd ever had.

Until she and Elizabeth went to the ladies' room. It wasn't like the cowboys could go with them. And the area where the porta-potties were located seemed like it would be safe enough. The carnival had security roving around, and no one thought there'd be any issues with the girls heading to bathroom by themselves.

Elizabeth and Callie had washed their hands in the portable sinks and were making their way back to where the guys waited for them. They never even saw the person hiding in the shadows.

"Don't scream, and don't call any attention on us," a man's voice said when he pointed a gun at Elizabeth.

Callie saw him less then a second before the man said anything, and she stepped back and pivoted. Before the man with the gun could even get Callie in his sights, she had swung back around with her leg and kicked the gun up in the air. It went off, and the man lost his grip on the pistol.

Everyone around them went running—except for those who were carrying guns of their own. Before their attacker could get the gun back in his hands, there were four guns pointed at his head.

"Whatcha gonna do, mister?" one woman with steely eyes said as she pointed her weapon at his head.

"I wouldn't mess with Bertha, she's a crack shot. And she's not afraid to shoot." A man in a black hat pointed his weapon at the man's chest and grinned at his prey.

Two more cowboys stood on the other side with their weapons aimed at the attacker.

He let out a string of cusswords and raised his hands. Two security guards pulled out plastic tie strips and basically cuffed the man and hauled him away.

"What's going on?" Callie asked as her eyes followed the security guards taking the gunman away.

Logan wrapped Elizabeth in his arms and held her tight. "I'm taking you back to the ranch now. Our night is over."

Elizabeth nodded but didn't say anything.

Luke put a hand on Callie's arm. "Are you alright? That was some kick."

Callie winced. "Yeah, I'm fine. These boots are great for kicking a weapon out of a man's hand and not hurting my foot. But why did someone pull a gun on Elizabeth? She's a regular veterinarian, right? You guys don't have a ranch of gangsters she's wronged somehow, do you?"

Luke chuckled. "No. This is Bart's doing, I'm sure."

Staring into Luke's eyes, she said, "But that would mean Elizabeth and your family are really messing with Bart's operation. I thought you only helped one woman get away from him?"

Matthew looked around. "Let's get in the truck before we talk more about this."

While keeping an eye on everyone and everything in their path back to the truck, the four of them left with Logan and Elizabeth on their trail. When they made it back to Matthew's truck, a deputy was waiting for them.

"Matthew, care to tell me what's going on?" The deputy took out his phone and stuck it in Matthew's face. "It seems your family is a magnet for danger this week."

They each took turns telling the deputy what happened, and finally an hour later they were all able to head home.

Callie twisted her hands in her lap, wondering how safe it was to do anything with the Mannings, even when there were guns around.

Matthew noticed her hands and put one of his on hers. "Don't worry, we'll keep you safe." He squeezed, and she smiled.

Luke piped up from the back. "It really isn't like this normally." He rubbed his chin. "Earlier, you asked about how much we had disrupted Big Bart's schemes."

Callie nodded.

"Well, we saved more than one lady. It's just that only one has come to stay with us so far. We've taken ten women from his control and sent them to various cities in the north. Some went straight home, but most are in other halfway houses, trying to find the help they need," Luke explained.

"W-what? You've helped get ten women off the street and back on the straight and narrow?" She knew they had done some nice things for the homeless, and that one had gotten off the streets, but she never in a million years thought they'd get ten women back into society.

"How long have you been working with the homeless in Bozeman?" Maybe they'd been doing it for years, and that was why they had such a high number? Impressive wasn't even close to what she was thinking. More like miraculous.

Matthew looked at Luke in the rearview mirror.

"I've only been home for a few months. I helped out last summer a little bit, but it's been mostly Elizabeth and Logan." John sat behind Callie so she couldn't see his face. The headrest on her seat blocked her view of him.

"Yup, it actually all started with Elizabeth and a few of her girlfriends. Then Chloe got involved at the same time as Logan did, and finally Mark, Luke, and I joined in when we heard about the trouble Big Bart was giving them. We've all discovered it's something we really enjoy doing." Matthew more than enjoyed it—it filled his soul, and his brothers had said the same thing when Elizabeth asked them why they kept helping her.

"Wow, it must be a huge project. I'd love to hear more about it and how it's working. But why does Bart care? That part makes no sense to me." Callie scratched the back of her neck and twisted in her seat to look at Luke.

"Bart runs the homeless population. And I mean the entire city of Bozeman's homeless. There are hundreds there. He's even imported them. We don't know exactly what they're up to, but one thing is for sure: every single dollar the homeless get from panhandling goes to Bart. They even have to run the clothes and food past Bart. He decides who gets what," Luke explained.

"Sounds like an extreme form of socialism. Like what I learned about the Soviet Union in college." Callie believed in sharing what she could with others who didn't have as much as she did, but disagreed that people should be forced to do it.

Growing up, her entire family would volunteer at the church and with local organizations like Christmas Angel. They would gather funds and toys to help kids in need. Giving assistance to children, especially, had always filled her with joy and a sense of accomplishment. God had given her so much in her life, and she believed He wanted her to share her excess.

Even the New Testament Saints had done it.

Just last month she had read in Acts about how the Saints sold their extra possessions and shared the money with the church—not by force. People gave of their own free will to help those who didn't have enough. While she didn't go that far, she did give money when she could, and definitely gave of her time.

Although, lately she'd been more focused on herself and her job concerns and hadn't volunteered at church in a while. She still went to services each week, but that was about all she did.

Matthew snorted. "Huh, I hadn't thought about it that way. But I guess Bart might see himself as a supreme leader. And he probably does think that everyone else should work while he sits back and directs them."

"But hasn't the crime rate gone up in Bozeman, too?" Luke asked.

"Not to mention the crime rate around here," John added.

Something about that didn't sit right with Callie. "Are you saying that just because there's more homeless in Bozeman than before, they're responsible for the crime going up?"

She understood that there were definitely criminal elements among the homeless, but not all of them were bad. Since coming to Beacon Creek and the Triple J Ranch, Callie had learned a lot just needed a helping hand.

Matthew shook his head. "Not at all. I think if the homeless are committing these crimes, it's because Bart is making them." He thought about his next words carefully. "I've been up to Bozeman a lot over the past year and talked with most of them that would talk to me, men and women both. Only a few are bad eggs. The rest want out, they just don't know how to do it."

"They told you they wanted out? Why didn't you take them all with you, then?" She couldn't believe Matthew would leave anyone behind who had asked him for help.

"Not in so many words, no. But I could see in their eyes when I asked why they stayed. Some stayed to protect friends who weren't ready to leave. Some had nowhere else to go, and most were afraid that Bart and his gang would find them and beat them to a bloody pulp. He's actually done that a few times." Anger permeated Matthew's entire being, and he gripped the steering wheel so hard his knuckles turned white.

"Sounds a lot more complicated than I ever imagined." Without knowing what to do to help these poor people, she said a quick prayer that God's will be done.

A whisper from Luke's side of the truck made it to her ears. "It really is."

No one spoke for the rest of the trip home. They all thought about what was happening and how they could stop Bart.

When they pulled into the long drive of their ranch, Matthew said, "I think Bart has help in the Bozeman sheriff's department."

Callie felt her breath catch, and she worried that Beacon Creek's local sheriff's office might also be on the take. "How well do you know everyone in your sheriff's department?"

"Our dad went to school with Sheriff Roscoe Blake, and I went to school with one of the deputies. The other two also grew up here on local ranches. I seriously doubt any of them would work with Bart and his gang." Matthew's confession helped to ease Callie's already shaken nerves.

Mr. Manning was already on the porch by the time they got out of the truck. "Sheriff Blake called me. Is everyone alright?" He looked his sons up and down, and then looked at Callie with concern evident in his eyes.

"I'm fine. Have you spoken with Elizabeth? She's the one who had the gun pointed at her."

Caleb Manning nodded. "Yes, she and Logan are on their way here. They went by her place to pick up some clothes and her truck. She's agreed to stay here until this is all handled."

"Good, it'll make it easier to protect the entire family if we're all together." Matthew walked up the steps and patted his dad on his shoulder as he walked past him.

"I think I could use some herbal tea. Anyone else want a cup?" Callie asked as she walked into the house.

Like the night before, it took Callie a long time to calm her brain so she could sleep. She prayed the loud, screeching fowl wouldn't be anywhere near her window the next morning.

Sadly, her prayer wasn't answered. Callie woke with a start when she heard the sound that was worse than nails raking down a chalkboard.

Knowing it would be useless to try and get back to sleep, she got up and decided she might as well get her day started.

After the incident with the gun at the carnival, none of them wanted to attend the carnival again, so they all stayed home the last night of rodeo.

On Sunday, Callie got up after a long night of sleep and got ready for church. Thankfully, Ol' Red wasn't at her window that morning. Did the rooster know it was Sunday and that they got to sleep in?

Once the entire family was inside the church, she realized they took up two pews on their own and chuckled.

Not that anyone actually had their names engraved on the pews, but it did seem like families sat in their own pews. She noticed a few people had left their Bibles on the pews, like they were saving seats. Callie wasn't sure if they had come in early and dropped off the Bibles to save their seats, or if they'd left them there since the last church service. Either way, it was the same in the end—they had their pew reserved.

Back in Louisiana, a lot of the octogenarians at her church liked to sit in the same exact spot each week. One week a new family was visiting, and they sat in Mrs. Pearl's spot before she arrived. The look Callie saw on her face was priceless, but she held her tongue and sat in the pew behind them. The next week, Mrs. Pearl was early and retook her seat. Maybe it was just that way in all small churches? Callie wasn't sure, since the church she attended in St. Paul was large and she rarely sat in the same spot each week. She sat in the same general area, just not always in the same spot. Most of her friends were the same.

The pastor of the Beacon Creek Baptist Church was a nice man, but he must have known what was going on. His sermon on vengeance belonging to God was very apropos.

Callie wasn't sure if the preacher was speaking directly to the cowboys in the church about Bart, or if it was just something God had told the man to preach on. Either way, she noticed several men squirming in their seats when the pastor read the passage in Romans 12:19. *Dearly beloved, avenge not yourselves, but rather give place unto wrath: for it is written, Vengeance is mine; I will repay, saith the Lord.*

On the way home from church, Matthew asked those in his truck if they had paid attention during the service. He, too, had thought the message very timely, and wondered if the pastor had chosen the topic after he heard about what was going on lately.

"Yeah, I heard," Mark grumbled.

"Me too," Luke added.

"Good, let's keep this in our hearts this week. I don't know what's going on, but since Friday night, we haven't had any issues with Bart and his gang."

Matthew had been out that morning checking the fence lines with his dad, and he didn't see any more issues.

The previous night, Mark and Luke had both taken a turn riding the perimeter and checking to make sure their bulls were in the right pastures. No issues so far.

"Do you think he's coming back for more trouble?" Callie asked.

"I don't know, but we have to be ready for anything," Luke answered.

The next few days went pretty much the same. She woke up early and spent her time with the Manning family, learning about working on a ranch in the morning, taking a nap after lunch, and then helping Mrs. Manning and Elizabeth make dinner in the afternoon and early evening. Usually at some point in the day she went for a ride with Luke.

Callie still hadn't had a chance to speak with Luke and Mark about their attentions, but if the past two days were any indication, she may not need to. Sure, they both liked sitting next to her whenever they got the chance, but they had stopped messing around and instead seemed to be in protective mode rather than competitive mode.

It was probably because of the situation. The danger made it a bit difficult to be amorous. And none of the brothers seemed to be playing jokes on each other, either. They were taking everything very seriously. While she hated the reason for their serious attitudes, it made her think Luke and Mark were both more mature than she originally thought.

They knew how to have fun, but they also seemed to know when to be serious and not mess around.

Chapter 13

Once Callie had been there for a week, she began to relax and think that maybe Bart had backed off. Two of his goons had been arrested, and one was arrested for threatening a woman with a loaded weapon. Bart had to feel the need to stay below the radar, right?

She hadn't been anywhere alone since she arrived, other than her bedroom. Which was starting to grate on her nerves; while she appreciated the protection all the family offered, she did wish to be able to roam the grounds by herself.

However, she was able to keep herself busy by applying for jobs online most afternoons. Her mornings were spent working on the ranch, and after lunch she'd be on the computer for a few hours searching for jobs.

On Wednesday, Luke came up to her halfway through the morning. "Hey, I know it's been really tense and crazy around here, but I have a surprise for you." He grinned at her while he kept his hands behind his back.

Callie tried to look around him to see what he was hiding, but she couldn't. "Whatcha got behind your back?" She raised a questioning brow.

He shook his head. "Nope, not yet. Come with me." Luke walked backward toward the barn.

She wasn't sure what he was up to, but she enjoyed his playful attitude. She'd actually missed this side of him the past few days. "Alright, I'll play your game."

He quickly pivoted around and tried to hide what he had behind him, but Callie caught sight of the edges of a basket.

"Is that a picnic basket?" she asked.

"Ah, smarter than the average bear, eh, Boo-Boo?" He chuckled.

"That was one of my favorite cartoons as a kid."

"Mine, too." Luke showed her the basket when he latched it to his saddle.

Sitting in the middle of the barn, all ready for a ride, were Whiskers and Midnight.

"Are you sure it's safe for us to take a ride?" She bit her lower lip and worried that Mr. Manning might not approve.

"Don't worry, my pa knows exactly where we're goin'. I'm sure we won't be alone for long." He shook his head.

Callie thought that it might be a good time to bring up her decision to keep things friendly. "Um, Luke. I think we should talk."

"Uh-oh. Whenever a woman says we need to talk, nothing good comes of it." He stopped next to her and offered up his hands to help her get in the saddle.

She put her hand on his shoulder and let him help her up. "I just think that I'm leaving in less than a week, and there's so much going on here..."

He interrupted her. "Don't say it. Let's just enjoy these last few days we have together and not worry about tomorrow. Let tomorrow worry about itself."

Callie wasn't sure that was smart, but if the two brothers didn't start fighting over her again, maybe she could just enjoy herself. That wasn't too much to ask, was it?

Luke led them out of the barn toward the shooting range. He had brought his shotgun, as he had every time he got on his horse over the past week, but he also had something a little extra special for Callie.

She thought about what he'd said for a moment before answering. "What about Mark?"

"We spoke last night and came to an agreement. No more honing in on each other's dates with you. We both know you aren't going to be here much longer, and we want to spend more time with you." The sincere expression on his face softened her heart.

"And if I only want to spend time with one of you?" she asked.

He nodded. "We talked about that, too. If you choose one of us over the other, we'll respect your decision. Mark said he'd back away and give us space." Luke grinned at her.

He thought he'd already won.

She shook her head. "And if I choose Mark?"

"Huh, he asked the same question." Luke chuckled. "If you can tell me you don't feel the connection between us like I do, then I'll back off and give you and Mark space." He would, too, but he was pretty sure Callie and Mark didn't have the same spark that she had with him.

Even with the tension over the past few days, he still caught her looking at him at times with interest in her eyes. Luke wasn't going to give up until she either told him to back off, or she left.

And maybe not even then. They had something, and he knew it.

"How about we just spend time together as friends, no strings attached? And no pressure. I'm leaving in a few days, and I don't want to leave my heart behind, or one of you with a broken heart." She doubted they wanted that, either.

But like most men, they probably weren't thinking a week ahead. They were only concerned with the here and now.

"Are you gonna tell Mark the same thing? Or is this your way of sayin' you're choosin' Mark?" Luke wasn't sure how he felt about that. When discussing it with his brother the night before, he was confident Callie would choose him. He wasn't prepared for her to choose Mark. At least, not yet.

"I am. I don't want to start anything romantic because I know it can't go anywhere." As much as she liked both cowboys, this really couldn't go anywhere. She lived too far away. Pain shot through her heart at the thought of saying goodbye, but she didn't live in Beacon Creek.

"Alright, how 'bout we don't put any labels on this"—he motioned between the two of them—"and we just let things happen naturally? We have less than a week together. Let's just enjoy each other's company."

She nodded. "Alright. But if I begin to feel uncomfortable, I'm going to ask you guys to back off." Callie thought she must be crazy to agree to spend time with two brothers at the same time. This wasn't a romance novel; these kinds of things never worked out. Plus, she never liked dating two guys at once. It always got too complicated.

"Deal." Luke kicked Midnight and sped up. When he looked back over his shoulder, he saw a huge grin on Callie's face. She kicked Whiskers into motion, and they took off at a nice gallop toward the range.

Luke wanted it to be a race, but he knew he'd win hands down. He did, however, enjoy getting Callie to ride out of her comfort zone. Pushing someone to do more, or better, was one way they improved. It was also a great way to see if Callie could fit in here at Triple J. He wasn't going to give up on her too easily.

She may not live here, but other than an apartment and some friends, she had nothing keeping her in St. Paul. There was no job there, and who said she couldn't find one here? Luke knew that Callie had been doing job searches in the afternoons, but he wasn't sure where she was looking.

If he got his way, she'd find a job here, or at least close by. Maybe Bozeman would have jobs for her career? Or could she find something different? He wasn't going to push, but he was going to subtly drop hints about finding a job locally.

Even though he was pushing Callie to go faster, he didn't let Midnight go too fast. He didn't want her to get hurt trying to keep up. Luke was getting the impression Callie might be a tad bit competitive. He grinned. Just what he liked, a woman with spirit.

The fact that the events of the past week hadn't caused her to break down or run away screaming told him that she was strong-willed and not easily spooked. While there was nothing wrong with a filly who spooked easily, that type of woman wouldn't be good for a rancher.

The more he got to know Callie, the more he liked her.

Luke pulled on the reins. "Whoa." He stopped next to the fence that enclosed their little shooting range.

Callie pulled up next to him. "Hey, cowboy. That was fun. Can we do it again?" Her hair was windswept, and her breathing heavy. The pink that tinged her cheeks wasn't from embarrassment, it was from excitement.

He chuckled. "For someone so new to horses, you seem to be doin' really well. If I didn't know any better, I'd say you've been ridin' for years."

"Nope, first time was with you. But it is something I've always wanted to do." She dismounted without his help.

She looked much more comfortable getting off horses without help than she had just three days ago. If they kept up their daily riding, she'd be right at home. Plus, she was getting better at getting into the saddle without a mounting block. He wouldn't be surprised if she no longer needed help before she left to go home.

His breath caught at that thought. Would he be able to say goodbye when she left? He shook his head. No, he couldn't think like that. They were having fun, and maybe the Lord would find a way to keep her close by. If they were meant to be, he had to trust in God's plan for them.

Luke pulled down a satchel from his saddle bag. "I have somethin' for you." He handed her the bag after they had tied their horses to the fence.

Her eyes sparkled when she looked at him, and his heart skipped a beat. Luke was in trouble.

"Thank you. You didn't have to get me anything." Callie was excited to see what it was. The bag felt heavy, and she couldn't imagine what it was.

When she opened the bag and pulled out the box, her eyes grew huge and she felt tears prick at the backs of them. "You... You got me a Taser?" She held the box close to her chest, then pulled it back and opened it.

Inside was a black Pulse+ with yellow lettering and highlights. Included in the box were two live cartridges and the manuals. Callie's hand hovered reverently over the expensive gun.

When she looked up, a tear fell down her cheek. "But this is so expensive. I can't pay you back for this." Her shoulders drooped. "You should return it."

While some might think it a boring gift, Callie saw the heart behind it. She didn't want to carry a real gun, but carrying a Taser while she was near the Triple J would keep her safe. Or at least help her to feel safe.

She had always liked gifts that were useful as well as heartfelt. For her, a Taser was both.

The only downside to using a Taser was the cartridges were one and done. The civilian model was designed to incapacitate an attacker for thirty seconds, giving the victim time to run away and seek safety. Having extra cartridges on hand would be helpful, although not as practical as a handgun.

Luke put his hand on top of hers. "Callie, it's a gift. My parents and I agreed this is a good idea. If you're stayin' here while we have these issues, you need to feel safe. And since you aren't a fan of handguns, even though you're trained in their proper use, we want you armed."

"I don't know what to say." She shook her head.

"You don't have to say anything." He shrugged. Luke wanted her safe, and if carrying a Taser would keep her safe, he'd feel better about her stepping foot outside the ranch house. Didn't matter if she always had a guard; he knew she'd never run and hide. She'd proven that the other night when she turned Mark's truck around on the road and jumped out to find out what was going on.

This would make him feel better. And her dad would probably be happy if he knew. Maybe he'd even approve of Luke as a suitor. Wait, was he a suitor? He did want more than just a few days with her, but how much more?

"Thank you very much." She leaned in and kissed his cheek.

Luke felt his heart pick up speed, and he gulped. If this little lady could get his heart pumping like when he used to rope, then there was definitely more than a little flirtation going on between them.

Chapter 14

The next afternoon, Callie was going through her email when her phone rang. She looked at the caller ID but didn't recognize it. "Hello?" With all the resumes she'd sent out, it was most likely a job recruiter. Or at least, she hoped it was. She hated telemarketers. It should be illegal for them to call cell phone numbers.

Callie didn't have an unlimited phone plan, so when telemarketers called, she just hung up. No sense in wasting her minutes on some hotel marketing scam or other such nonsense.

"Callie Houston?" the pleasant female voice on the other end of the call asked.

"Yes, this is she." Her stomach flittered around, and hope sprang up.

"This is Barbara, and I'm calling from Axiom Placement Agency. I saw your resume online."

It wasn't for a job she had applied to. Instead, it was an agency probably calling about something she wasn't even qualified for. She had already received a dozen emails about jobs that had nothing to do with her qualifications. Why couldn't these agencies actually look at her resume instead of going off a bot that only picked up on keywords?

One part of her wanted to hang up right away, but another told her to listen to what the person had to say. Maybe since it was a human calling, they had looked at her resume and it was something that might fit with her qualifications.

"Yes?" Callie waited for the lady to say more.

"I have a Fortune 500 customer in Washington State looking for a temporary Contracts Specialist, Senior. The role would last at least six months and could turn into something permanent after the first of the year. Would you be interested?" Barbara paused.

She was about to jump on the chance, and then remembered her bad interview from last week. "Is this with Longston Tech?"

"Yes, it is." Barbara sounded surprised she knew her client's name.

"No, thanks. I'm not interested in that company. But if you have anything else, I'd be interested in hearing about it." Callie tried to stay chipper, but her experience with Longston came back into her mind and she shivered.

Barbara tried to get her to at least let her send her resume in, but Callie finally told the lady about her experience, and Barbara abruptly ended the call.

"Well, I guess that agency won't be looking at my resume again." She chuckled and put her phone down. If a female recruiter sided with a disgusting pig, then she didn't want to work with her, anyway.

"Bad news?" Mark walked into the room Callie was using for her job search.

She was startled out of her reverie. "Huh? Oh, just a bad recruiter. No biggie." She didn't want to make a big deal out of it. It wouldn't do her any good to complain about something she couldn't change, and about someone she'd never see again.

"Any luck finding a job?" Mark asked. He, too, was hopeful she'd stay. They hadn't spent much time together over the last few days, but he did still want to get to know her better. How could he not? She was beautiful, intelligent, and had spunk. What man wouldn't want her?

"Not yet, but it's only been a week. I'm sure something will turn up soon." She smiled weakly. "What can I do for you, Mark?"

"I came to rescue you from the doldrums." He raised his brows once and put his thumbs in his front belt loops.

She tilted her head and gave him a coy smile. "Oh, really? What gives you the idea that I'm bored?"

"Looking for a job is boring." He laughed.

"True, it is." She stood up. "What did you have in mind?"

For the past few days she had taken regular rides with Luke, but had only gone on one ride with Mark so far. As much as she loved the ranch and riding, she really did want to do something else. However, she also knew that dangerous men were out there.

"Have you ever been four-wheelin'?" Mark asked.

Her mouth formed an O. "No, I haven't. That sounds like a blast!" She rubbed her hands together in anticipation of trying another new experience. So far, this trip had been all about new experiences. Some she may not want to remember, but most have been indelibly etched into her memory. She couldn't wait to try another fun adventure.

"Then let's go." He led her out of the room once she closed up the computer she was using.

Out behind the barn was a smaller outbuilding that housed four-wheelers and dirt bikes, along with a few trailers that looked to fit behind the four-wheelers.

"Wow, is this what you use to carry stuff around your ranch?" Callie walked through the small building that was no larger than a three-car garage.

"Yup, we mostly use them when fixing larger sections of our fence line where our trucks don't fit as well." He winked. "And I use them when taking pretty ladies out for a ride."

She chuckled. "Such a flirt." Callie noticed her heart didn't seem to flip like it had before. Mark was a very attractive man, but she wondered why her heart wasn't in it. Could it just be that she was upset about the lack of job prospects? Or was her attraction to the cowboy waning?

Or had Luke somehow stolen her heart without her even knowing it? Luke wasn't the perfect model of who she wanted. For one thing, he was a couple years younger than she was. And for another, he still lived on his family ranch and didn't seem to have any ambitions of leaving the ranch.

Mark was the same. Well, except for the age. He was two years older than her twenty-four years. His age was perfect, in her mind. But again, he still lived at home.

She shook her head. Thinking along those lines did no good, anyway. She wasn't going to have a long-distance relationship with either of them. A little flirtation was all she could do. So really, it didn't matter.

"You know it." He laughed as he walked to a shelf along the back wall that housed helmets and other gear. "Here, try this on." He handed her a black helmet.

She put it on. While it wasn't going to be something that won her any fashion awards, it wasn't bad. Her hair would be flat when this was all done, but that didn't matter. Safety was more important than nice hair.

Mark guided one of the four-wheelers outside. "For your first time, we'll just take out one. You can ride on the back with me until you get a feel. Then I'll let you drive."

She nodded.

He explained what the different knobs on the off-road vehicle meant, and how to brake and give it gas.

She noted that he had strapped a shotgun to the front of the handlebar. None of them were going to be out on their own property without some form of protection.

"Alright, get on behind me and hold on tight," Mark said over the roar of the engine.

She complied. When she wrapped her arms loosely around him, he took her hands and wrapped them tighter around his mid-section.

They took off slowly as he maneuvered through their backyard. Once he was past the paddock and far enough away from the animals, he gave it some more throttle and they sped up.

"Woohoo!" Callie yelled as the wind blew her blonde tresses behind her.

Mark sped up when he could, and slowed when the terrain required it. They crossed a stream, and muddy water caked her pant legs.

She closed her mouth before she could get any mud in it. And just in time, for she felt a splatter of something wet on her face.

Callie had decided that four-wheeling was something she would have to do again. The energy rushing through her body was exhilarating, and the beauty of the ranch took her breath away.

They went through a couple different pastures. Each time Mark stopped by a gate, she got off the back of the four-wheeler and opened it so he could go through. Once Mark was through the gate, she closed them without him even having to ask. She had learned the importance over the past week of ensuring each gate was always kept closed, unless they were herding the cattle from one pasture to the next. If thy left a gate open, it was possible cattle could get lose, or an ornery bull could get in.

Callie's eyes grazed the fence line whenever she was in eyesight of one. It was becoming second nature to her to make sure there weren't any holes or weak fence posts as they went through the ranch lands.

After forty-five minutes, Mark pulled over by a large oak tree with a wooden table underneath it. They had all eaten lunch more than two hours earlier, so she knew they weren't on a picnic.

"What do you think?" Mark asked when he took his helmet off.

"I love it. I think I love four-wheeling almost as much as riding a horse." She beamed.

He chuckled. "Yup, you're a rancher at heart, Callie."

"You think?" She scrunched her nose. "But I still don't like mucking out stalls." She had helped in that area even though she didn't like it.

"Yes, ma'am. No one likes muckin' out stalls. It's just what you do when you have horses." He shrugged. "Alright, you wanna try?" He waved to the front of the seat.

She grinned and straddled the machine.

Mark ran her through the various parts again and showed her how to shift gears, accelerate, and brake.

Callie repeated out loud everything he told her while running her hands over each part. "I'm ready." She bounced on the seat, excitement running through her veins.

Mark chuckled. "Alright, get goin'. But start slow." He backed away and watched her hands closely to make sure she was doing it right.

Callie twisted the handle, and the four-wheeler stuttered forward. She pushed the brake and started again. This time her forward movement was a bit smoother, but still jerky. After a few attempts she got a smooth start and went down the dirt road she was on, gaining momentum before she put on the brake and did a slow turn.

When she turned around and headed back to Mark, she gave it too much gas and whizzed past him, screaming.

"Brake!" Mark yelled as he ran to catch up to her. "Put on the brake!"

Her mind clicked, and she hit the brake a bit too hard. The ATV stopped so quickly, it spluttered and died. Callie laughed. "That was fun! Let's go again."

Mark chuckled. "This time I'll be on the back with you to make sure you don't get going too fast again." He sauntered over to the four-wheeler and helped her restart the engine. Then he jumped on behind her and wrapped his arms around her waist tightly.

"Ya ready?" Callie called out.

"I was born ready!" he returned.

When she gave it gas, it inched forward, and she gave it a bit more until the vehicle was moving at a speed she was comfortable with.

Mark let her drive the entire way back with only a few directions on where to go and one suggestion about the placement of her hands on the controls.

She slowed down when she saw the top of the outbuilding where they kept the toys. No matter what Mark said, the ATV and other items in the building were toys. Mark may have said they were used for work, but she knew the truth.

Callie stopped a few feet from the door. "Well, that was fun. I hope I can do that again."

"Next time, we'll take out two four-wheelers and you can drive your own." Mark took off his helmet and grabbed Callie's out of her hands. "I've gotta wash it before putting it away. Why don't you go back inside?"

Even though Callie didn't want to wash the ATV, she also didn't want to be sent inside like a little kid. "Mark, I helped get it dirty. I can help clean it." She put her hands on her hips.

He held his hands up. "I'm not gonna turn down help. I was just tryin' to give you a little extra time to clean up before supper."

She looked at the time on her phone. "Yikes! I didn't realize we had been gone so long." Callie considered her next move. "Alright, thanks. I'm supposed to help your mom with dinner."

He waved her off, and she took off to the house.

As she hurried back, she thought about the afternoon. While she'd had a great time, she wasn't sure there were any real romantic moments between her and Mark. He was a great guy and a lot of fun, but did she want more than friendship with him? Or were they just having a fun flirtation like she'd originally said?

Then what about Luke? That cowboy confused her.

The next afternoon after her daily ride with Luke, she got online and checked emails. There was a legitimate email regarding a possible job offer. The recruiter had a few questions for her, so she responded and prayed God would turn this into something real. She needed it.

As she finished up, she heard some loud voices in the living room. Callie hadn't heard anyone doing any real arguing since she arrived, so she thought something must be going on. She closed up her computer and went to investigate.

"I don't want you going to Bozeman. Not now, while Bart and his crew are acting up like this. We aren't the only ones who've been targeted." Logan was pacing back and forth in the living room.

Elizabeth sat primly on the sofa and watched her fiancé as he ran a hand through his messy hair. "Logan, now's exactly when we need to go up to Bozeman in a large group. We have to show Big Bart that he can't intimidate us. We aren't going to stop helping those women just because that cretin threatens us."

"But he had someone try to take you at gunpoint!" Logan threw his hands in the air.

"And Callie was there to stop him." Elizabeth stood up. "Darlin', with all those cowboys and cowgirls packing heat at the carnival, do you really think that idiot had a chance of doing anything? Besides, he hasn't said Bart was his boss." She shrugged. "Maybe it's someone else who's doing all this stuff. Or maybe I was just in the wrong place at the wrong time."

Logan harrumphed.

"Hey, maybe he wasn't after me specifically. It's possible." She put a hand on Logan's arm. "Those women need our help. I doubt they get much food. All I want to do is bring them all a bagged lunch. Unless someone asks me to take them away, I won't try to remove any of them...this time." Elizabeth hated not getting all the women off the street, but she recognized that it wasn't safe at the Triple J right now.

"Lizzie, I don't know what I'd do if anything happened to you before we got married." He pulled his fiancé in a for a long hug.

Elizabeth pulled back. "So, once we're married it's alright if something happens to me?" The edges of her lips curled up. She tried to hide her amusement, but failed miserably. She knew Logan loved her very much, and no matter what their marital status, he'd be crushed if something bad happened to her.

Callie felt like a creeper listening to them. She cleared her throat. "Um, is everything alright?"

Elizabeth and Callie had spent the evenings playing games and chatting, since Lizzie was still staying at the ranch each night. Logan was there for dinner, but he left after dessert and went back to his house with his family. Callie was worried their fight might be serious enough to cause a rift between them. Since she had grown close to Elizabeth, she also felt protective of the woman.

"It's fine." Elizabeth smiled at Callie and waved her into the room. "Logan's just being a Neanderthal, that's all." She shook her head.

Callie chortled. "Neanderthal?" She raised her brows and turned her gaze to the man.

He laughed. "Lizzie hates it when I get overprotective. Or when I tell her she can't do something."

"Neanderthal sounds about right," Callie agreed. "But he might be right in regard to Bart." She was a very independent woman herself, but she also knew when to stay away from danger.

Elizabeth threw her arms in the air. "What if it isn't Bart who's behind it all?"

"Bart is the number one suspect right now." Logan turned to look at Lizzie. "You know he's dangerous. And he's threatened you a few times. Not to mention the times they tried to attack you out in the open."

"Exactly!" Elizabeth pointed at Logan. "It's always been out in the open. This sneaking around doesn't seem like Bart's M.O."

Callie scratched her cheek. "Criminals do change up their tactics when they escalate. The attacks on the ranch, and you"—she pointed at Elizabeth—"are consistent with a perp escalating. What does the sheriff say? Has he been in touch with the Bozeman sheriff?"

Logan nodded. "Yes, but the Bozeman sheriff agrees with Lizzie. He said it doesn't sound like Bart." He sat down on the sofa. "Bart's all about controlling the homeless population in Bozeman. They're most likely committing petty crimes, but nothing too serious," he held up his hand to stop Elizabeth from interjecting. "Besides beating up the women who want to get away."

Callie scowled. "But if it isn't Bart, who could it be? Both of the men who've been caught appear to be homeless, don't they?"

"The sheriff said it would have been easy for anyone to hire out the criminal element in Bozeman to do the work here. Or even bring someone in from another city. There's no proof those two men were ever in Bozeman," Logan said.

"Okay, I know I haven't been asking questions, but now I'm curious." Callie sat on the recliner across from Logan. "Who else around here is having problems?"

Elizabeth blew out a breath and took the seat next to Logan. "It seems there's at least six other ranches in the area who have had issues. Some have even lost cattle. One had a horse stolen along with its tack."

"It does sound like whoever is behind all this is escalating their crimes. While it could be Bart expanding his repertoire, I think it might be someone else." Callie leaned forward. "I agree with Elizabeth—it's time to take a trip into Bozeman."

Logan jumped to his feet. "What? Are you nuts? You just said whatever is going on is escalating. If it is Bart, then his guys have guns now."

Callie shook her head. "One guy had a gun. It's not too difficult to get them. Especially around here. In fact, I wouldn't be surprised if that gun was stolen."

Callie had heard about this before. Many of the guns used in crimes had been stolen from law abiding citizens who didn't lock up their guns.

Her dad used to come home and talk about some of his cases with her. He thought it would be good to help her develop her skills of deduction, which would help in any career she chose. Although, she knew her dad had hoped she'd eventually choose to join him on the force. Police work was never something she considered, even though she loved solving the puzzles of his cases.

Elizabeth agreed. "Plenty of people have extra guns in their houses. It's very possible that he stole it and the owner hasn't even noticed yet." She looked at Logan. "Do you know if they've run the serial number on the weapon yet?"

He nodded. "Yes, it's an older gun, and the owner of record died six years ago. They don't know who ended up with the gun after his death. But they're looking into it."

Callie bit her lip. She knew her dad would love this case. She should call him and tell him all about it, but he'd be upset that she didn't tell him sooner about the local danger. She had called him and told him about her car breaking down and being stuck in Montana for two weeks, but she hadn't told him about the almost-attack on Elizabeth and the possible cattle rustlers. Maybe it was time?

Luke entered the room. "Talking about Big Bart and his goons?" He sat in the recliner closest to Callie.

"Elizabeth and Callie think now's a good time to head into Bozeman and hand out bagged lunches to the homeless." Logan motioned with his hand to the two girls.

Luke's eyebrows rose. "Really? Now? Don't you think it's too dangerous?"

"Now would be the perfect time to get a bead on the situation with Bart and his gang." Callie looked to

Luke with a small smile. "I think if there's a chance it isn't him, we should find out." She knew that a direct confrontation might happen, but it could give her a chance to see if Bart knew what was going on. If she could read him, she'd be able to tell if he was responsible for the attacks and sabotage.

But she didn't think it sounded right. If the only attacks were on the Mannings, then it would make sense to suspect him. But with other ranches reporting issues, it sounded like a bigger issue.

"How often do you have to deal with cattle rustlers?" With the fence issues and stolen horse, Callie thought it might be a few crooks who were trying to upgrade to cattle rustling. With the high price of beef, it was a very possible scenario.

Luke thought about it for a moment. It had been a while since he'd heard of any cattle rustlers in their area. "Actually, a friend of ours, Hank Walton in Wyoming, did say that they had some rustlers in the area a few months ago. It's something ranchers have to keep an eye out for, but it's not a common occurrence."

Callie stood up and began to pace the room. "So it is possible that these issues are from a new band of cattle rustlers. If that's the case, then we need to follow up with Bart and confirm his guilt, or innocence."

Elizabeth stood up. "Hold on, Bart's not innocent. I never said that."

Callie put her hands up in front of her in a placating gesture. "I don't mean to say Bart's innocent in general, just of the current crimes."

Elizabeth's shoulders relaxed, and she re-took her seat. "Alright, as long as you understand Bart's a really bad guy, even if he isn't part of the current issues here in town."

"Understood." Callie nodded. "I'd like to go with you all. I've been curious about your volunteer group since I first heard about it."

Elizabeth smiled. "Yes, you must come with us. I think you'll be shocked when you see how many homeless are in such a small area." She put a finger on her chin. "Maybe you can even provide us with a different viewpoint and help us figure out what Bart's endgame is."

"Sounds good. When do we leave?" Callie stood up, ready to leave right then and there.

Chapter 15

The next morning after breakfast, the Manning kitchen was full of women making sandwiches. Elizabeth had called her friends who regularly helped her with feeding the homeless, including her best friend, Harper Bensen.

"Lizzie, what can I do to help?" Logan asked. While he was against them going to Bozeman, he wasn't about to let his fiancé run into danger without him backing her up. So he called a few friends to join them.

The house was full of cowboys who felt it was their duty to protect the cowgirls of Beacon Creek.

"Find the coolers we have out in the shed. We'll need them to keep the lunches cool before handing them out." Elizabeth gave Logan his orders, and he took Mark to go searching for the items.

The rest of the cowboys were in the living room, discussing what they'd heard about the shenanigans happening on the various ranches.

Drake Addison was holding court with the men and telling them about the Miller ranch. "I heard he lost two hundred head of cattle two days ago."

Noah Westin added, "I heard it was over three hundred head."

The girls in the kitchen could hear the guys, and Callie shook her head. "Is this an example of the Diner Divas?"

Elizabeth laughed. "Probably. Mr. Miller is one of my clients. I saw him yesterday and he said he lost ten head, as far as he could tell."

"Ten, two hundred, or three hundred? It's all the same, right?" Harper winked at her best friend and laughed.

"If you ask Cindy Macon, it probably is all the same. But it's not. Ten head of cattle could just be a counting error, but three hundred? That's definitely a rustler." Elizabeth scrunched her nose. As a rancher and a vet, she disliked cattle rustlers with a passion.

"So, you think it could just be an accounting error?" Callie asked.

She doubted missing ten head of cattle, and reporting them missing, was a mistake. She could see Mr. Williams being off by one or two, but not ten. Unless he had tens of thousands of cattle? She doubted anyone had that many around here.

"No, I do think someone stole from him. But ten tells me it's someone looking to feed a small group. Probably a couple families on the run." Elizabeth considered the possibilities.

"Or a large group of homeless?" Harper added with a pointed look at Elizabeth. The nurse thought all the issues lately had to do with Bart and his gang, but she still wanted to go and help the women. She agreed with Callie—heading out to Bozeman and confronting Bart and his gang would give them a good idea if he was involved or not.

"Huh, that could be it," Callie mused. If Bart was responsible for a large group of homeless and he couldn't feed them all, they would stop working for him. They might even gang up and go after Bart. He had to at least feed his troops. And if food was scarce, some would be willing to do whatever they needed to eat.

They finished making the sandwiches and added a small bag of chips and an apple and banana to each bag before putting them in the cooler for transportation.

Elizabeth handed Callie a backpack. "We put several bags inside these and go out and hand them out. When we run out, we go back to the truck for more."

"And if there are extra bags, we find those who look like they haven't eaten in a week and give them a second one," Harper added.

It sounded like they had a good plan, one Callie really liked. She couldn't wait to join the group on this adventure and do what she could to help brighten someone's day, even if it was only a sack lunch. For the average American, that wasn't anything special. But for someone who was so poor they had to sleep on the streets, it probably meant the world to them.

Noah Westin came into the kitchen. "Alright, everyone needs to get a battle buddy." He eyed the girls. "And each of you need to be paired up with a guy, for safety's sake." He turned to Harper. "How about you and I team up?"

Harper smiled and agreed.

Callie looked to Elizabeth. "Battle buddy?"

"It's a military thing," Elizabeth explained. "Noah served in the Iraq war. No one ever goes into a dangerous situation alone."

She nodded and patted the Taser on her belt. Her battle buddy was her weapon, but if it was part of their procedure, she'd team up with one of the guys.

When she turned around, she found Luke smiling at her. "Hey there. Wanna team up with me?"

Her stomach somersaulted, and she knew it was a bad idea to team up with someone so distracting, but she couldn't say no. "Sure. Sounds good." Callie was going to have to learn how to play nonchalant around Luke if she wanted to keep things cool. He was just too good looking, and nice.

"Great, I'm driving one of the trucks. You can ride with me." He took her backpack and his and walked her to his truck. All the Mannings drove Fords, and his was a newer F-150 model with an extra cab and plenty of space for three adults in the back seat.

Luke opened the door for Callie and helped her up into his truck. He had large tires and had lifted the chassis so it was higher off the ground. There was a step bar to help her, but Luke wanted the honor of assisting her inside his truck.

Once she was safely inside with her door shut, Luke ran around to the driver's side. He started the truck and turned to a country radio station that had Garth Brooks playing in the background. They sat in companionable silence listening to the country crooner while they waited.

Logan and Elizabeth joined Luke and Callie in their truck. A silver disk was thrust from the back toward the CD player. "Here, Luke. Play this one."

Luke chuckled and complied with his sister's demand. "Please don't tell me it's more bands sending you their samples?" He turned his head toward Callie before he backed out of his parking spot. "The last time she gave me a CD to play, it was of high school kids wanting to try out for her reception."

Everyone but Callie laughed.

"What? Weren't any of them any good?" She looked back over her shoulder at Elizabeth and Logan.

The couple shook their heads.

"Not at all," Elizabeth replied.

Logan wasn't quite as nice. "Most sounded like someone was scratching a chalkboard with metal nails." He chuckled.

When a distinctive violin riff came through the surround sound in the truck, Callie couldn't help but smile. "She's one of my favorite country singers."

"You into chick music?" Luke asked.

"Some, but Carrie Underwood has just always done something for me. When 'Jesus Take the Wheel' first came out, it was what all my girlfriends listened to. We would play it over and over. And this song"—Callie pointed to the car radio—"I didn't hear until I bought the CD. It's a sad song, but also good in the end." She was talking about the song "Wasted." The lyrics came over the radio, and Callie eyed Luke from the corner of her eye. "Why, don't you like them?"

He held one hand up. "Oh, no. I love Carrie. She's fantastic."

Elizabeth said, "If you two don't pipe down, we'll have to restart the CD." Then she started singing with Carrie Underwood.

Callie joined in, and before long all four of them were either singing or laughing. It made for a very short trip to Bozeman.

Once they arrived, Matthew pulled up next to Luke, and he exited his truck with his brother Mark, Leah, and Sophia. It seemed all the vehicles had two sets of cowboy/cowgirl pairs. Callie hadn't thought about it before they left, but there were the same number of women as there were men. She figured Elizabeth and Logan must have planned it that way, since they did all the inviting.

Roman and John had to stay home with their parents because someone needed to stay back and help watch the place. Other than Chloe, who was in another town, the rest of the Manning siblings had come along.

Before Callie could get her bearings, Luke was next to her and guiding her to the back of the truck where he had stowed the coolers. Logan had pulled all four of their backpacks out of the back seat and was handing them around.

When she looked up, Callie saw they were in the parking lot of a fast food joint. The rest of the group's trucks where there with them. The various teams exited their vehicles with smiles and laughter. No one seemed too worried about their safety. A couple of the guys did wear pistols strapped to their belts, but it looked more like it was part of their daily accessories than something they had done for safety's sake.

Drake's holster was made of a worn, soft-looking leather. His pistol was strapped in on his right side, and when he moved his arm he naturally avoided touching the weapon. Callie got the impression he wore it all the time.

Most of the men looked very comfortable with their sidearms. Even most of the cowgirls did. Callie thought for sure she stood out with her large Taser on her right side. The sleek pistols weren't as thick as the stun gun. But she didn't care; a non-lethal weapon was what she preferred, and it was a gift from Luke. There was no way she was going out without it.

After she let out a deep breath, Callie asked, "So how does this work? Do we take different streets and meet up at the end?"

Elizabeth shook her head. "Not anymore. After all the issues we've had with Bart, we all stay close by on the same street." She pointed to the side street across from them. "We usually start there, and then end up one block to the left before coming down and around to Smith Street."

"I'll just stick close to Luke and follow your lead." Callie was good with directions, but she was so busy having fun singing on the way to Bozeman, she'd forgotten to look up the area and get a feel for the streets. After one trip, through, she'd remember for next time.

"That's a good idea. But"—Luke looked straight in her eyes—"if anything happens, run back here to the fast food place and wait inside. Call the cops if you think it's necessary, but I don't want you wandering around the area where the homeless live. Most are harmless, but you don't know who is and who isn't yet."

"Got it." Callie put a comforting hand on the butt of her Taser.

"Move 'em out," Logan called.

Luke walked next to Callie while Mark was walking next to Leah. They were chatting about one of the women they'd spoken with last time they came by, which gave Callie the thought that the two of them must partner up a lot.

Part of her wanted to ask Luke about it, but then she realized that wouldn't be cool. Technically, Mark was Luke's competition. Although Callie was starting to realize she needed to say something to the guys.

Mark was a nice guy, but all she seemed to feel was friendship for the cowboy. She wasn't even jealous of the attention he was giving Leah, and the attention she was giving him. Did they have a thing starting before she'd arrived? That would make things simpler all the way around if they did.

Now Luke, he was a totally different story.

Chapter 16

Most of the group had moved on to the next street. But Luke and Callie were in the back and talking with a woman Luke seemed to know.

Luke put a hand on the older woman's shoulder. She looked like she was in her forties. However, Callie knew that a hard life could age a person too fast. For all she knew, the woman was only a few years older than she was.

"Margie, the offer still stands. If you want out, we can help." Luke's soft-spoken words reminded Callie that what they were doing was dangerous.

Elizabeth had told her that morning that some of the people on the street watched and reported anything of interest to Bart and his goons. And them showing up would be of interest.

If Bart was attacking the Manning family and their neighbors, she doubted he'd hold back right now if they took Margie with them. But she also thought it was weak to back down from Bart. If Margie wanted to go, she'd fully support bringing her back to the ranch and doing whatever she could to help them.

God's will would prevail. Even if it meant they would get into more trouble, she wasn't about to get in God's way.

Callie knew that doing God's will didn't necessarily mean they would be safe. Even missionaries and preachers died working for God. But if she let fear of death get in her way of doing what she knew God wanted, then she'd have to answer to God when she got to Heaven. Who wanted to be confronted by God and asked why she said *no* when He asked her to do something?

Fear of death was healthy, but she didn't fear what happened after death. She knew without a shadow of a doubt where she was going.

Callie looked back at Margie, who was shaking her head. The poor woman's eyes were so wide, it had to hurt. She could feel the fear coming off Margie in waves. Bart had a strong grip on this one.

It broke her heart to see in person what was happening to the people society had forgotten. No matter what happened, she was glad she went.

When she got home, she'd have to find a way to do more for those who truly needed a helping hand. And while she was here in Montana, she'd do whatever she could to help.

Callie pulled an extra bag of food out of her backpack and handed it to the scrawny woman. Everything inside her screamed to grab this woman and run, but she couldn't do that. Forcing someone to leave wouldn't help, it would only make matters worse. Margie would be in her daily prayers until she heard the woman got out.

"Hey, what have we said about coming around our territory?" A loud voice was followed by another one with a string of expletives that would make even a drill sergeant's ears hurt.

Luke stood up and pulled Callie behind him. "That's Bart's gang. Stay behind me," he whispered.

Callie looked around as five tall men dressed as though they didn't live on the streets walked up. One smoked a cigarette, and another spit chew at Margie's feet. She also noted that most of her group was already gone. Only one team was left on their street—Noah Westin and his teammate, Sophia Campbell.

Cigarette man yelled at Margie, "Ya know better. Ya need to skedaddle before ya get 'nta more trouble." He pulled his arm back as though he was going to hit her, and she scrambled away.

Callie put her hand on her Taser and unlatched the holster. She wouldn't taze any of them unless they attacked first. Besides, she only had one shot with the Taser. She needed to save it for when it was most needed. But her blood was pumping, and her adrenaline had kicked in big time.

"Steve, so nice to see you again." Sarcasm dripped from Luke's voice. "Where's your master?"

If Luke wanted to cause a scene, he was doing a great job.

Steve's face turned red, and he walked up to Luke and stuck a finger in his face. Which was kinda funny since Luke was taller than Steve, and built better than Steve. "Look, Manning, you've got enough troubles of your own to deal with from what we've heard. Don't go startin' any more." Steve tapped the brim of Luke's hat and stepped back before he started to chuckle.

Callie's eyes narrowed, and she wondered what all Steve had heard about their troubles. Just before she could step to the side and say something, Noah stepped up next to Luke and Sophia stood behind him, next to Callie.

Sophia leaned over and whispered in a conspiratorial voice, "We're their backup."

Callie tried to keep her laugh inside, but she did a horrible job. She tried to cover it up with a cough, but she caught Steve's attention, and he leaned around Luke.

"Oh, what do we have here? Another new girl?" Steve looked her up and down. "When you're ready for a real man, come and see me." He winked.

Callie gagged and tried to stay quiet, she really did. But the disgusting pig deserved a reply. "Don't you mean when I'm ready for the trash pick-up to call you?" It wasn't her best comeback, but she doubted he'd understand anything too high-brow. She could have gone with the old southern standard of, "Aren't you so sweet." But she doubted he'd get the cheeky reply.

Steve took a step to the side to get a better look at her. "Listen here, you better show some respect. We own this town, and everyone in it."

She put a finger to her lips. "Hmm, I think you own less than you realize." She arched a brow. "Isn't Bart in charge? And don't you just work for him? Like all these poor people on the street?"

Luke put up his hand. "Steve, she's new, like you said." He didn't want Callie starting a fight. The idea was to get them to reveal if they were involved or not. It wasn't to cause any more trouble.

"You better keep your little lady on a tighter leash. We don't take too kindly to women disrespectin' us." Steve's hands fisted at his side.

"Oh, is that why you had to use a gun on Elizabeth?" Callie countered.

Steve's brows furrowed in confusion. Then his face went blank. "Whatever it takes to keep women in their place."

Either Steve didn't know what Bart had done, or Bart didn't send that guy after Elizabeth. Callie was sure of it. She now knew that at least one of the crimes was someone else. But that didn't mean they could all be attributed to someone else. The gun-totin' criminal at the carnival could have had nothing to do with the fence line issues, or any of the other ranch's issues.

"Luke, if you know what's good for you, y'all put a leash on that one sooner rather than later." Steve grinned; his brown teeth looked as though he hadn't brushed them in a decade.

Callie shivered. Not from the threat, but the grossness of the sorry excuse for a man.

Noah had stayed quiet, but he spoke up now. "I think Matthew and the rest are already done. We should go and catch up."

Luke nodded and took Callie's hand. They walked backward away from Steve while Steve and his cronies did the same.

Callie hadn't realized it, but she still had her hand on her Taser. When they turned the corner, Luke sagged.

"What was that about?" Noah asked.

Not wanting to discuss this where anyone else could hear, Callie said, "Let's get out of here first."

The four of them turned down the street heading back toward the fast food joint and the rest of their team.

"Well, Luke. You sure know how to show a girl a good time," Callie joked.

The tension surrounding the four began to break, and they all chuckled.

"Let's get out of here. I don't think they're going to allow us to talk to anyone else today." Noah led the group down the next street.

The rest of the teams were waiting at the end of the street, across from the fast food restaurant they'd parked at.

Matthew walked up to them. "What happened? I was just about to go back looking for y'all."

"Steve." Luke knew he didn't need to say any more.

"Ah. Yes. Are we ready to head back?" Matthew looked over Luke's shoulder and saw Bart had come, and had Steve and his band of merry thugs all staring at them.

Bart held of their brown bags in his hand. He crushed it between his hands and threw it on the ground. Then he stomped on it a few times. When he was done, he pointed to Luke and Callie.

Not wanting to let him think he'd cowed her, Callie smiled and waved back. The rest of her group laughed, and they all moved to get into their trucks.

On the way home, Callie told those in Luke's truck her thoughts about Bart.

"You know, I think I agree," Elizabeth said. "I mean, the guy who had the gun on me last week wasn't someone I'd seen before. And I've seen all the guys Bart employs. He wasn't one of them." She screwed her lips as she thought back to that night.

"Just because you didn't recognize him doesn't mean he wasn't a new recruit for Bart's gang," Logan added.

Luke had remained quiet the entire time. "Actually, I think I agree with Callie. None of Bart's gang had guns on them. At least, not out in the open. And the way Steve reacted when Callie brought up the event—he really didn't know about it. I'm sure of it. He's the kind of cretin who would have taunted us if he knew what happened."

"He didn't say anything about it?" Elizabeth asked.

"No. In fact, he had a confused look on his face, and then he went blank. Like he had no comeback." Callie rubbed her neck. The adrenaline was making its way out of her system, and her neck ached from the tension of the encounter. She might even want a nap when she got home.

Home. Since when had she thought of the Triple J as home?

Chapter 17

"I think we should go see the sheriff and tell him about yesterday," Elizabeth announced when she sat down to breakfast the next day.

"What do ya think he's gonna do?" John asked.

He had been fairly quiet since they arrived home yesterday, so Callie was surprised to hear from him. Although, to be fair, she guessed he was a quiet type in general. He hadn't said much to Callie since she arrived. He wasn't rude, just not very friendly. Or at least, not as friendly as his older brothers. Maybe he was just too young? Callie didn't buy that. He was twenty-one, only a few years younger than her.

No, the more she watched him, the more she saw the anguish in his eyes. Something had happened to him. She wondered if the rest of the family knew. It was probably the real reason he'd come home from college early.

"Well, I think we need to inform him of Steve's confusion when Callie mentioned my almost-abduction," Elizabeth said. "We're all under the assumption that the gunslinger was after me in particular because of Bart. What if he doesn't know Bart, and I wasn't the actual target? What if it was someone else?" She put cream and sugar in her coffee and sat back to take a drink.

Once everyone had finished up with breakfast, Callie, Elizabeth, Luke, and Matthew all went to see the sheriff.

Logan was waiting for them in front of the sheriff's office when they arrived. "Sheriff Roscoe is inside waiting for us. I saw him when I arrived and told him we had some more information for him." Logan walked over and kissed Elizabeth's temple.

She loved it when he did that, so he tried to do it whenever he could.

Luke took Callie's hand and put it through the crook of his arm. She smiled at him and noticed the black of his pupils had chased away most of the brown and green of his eyes. Was he really interested in her? Or was all this just a competition with his brother like she'd originally thought? It would be easier to walk away if Luke was only trying to beat his brother.

Her stomach somersaulted, and she had to avert her gaze. Staring into Luke's eyes could be dangerous to her heart. She had to protect that very fragile part of herself from being hurt again. There were only a few more days to go until her car would be fixed, and then she could leave and everything would go back to normal. She doubted Luke would even want to call her or write once she left. Who wanted an absent girlfriend?

It wasn't like they could pop over to each other's place for long weekends whenever they wanted. It was a two-day drive—that would take up the entire long weekend. No, it was time she girded her loins, as her favorite literary heroines would do, and put up a barrier around her heart.

The sheriff stood up and walked out of his office when the group stepped into the reception area. "Please, join me in the conference room. I have some information to share with you as well." He led them to the side of the building, where they came into a conference room designed for ten people.

Everyone took seats around an oblong wooden table and waited for the sheriff to start. Luke helped Callie into her chair like a gentleman, and Logan did the same for Elizabeth.

Callie's heart pitter-pattered again, and she prayed her car would be done faster, but then she also prayed it would take longer. Leaving Luke was going to be agony, and staying longer would only delay her inevitable heartbreak, but she wanted more time with the gentleman cowboy.

She needed to make up her mind and stick to it. Either she wanted more time with Luke, or she needed to get as far away as fast as she could.

The sheriff cleared his throat, and all eyes went to him. "We've discovered who our mysterious gun-toting vagrant is."

Everyone in the room sat stock still, hardly breathing.

"Turns out he's from our neighbors to the north. But he spent some time in Northern California. They have a very large homeless population there. The state recently completed some sort of census, and the data hasn't been uploaded to the national registry yet." He rubbed the scruff on his face. The sheriff looked like he'd been up all night working and hadn't gone home yet. His uniform was mussed, as was his hair. The normally clean-shaven man had more than a five o'clock shadow.

"Why's he here in Beacon Creek?" Matthew asked.

"That's the million-dollar question. But his name is George Anderson. And he's stayed past the six months allowed to Canadian nationals. We've been ordered to send him to a Department of Homeland Security office."

Callie's eyes widened. "Not ICE?"

"Nope, this fella here's gonna get some special treatment." The sheriff stood up and walked around the conference table. "I think we've stumbled upon something much bigger than a gang of homeless outlaws. As does DHS."

"So, unless Big Bart has made a serious jump, he wasn't involved with the attack on Elizabeth." Logan looked at his fiancé, who smiled back at him. "Does that mean she's still in danger?"

The sheriff shook his head. "Probably not. But Elizabeth, you need to continue to stay with your parents until this is all solved."

"But you just said it wasn't about me." Elizabeth rubbed the gooseflesh rising on her arms. "Doesn't that mean I was just an opportune target? Or looked like someone else?"

"The latter, I think." The sheriff scratched under his chin. "I think you look like someone he was after. George didn't seem to know your name, and was surprised when I called you Elizabeth in the interrogation, meaning he was after someone in particular who either looks like you, or was dressed like you."

Logan took Elizabeth's hands. "I agree with the sheriff. Please stay with your folks until this is all settled."

She nodded her agreement.

"What about the other issues?" Matthew asked. "Do you think they're tied to George?"

Callie interjected, "That would make sense. The scruffy guys who have been seen around here lately could all be criminals from Canada or Northern California. I'd bet that someone else is running this new gang and they're learning how to be cattle rustlers. While someone else with more experience is running the gang, he may have recruited from a group of homeless people who are open to committing any type of crimes."

"Not all homeless are criminals," Elizabeth added.

The sheriff held up his hand. "I agree, Miss Elizabeth. But you yourself have seen that there's a criminal element who likes to hide on the streets. Living on the streets adds a layer of anonymity for them. When criminals live within society's bounds, they're easier to track."

"But those who live off the grid don't leave digital fingerprints." Callie stood up and began to pace her side of the office.

Sheriff Roscoe pointed to Callie. "Exactly." He narrowed his eyes. "You seem to know a lot about how criminals operate."

"Her dad's a detective in Louisiana," Luke informed the room.

The sheriff smiled. "What else can you tell me about this case?"

Callie stopped and blinked. "You want to know what I think?"

He nodded. "Of course I do. If you grew up with a cop for a father, you've probably picked up a few skills."

Luke sat up taller. "Her dad trained her to think like a cop while she was growing up. He'd tell her about cases and work with her to figure out the criminal's motives and actions." He looked as though he was her proud papa, with the way his face radiated and the way his eyes stared intently at hers.

"Oh, like that TV show!" Elizabeth exclaimed. "You know, the one where the dad was a cop in some beach town and his son used his powers of deduction to work as a psychic detective."

Callie jolted and realized everyone in the room was looking at her, not just Luke. She felt the tell-tale signs of heat creeping up her neck, and she looked down at her hands on the table. "Something like that. But I'm no psychic."

Luke put a comforting hand on hers. "But I bet you're a fantastic detective."

A feeling of unease spread over her. She wasn't used to getting so much praise or attention. When Callie felt like she could talk, she cleared her throat. "I think we should look at the different events taking place around each ranch that has had problems. Track it all back to see when it started. Then canvas the area and see if anyone has noticed strangers around. This is a small town, and I'd bet any stranger would stand out like a sore thumb."

Matthew rubbed his chin. "I agree. With the exception of the rodeo and carnival, there hasn't been anything going on around here to attract many visitors since Christmas. I doubt these events go back to then."

"Agreed," the sheriff said.

"I think our problems started just over a month ago," Luke added.

The sheriff took his seat again. "From what my deputies have discovered, I'd say our unwelcomed guests arrived sometime within the past six or seven weeks."

Everyone at the table began to list off the various problems they knew about. Even Logan's family had had some issues, and they only had a couple milk cows, three pigs, and some horses. They did scare someone off who had been trespassing on their small property. Since the perpetrator didn't take anything, they never reported it.

They spent most of their time at the store, so they didn't have the ability to run a full ranch. However, two of those pigs would be going to slaughter soon and filling their freezer for the next year. They did sell some milk and on occasion cheese, if they had extra.

The bulk of the problems seemed to be focused out near the Manning ranch. They were on the west side of the town, and the other ranches in their vicinity had all reported issues. The latest issues showed an increase in the number of cattle they'd stolen, and the bandits were moving east.

With as sloppy as they were being, Callie figured they could deduce what ranch would be hit next. With that in mind, the sheriff called for an old-fashioned posse. Most of the ranches sent at least one cowboy, if not two, to join.

The next afternoon with the sheriff's station full of volunteers, Sheriff Roscoe deputized the lot of them, including Callie and all the Manning brothers. Elizabeth wanted to join the posse, but Logan put a kabosh on her desire to help.

"When are you going to find time to go out with us and search, or lie in wait for them to strike again?" Logan knew that Elizabeth could take care of herself, but he still worried for her safety, especially since they still didn't know why she was targeted.

"I could join the team after work a few nights a week," she protested.

"And when would you sleep?" Logan asked, arms crossed over his chest.

Callie was a little bit uncomfortable with the way this was going, but she kept her mouth shut and stayed out of the argument.

Luke whispered in her ear, "Don't worry about them. They'll be kissing and making up just as soon as Elizabeth realizes she really doesn't have time for this."

Not wanting to eavesdrop or discuss the cute couple any longer, Callie directed Luke away from them. "I heard from Mikey right before the meeting started."

Luke's blood ran cold. This was it. Her car was probably fixed, and she'd be leaving tomorrow or the next day. He knew the time was coming, but he'd never expected it to be early. "And?"

Callie sighed and crossed her arms over her chest. She wasn't sure if it was good news or bad. "There's been another delay. Something about a key part from South Korea not shipping on time. I don't know all the details, but Mikey said it'd be another week, maybe longer."

Luke really did try to hide his grin, but he felt the smile from ear to ear. If Callie hadn't been in the room, he would have pumped his fist in triumph. "I'm sorry. I know you want to get home."

His joy was contagious, and a small corner of Callie's lips quirked up in an almost-smile. "You're enjoying this, aren't you?"

"You're darn tootin' I am. This gives me more time to get to know you, and for you to find a job here, or close by Beacon Creek." He hadn't heard of anything in the area that Callie might be qualified for, but he'd keep checking with his contacts until he found her a job.

"I guess I can keep helping out with the search for those guys." Callie wasn't sure how she felt yet about having to stay another week. Mr. and Mrs. Manning had told her she was welcome for as long as she wanted to stay. Even after everyone left and rooms opened up at the hotel, the Mannings still wanted her to stay with them.

She had enjoyed life on the ranch, and would be very sad when the time came to leave. Although, getting to stay an extra week just might get her need for country living out of her system... along with a certain cowboy.

She still hadn't had a talk with Mark, but ever since the trip to Bozeman, he'd been a little distant. Or maybe he was distracted? She wasn't sure, but he had gone into town every day since then, and they hadn't had any time alone. Not that she was complaining; it gave her more time with Luke.

Although, more time with Luke wasn't necessarily a good thing for her heart health. Too bad she couldn't take Cheerios, or something else to help strengthen her heart against a break.

Chapter 18

"Listen up!" a loud voice bellowed in the sheriff's office. "I want to set up teams of four to take shifts at night, driving around looking for people who don't belong, as well as a couple teams to keep an eye on the ranches we suspect might be next." The sheriff put up a list on the cork board in the meeting room.

With so many cowboys and cowgirls volunteering, the deputies pulled out the big conference table that had been in the largest room of the sheriff's station. Now, everyone stood mostly shoulder to shoulder and waited to see what their assignments were.

It was no surprise to Callie that she had been teamed up with Luke, Matthew, and Logan. However, she was surprised that Mark hadn't been on her team. But since it was teams of four, that made sense.

Mark had been teamed up with Leah, Logan's sister, along with Noah Westin and Sophia Campbell. When Sophia saw who she was teamed up with, a small smile graced her face, but it left just as quickly when she saw Callie looking at her. Noah and Sophia made a cute couple, and Callie wished them well.

Luke made his way up to the schedule and took a picture with his camera, then shared it in a group text with his team. When he made his way back to Callie, she was talking with Matthew about what they'd need for their turn keeping watch.

"I know you don't like real guns, but it would be smart if you at least carried a shotgun while on patrol. It has a longer range than your Taser does, and you may need it." The oldest Manning's face wasn't harsh, but he wasn't smiling, either. Luke figured he and Callie had been arguing over what she should use.

Callie bit her lip and winced. "I do think a shotgun would be wise. You're right about that. I'll agree to carry that as long as you're fine with me choosing to use a Taser before the shotgun if the perp is close enough."

Matthew held up his hands. "Hey, I don't want anyone killed, not even the bad guys. If you can bring down an attacker by tasing him, I'm all for it." He put his hands down. "I'm not out for blood, I just want to stop the bandits and get the guys who are running this show before they move on to another area and hurt more people."

"Sometimes," Luke interjected, "all it takes is to show the weapon and criminals will stop. I don't think my brother expects you to take down a target who's fleeing unless it's absolutely necessary."

"You mean, if he's already shot someone and is on his way to shoot another person?" Callie asked. She could do it. If a rustler was shooting people, she could shoot back.

"Or in case of a shoot-out. You might need it to just defend yourself," Matthew added.

Callie's sardonic chuckle caused a few people to look her way. "I guess it really is still the Wild West out here, isn't it?"

Sheriff Roscoe walked up. "Yes, it is. It's best to stay safe and watch your back. You can't let your guard down for one minute as long as we have dangerous criminals on the loose."

Callie nodded, and knew her dad would say the same thing. Maybe it was time to tell him what was going on. She dreaded the phone call to him, but it had to be made. If anything happened to her and she hadn't told him about the dangers here, he would be so mad at her for keeping him in the dark.

"Alright, so we're all on the same page?" Luke asked.

Logan, Matthew, and Callie all agreed.

"Great, because we have our first shift tonight at midnight." With the picture showing on his phone, he passed it around for his team to see their schedule. "I also texted it to you in case you hadn't seen it yet."

The rest of the team pulled out their cell phones and opened up their text message.

"Logan, do you want to come to our house and drive with us? Or do you want meet up at the Chandler ranch?" Their first assignment would be to patrol the Chandler ranch's borders. That was the most likely next target. At least, it was next in line if the rustlers were going in order.

"The Chandlers don't have a regular road around all their borders. We might need to patrol on horseback." Logan had been out to their ranch many times over the years, delivering feed and grain. He'd seen their land and knew that even with a 4x4, they'd have some issues getting close to all the outer fence lines.

Matthew rubbed his chin. "Good call. We'll bring horses and meet you there just before midnight."

They all said their goodbyes and took off back to their homes. Each rancher would be responsible for watching their own place during the day, but at night, everyone would take turns watching the places the sheriff thought might be the next targets.

Mark had the Wilson farm for his first assignment. Since there were enough volunteers, there would be two shifts per night – eight PM to midnight and midnight to four AM. And they would only have to volunteer every other night. Then the ranchers would have their own hands begin their patrols just before dawn.

When Callie got back to the Triple J, they had a family meeting to discuss everyone's assignments. With so many of the Mannings volunteering, they'd have to re-work their own schedules. Each group of Mannings were on a different schedule from the rest. Roman and John had been paired up with Deputy Chris Deacon, along with Mr. Johnson. They weren't on duty until the next night.

"Do you think they're done trying to get your cattle?" Callie asked. Since the rustlers had tried twice already, it made sense that they would move on to another ranch. With the Mannings warned, any crook worth his boots would know that the Triple J wasn't a place to target anymore. They'd have to know the Mannings would be on the lookout.

Mr. Manning shook his head. "I don't know. We need to keep our eyes and ears out just in case they do try to come back. When y'all are out on the roads each night, be sure to drive slowly by our fence lines and keep a good eye out."

"Yes, sir," Matthew said.

Callie had already decided she'd be keeping an extra eye on the fence line whenever she drove by—or rode by, as the case may be. With the quality of crooks this new gang employed, they might not be smart enough to move on.

She sent up a quick prayer asking the Lord to keep everyone safe and to deliver their enemies into their hands without injury.

"That's a good idea." Mr. Manning pointed to Callie as she prayed. "Let's all pray as a family before each night begins, and then again in the morning."

"We should ask the pastor to get the prayer chain going, if he hasn't already," Mark suggested.

Mrs. Manning had been quiet this entire time, but now she spoke up. "I already called the pastor's wife. They started the prayer chain earlier today. Pastor Baker even called the other clergy in the area, and all of them have their prayer chains going."

Callie breathed a sigh of relief. No matter what happened, God would have his hand in the coming events. She wholeheartedly believed in the power of prayer. Even if God's answer wasn't what she wanted, she knew His answer would be the right one.

She thought of the country song about how sometimes it seems like God doesn't answer prayers, but sometimes those unanswered prayers really are answers in themselves. We can't always know or understand what God has in store for us, but as long as we give it all up to him, then we shouldn't be worrying about it. Let God worry for us. He wants to carry our burdens so we don't have to.

"I want to read a verse from the Bible. I think this is something we need to be reminded of today." Mr. Manning pulled his phone out of his pocket and opened up an app. "In Matthew 11:28 – 30, Jesus tells us: *Come unto me, all ye that labour and are heavy laden, and I will give you rest. Take my yoke upon you, and learn of me: for I am meek and lowly in heart: and ye shall find rest unto your souls. For my yoke is easy, and my burden is light."*

It was as though Mr. Manning was reading her mind. He went right to the passage of scripture she was trying to remember so she could study it more that night. Callie took her phone out and opened up the verse and marked it for further study. The heavy pressure she felt on her spirit began to lift as she considered the verse and prayed again to give it all to God.

"Thanks, Pops. That was exactly what I needed to hear." Luke lowered his head and began his own prayer. Prayer for strength, and for safety. Luke trusted the Lord in all His ways, but that didn't mean Luke wanted to see anyone injured. If God was open to requests, he was going to lay them down at his master's feet.

As Luke prayed, his shoulders relaxed and the furrow between his brows relaxed. Jesus was right—when he laid his cares at the Lord's feet, God was gracious and took them on his back. There was no need for Luke to worry about what he couldn't change.

The cattle rustlers were in town, doing who knew what. It was his job to protect his family and neighbor's property. He'd do what he could, but he wouldn't stress over the situation. The outcome was ultimately in God's hands.

When Luke lifted his head, he noticed that everyone in the room was either praying or looking at their phones—probably looking up verses, or re-reading what his father had read to everyone. His spirit soared when he saw Callie's head bow again. Knowing she was a woman of faith only strengthened his resolve to spend more time getting to know her. She was exactly the type of woman he wanted to court.

If only she lived closer to Beacon Creek.

When Callie finished her prayer, she looked for Luke. "I think I need to call my dad now. Is there anything I should do before helping your mom fix dinner?"

Luke shook his head. "Nah, I'll have your horse ready to go by eleven o'clock tonight. We can load them up into the trailer and drive over to the Chandler ranch. You do what you need to, and I'll see you at dinner."

She put her hand on his forearm and smiled before heading off to her room to have that scary call with her dad.

Callie's dad wasn't mean, but he was very protective of his girls. He had trained them all, including Callie's mom, to take care of themselves, but that didn't stop him from being overprotective of those he loved dearly.

She closed the door behind her and called her dad.

"Callie-bear! Good to hear your voice. Please tell me you have some good news?" Callie's dad, Paul Houston, had called her Callie-bear since she was a little girl carrying around a beat-up teddy bear everywhere she went.

"Hi, Dad. Is Mom around?"

"Sure is. Do you want me to put you on speaker phone?"

"Yeah, it'll probably be best if I tell you both at the same time." Callie was sure the trepidation she felt was coming through the line. Especially when he answered.

"Tell me everything's alright?" Her dad sounded a little farther away than before, making Callie think he had put her on speaker already.

"I'm fine. I just want to start out by letting you know I'm not injured or anything like that. But"—she took a breath—"there are a few problems here."

"Honey, if it's money, just tell us what you need and we'll put it in your account right away," Crystal Houston, Callie's mom, said.

"Thanks, Mom. But it's not money issues. First, my SUV won't be ready for at least another week." Callie waited to hear what they had to say.

"That's not too bad. Can you afford to stay there? Or do you want to fly home until the car's fixed?" Paul asked.

"No, I'll stay here. I just wanted you to know that it will be a while longer. But there's more." After a dramatic pause where her parents stayed quiet, she continued, "The real problem is cattle rustlers."

"What!" Paul bellowed into the phone.

"Calm down, Daddy. Like I said, I'm fine. But there have been issues here in town lately and on some of the ranches, including the Triple J." Callie continued on and told them what had been going on, and how she was deputized earlier that day by the local sheriff.

When she was done, she waited with bated breath before her dad said anything. She knew her mom wouldn't speak until after her dad said his piece, since it was a police matter. So she was surprised when Crystal spoke first.

"Honey, what are those Manning people doing to keep you safe?"

"Luke bought me a Taser, and Mr. Manning has given me one of his shotguns to use. I'm not allowed to go anywhere without backup and a gun of some sort."

Her dad snorted. "You could probably take better care of them than they could of you. But I approve of their methods. I want you to be safe. Please don't be a hero. Stick with the men there, and always carry a gun besides the Taser." Her dad knew how she felt about guns, and he generally approved of her stance.

"I know, Daddy. I'll be safe. Tonight, it will be four of us together as we patrol the next suspected target ranch. We'll be on horseback, too." Callie wasn't sure what her parents would think about that. She'd told them how she had been riding lately, and how much she enjoyed it.

"Callie, I hope you're wearing those helmets horse riders wear. You haven't even been riding for two weeks yet." Crystal's worried tone caused Callie to stop and think.

She hadn't seen any helmets for horse riding in the barn. Did the Mannings even have such a thing? The helmet she used for riding the ATV wouldn't work—it was too big and bulky.

"Speaking of safety equipment, I'm going to overnight you a bulletproof vest. I want you to wear it any time you're outside the house. Do you hear me?" It wasn't a request; her father was giving her an order, as though she was still a kid living in his house.

Callie sighed. She hated those vests. They got so hot when you wore them all day long. "Fine, but can you send me one that's designed for use in the Sahara Desert?"

Her parents chuckled. "Of course, sweetie. And I want you to text me before you leave and when you come back to the ranch after any of your shifts, got it?"

Even though her dad was being a bit overprotective, she smiled anyway. "Of course, Daddy. I will."

"Sweetie"—her mom took the phone off speaker and spoke directly into the phone— "please be extra safe when you're out there. You don't know the area well. Stick close to the Mannings and don't go running off after anyone. Okay?"

"Yes, Mom. I'll stick close to Luke. He's been assigned to me for these shifts."

"Luke, huh? Is he cute?" Her mother had been trying to get her married for the past two years. Any time she mentioned a guy, the first thing her mother did was ask if he was cute or single. As though she couldn't have a guy friend; all men who were single had to be dating material.

At least her father wasn't asking for Luke's credit report.

"Do I need to pull his credit and check for a criminal record?" Too late—her father was already asking.

He'd do it, too. When her ex, Chet, had started dating her, instead of cleaning his gun when Chet came around, he ran the boy's credit and background. She was mortified. Since then, she had kept her dating life—what there was of it—as far away from her parents as possible.

She laughed. "No, Daddy. It's not like that. He lives here in Montana, and I'm in Minnesota."

"That's not a no," her mother commented.

"You know, you could get a job anywhere," her dad said. "If this boy's a decent fellow, maybe you should start looking for a job near his ranch. That is, if those rustlers get taken care of soon." Now her father was trying to get her married off.

What was with her parents? It wasn't like she was old enough to feel her clock ticking or anything.

She'd only been out of college a couple years. Now was the time to date around and figure out what she wanted. It wasn't time to move near a guy who flirted with her. She didn't even know how Luke felt about her, not really.

She sighed. "Dad, Mom, let's just focus on getting my car fixed and me finding a job. I'm open to anywhere, but I seriously doubt I can find anything in my line of work anywhere in this state."

"I'll be praying for you, dear," her mom said when she took the phone back from her dad.

"Alright. I've got to go help Mrs. Manning get dinner ready. We're going to eat early, and then I'm taking a nap before we head out for our shift. I'll text when you I get home tonight. I love you."

"We love you, too," her mom said before she hung up.

Callie plopped down on the bed and rested a hand over her eyes. Her parents were great, but sometimes they could be a handful. Most parents would have been screaming for her to come home. Probably insisting she do so. But not hers. It probably had something to do with all the cases her dad had solved during his career. They both were almost immune to the violence out there these days.

Maybe it was good?

Chapter 19

A few minutes before eleven o'clock, Callie walked out of the house yawning. She carried two thermoses of coffee for everyone, along with four cups, stir sticks, sugar, and packaged creamer. Luke was next to her, carrying two sacks of snacks in case they got hungry.

Callie didn't know how they'd get hungry, not after the huge barbecue steak dinner they had. Since coming to the Triple J, they'd had some sort of barbecue at least three nights a week, and everyone was right: they had the best beef! Matthew made his own barbecue sauce that was tangy and a little bit spicy, just the way she loved it. Just thinking about their dinner had her rubbing her still-full belly.

Once the horses were loaded into the trailer and the snacks and equipment loaded into the back of the truck, she, Matthew, and Luke took off in Matthew's F-250 truck.

They arrived about ten minutes before Logan, and they got the horses out and saddled. Callie hadn't ridden with a shotgun before, and the way it was holstered to her saddle was odd. The scabbard was positioned under the leg strap, and when she mounted, Luke adjusted the scabbard to fit under the bend in her knee so it didn't rub her thigh or calf. Having it under the knee would be the most comfortable position, he explained, as well as the best to keep from getting rugburns.

The team assigned to the ranch before them came around to the front of the house where they had all parked. Drake Addison was in the lead. "Ho, Mannings. Nice to see you all here."

Matthew waved and brought his horse closer to Drake. "Any issues tonight?"

"None, as far as we can tell. Everything seems quiet." Drake moved on past Matthew, then turned around in his saddle. "There's a pack of coyotes out there somewhere. We couldn't see them, but we could hear them."

"If this ranch is a target, and the rustlers are new, they might be scared off tonight by the coyotes," Callie interjected.

Drake scoffed. "If the coyotes scare them, then they're in the wrong line of business."

His team laughed with him, and they all went to their trucks to put their horses away and leave.

Matthew and his team headed out back and began the process of scanning the fence lines. The night was fairly dark—only a little over a quarter of the moon shone—but they all had high-powered flashlights.

Once they had made one turn around the outer fence line, they stopped to have some coffee.

"I didn't hear any coyotes, did you?" Callie asked when she handed Logan a cup of coffee.

He shook his head and added cream and sugar to his coffee before stirring it. "They could have moved on by now. It is pretty late. Even coyotes sleep at night," Luke added.

The next few hours were quiet, except for their chatting. They talked about the case and rehashed what everyone already knew. Then Logan began asking Callie about her dream wedding.

"Why do you want know about my dream wedding?" Confusion was written all over her face.

The cowboy was riding next to her, with Matthew and Luke right behind them. "Because our wedding is turning out to be a disaster."

"Did you hire a wedding planner?" Callie didn't know much about weddings, but she did know that if you were going to have a big wedding, a planner was a must-have.

"Not until right before you arrived. We tried to keep it low-key and do it all ourselves, but it turned out to be too much for us to handle. We're both working fifty to sixty hours a week, and there just wasn't time during our day to take care of it all." Logan sighed and slouched in his saddle.

"Well, it's early summer and you still have, what, five months before your fall wedding?" Callie asked.

Logan nodded.

"Then your new wedding planner should be able to handle all the issues you've had. How's she do-ing?"

He shrugged. "I think she's taking care of it all. It's been so crazy around here, and I just wondered if it was worth it? Maybe we should just do a small family-only wedding in the backyard?"

Callie pulled on her reins. "Don't you dare suggest that to Elizabeth. She's super excited about her plans for the wedding." She started moving again when she heard Luke right behind her.

"Hey, no stoppin'. Get 'r goin', Houston."

Whiskers whinnied and started to get antsy. Her hooves scraped the ground, and she moved back-ward.

"Whoa, Whiskers." Callie's heart began to race, and she tried to get the horse to stop moving. She couldn't understand what was going on until she heard a loud mechanical sound.

Their shift was coming to an end, so it had to be almost four in the morning. What type of sounds would come from a ranch so early? She couldn't think of anything good.

Luke saw Callie's horse get antsy only a few sec-onds before his Midnight did the same. When he heard the sounds of metal grinding on metal, he knew exactly what was happening. "They're here." He pointed his light out into the pasture, but didn't see anything.

"I think they're up ahead." Matthew looked to Callie, and then to Luke. "Stay here with Callie and help get her horse under control. Whiskers isn't used to working cattle, so she might need help. Logan and I will go and see if it's them. You call the sheriff."

"No, you aren't to leave anyone behind. Even if you think it's safer for us to stay here, it isn't. We all ride together or not at all." Callie gave each cowboy in her company a pointed stare. "Got it?"

Matthew thought Callie did a great job of impersonating his mother. "Yes, ma'am. But I want you and Luke in the back."

She nodded. What would it hurt to take up the rear? Either position could be dangerous. The enemy could come up from behind to try and ambush them.

Luke pulled his horse closer to Whiskers and tried to calm her. "Shh, it's alright, Whiskers." He was close enough to pat the horse's neck. "Rub your hand down her neck and whisper to her like you would a frightened child. A soothing voice will help her."

Callie did just that, and Whiskers began to calm down before they urged the horses into a gallop. With one hand on the reins, she used her other and pulled the flashlight out of her jacket pocket.

She aimed it ahead of them and realized they were coming up on the ranch house. "Would rustlers steal cattle so close to the house? Especially considering how loud they are?"

Luke's ears perked up, and his idea began to change. It wasn't rustlers. Callie was right—they were too close to the house.

Matthew must have thought the same thing; he pulled back on the reins and slowed his horse down. The rest of the team did the same, and they trotted into the paddock area of the Chandler ranch.

Sitting in the middle of the paddock was a semi pulling a trailer. The noise they heard must have been the ramp being let down and then the sound of hooves clomping down and out of the metal trailer. Not cattle being led into a trailer.

Luke noticed the symbol on the side of the semi cab. It was the Chandler logo. Mr. Chandler's foreman must have been bringing in some new horses.

Matthew rode up to the man standing next to the back of the empty trailer. "Howdy, Mack. Awful early to deliver a load, isn't it?"

Mack nodded. "You got it, but Mr. Chandler said to come straight in. Said there was some funny business afoot, and he didn't want me sleeping on the side of the road so close to town."

Logan scratched the stubble on his chin. "Yeah, we got rustlers 'round here now. The sheriff figures this place is next on the list."

In the dim light, Callie could see the wide-eyed stare Mack gave Logan. "No kiddin'? Geez, I go away for two weeks and this is what I come home to?" He shook his head.

Mr. Chandler came out back and walked toward the group. "Mack, good to see you. Once you get everything put away, hit the rack. Come find me when you wake up and I'll explain it all."

"Sure thing, Mr. C." Mack tipped his hat and went back to work.

"Gentlemen, ladies." Mr. Chandler nodded to Callie. "Thank you for keepin' an eye out tonight. I really appreciate it. Did you see anything out there?"

"No, sir. The only sign of anything other than cattle sleepin' was when Mack rode in." Matthew looked to the semi and watched as two ranch hands led the last of the horses away into the barn.

"Good, good." Mr. Chandler nodded. "I was hopin' we wouldn't get targeted tonight."

"Just because they didn't come tonight doesn't mean they won't still try." Callie stared at Mr. Chandler. "Stay vigilant. The moment you let your guard down is when they'll strike."

"You sound like a cop," Mr. Chandler chortled.

"Her dad's a detective in New Orleans," Luke stated.

Mr. Chandler's eyebrows rose. He nodded and looked impressed.

"Well, if you're up and taking over, we need to get home before the sun comes up." Luke said goodbye to Mr. Chandler and led his team back to the front of the house.

"Huh, that was a dud. I wonder if anyone else had any luck." Callie took the empty bag of snacks, which the guys had eaten, and put it in the truck. While she was glad they hadn't come across any cattle rustlers, she hated that it wasn't over.

"Maybe someone else caught them? We did have teams over at the Wilson farm tonight," Logan added.

"I only hope they didn't target a ranch we weren't looking at." Matthew closed up the ramp to the horse trailer and said goodbye to Logan.

They were all back home within twenty minutes, but Callie had dozed off once they got out of the Chandler ranch. She felt someone pushing on her shoulder.

"Callie," a soft voice called to her.

"Hmm?" She blinked a few times and stretched her arms. "Are we home already?"

Luke chuckled. "Yes. Do you need help getting inside?"

She shook her head. "No, I'll help you guys put the horses away."

"Nah, go inside and hit the hay. We'll take care of them. I doubt I'll be able to get to sleep again, anyway. It's almost time for the sun to rise." Luke rubbed her back once she was out of the truck.

Without even thinking, she turned into Luke and gave him a hug. "Goodnight," she whispered into his shoulder.

Luke was momentarily stunned. Sure, she'd taken his arm and they had been close, but she'd never hugged him. When he got his head cleared, he wrapped her in his arms and held her tight. She smelled like vanilla, lemons, and horse. He smiled into her silky hair and took a deep breath. He could get used to this.

"Come on, Luke," Matthew yelled.

The sound of Matthew's voice must have woken Callie from a dream. She jumped back from Luke and felt the heat rise from her neck into her face. What had she done? She was hugging Luke. And she really liked it.

His masculine scent of leather, horse, and some spice she couldn't name—possibly ginger—wrapped around her entire being, and she almost went weak in the knees. As she drooped a little, she felt his arms tighten around her.

"I have to go. Will you be alright?" His soft, masculine voice was next to her ear, and shivers went down her spine.

It was all she could do to keep from moaning. She had to wake up and take control of her emotions. Callie's mouth felt like a cotton ball was stuck inside. She could only nod. Then she pulled back and averted her gaze.

"I'll see you in a few hours. Sleep tight." Luke kissed the top of her head; he couldn't help it. At least he didn't try to kiss her on her lips. With his luck, she'd slap him.

He stepped away from her and backed up a few paces before he turned around and joined his oldest brother. Before he turned the side of the house, he looked back and caught Callie watching him.

The look on her face confused him. She had her head tilted and her brows furrowed, as though she was trying to figure something out.

Chapter 20

When Callie woke up, the sun was already a quarter of the way in the sky. "Yikes!" She wondered how late she'd slept, then relaxed when she saw it was only ten in the morning. She hadn't slept in too much.

The memory of Luke holding her before he said goodnight haunted her memories as she lay in bed, analyzing what her heart and head wanted. It seemed they weren't in agreement at the moment. Her head said to stay away from the handsome cowboy, but her heart was screaming at her to go for it.

Why couldn't her heart fall in line with her head? This made no sense whatsoever. Sure, Luke was a very good-looking gentleman cowboy, but they lived too far apart. There were no jobs available anywhere in Montana for what she did; she'd even looked one day, just out of curiosity. The closest job posting was over four hours away, where she knew absolutely no one.

Callie put the pillow over her face and screamed into it. "Argh! This shouldn't be so difficult. I *have* to put a wall around my heart."

"Are you alright?" Elizabeth's concerned voice broke through her tantrum.

Callie sat up straight and threw the pillow down. "What?"

Elizabeth smiled. "I take it you're having trouble protecting your heart from my brother?"

With a sigh of defeat, Callie lay back down.

Elizabeth sat on the edge of her bed.

"Yes, I am. And I don't know what to do." Callie threw her hands in the air. "It's not like I can avoid him or leave town yet."

"I don't think that's the wisest way to go about it, anyway." Elizabeth pursed her lips. "Remember the verse my dad read last night? Give it over to God and let Him worry about it all. You just need to keep moving and doing what you believe God has led you to do."

Callie bit her lip.

"Do you think He wants you to leave now? Or wait for your car?"

Thoughts of all the different scenarios went through Callie's mind, and she thought on it. Only one felt right in her spirit. "I think He wants me to stay until my car is fixed. For some strange reason, I was brought here to your house. It could be that

I'm going to help solve this case, but it could also be something else." She shrugged.

The corners of Elizabeth's mouth tilted up. "I think you're here for my brother. I don't doubt that you'll help us solve the case, but there's much more to it than stopping cattle rustlers." She patted Callie's hand. "Come on, it's time to get up. Ma's got some breakfast waiting for you."

After Callie had showered and gotten ready for the day, she walked into the kitchen with a hot plate of chocolate chip pancakes, bacon, and warm syrup. "Oh Mrs. Manning, this is fantastic! Thank you very much." She sat down, and after saying grace to herself, dug in.

The clacking of boots on the linoleum kitchen floor sounded behind Callie, and she turned to see who'd come in. Before she got halfway around, large, callused hands lightly touched her shoulders.

"Good mornin', sleepy head." The husky voice next to her ear sent shivers of excitement through her body.

"Good morning, Luke. Did you get any sleep after we got back?"

"Nope, I've been workin' all mornin' while you wiled away the day in bed." He chuckled.

The heat on her cheeks made her even more embarrassed. She should have woken up sooner and helped out around the ranch. "Yeah." She dragged the word out. "I'm sorry about that. I should have set an alarm. I really didn't think I'd sleep so long."

He rubbed her back. "Don't worry about it. We're used to gettin' up in the middle of night and not gettin' back to sleep. When the horses foal, that's a normal night fer us."

"I guess I'm not a rancher after all, huh?" She looked down at her plate and mentally berated herself for not thinking ahead enough to set her alarm.

"Hey, it's fine. Don't even worry. You needed the sleep. I'm sure I'll be fallin' asleep at the supper table tonight, myself." His light laugh warmed her from the inside out.

"Thank you. I'm done. Just let me take care of the dishes, and I'll come out and help." Callie stood up and cleared her place setting.

Once the dishes were done, she went outside where Luke was waiting with Whiskers and Midnight all saddled up.

"I thought we could start the day with a ride around the perimeter. We still need to stay vigilant, even if they didn't make a move last night." Luke moved to help her into her saddle.

She put up a hand. "I think I've got it. Let me try." Callie put her left foot in the stirrup and grabbed the saddle horn. She pulled herself up and swung her right leg over the horse. Her seat wasn't as firm as she had hoped, but she adjusted and then sat comfortably in the saddle.

Luke clapped. "Nice job. I think you're totally on your way to bein' a rancher."

Blasted red cheeks. She turned her head to hide her embarrassment over his praise.

He mounted up quickly, and they were off.

"Tonight, it's Roman and John's turn to watch the Chandler ranch." Luke sounded worried. His voice was strained, and he looked away from her when he spoke.

"I don't think you need to worry. They'll be with Deputy Deacon and Mr. Johnson. I'm sure they'll be just fine." She bit her lip and sent up a quick prayer of protection for the group.

He nodded but didn't say anything for a while. "So, any news on your Honda?"

During one of their rides, Callie had told Luke what the tow truck driver said about Hondas and Hyundais being no different, and he liked to tease her about it.

"Hardy har, har. And no, nothing new." She sighed.

He smiled. If Luke's prayer was answered, she'd be staying a long while, if not forever. He wasn't going to tell her about his request to God he made every night before going to bed. She wasn't ready to hear exactly how much he liked her. Not yet.

Besides, with all the danger, it wasn't right to be talking about their possible future. Not when so much was up in the air. His plan was to keep getting closer and closer to her. Eventually, she'd fall just as hard for him as he had for her. He just had to be patient and take his time...or God's time.

Halfway through the property, Callie noticed something in the distance. It wasn't on their property, but on Mr. Johnson's. She pointed. "Look. What's that glint?"

Luke took a pair of binoculars out of his saddle bag and looked in the distance.

Callie's nerves were beginning to fray. She had pulled out her cell phone so she could call it in if it was the rustlers. Whiskers must have been in tune with her, because she pranced about, just waiting for a chance to go after something.

He put the binoculars down. "It's just Mr. Johnson. He's fixing a part of his fence."

"Do you think someone broke it?"

Luke shook his head. "Probably not. He hasn't been the best at mendin' his fences inside his property. That fence is just one of the inner pastures. If it was broke, the only thin' that could have happened is a bull gettin' into where he keeps his heifers."

She chuckled. "Like when I first arrived?" The memory of the stampede flooded her mind. It seemed like so long ago. She had learned a lot about riding, and so much had happened that the stampede seemed tame compared to what they were going through now.

When he looked at her, his smile was warm. "That was fun, wasn't it?"

The heat suffused her cheeks again, and Callie wondered how long it would be until she stopped blushing at his flirtatious comments. "Not at first."

She straightened her shoulders and decided it was time to give him back a little bit of his medicine. She winked and kicked Whiskers in the flanks, and they took off.

"Hey!" Luke called, but accepted the challenge and kicked his horse into gear.

She did her best, but she knew that Luke let her win by a nose. There was no way she could beat him, even cheating. Maybe one day she'd be able to beat him for real, but for now she'd enjoy the win. "Thanks."

He laughed and led them back toward the barn.

Chapter 21

Last night when Roman and John went out for patrol, nothing happened—again. At breakfast, Roman told everyone he thought that maybe the rustlers had heard about their patrols and moved on to another town.

Callie didn't think it too likely. Not yet. They hadn't scored anything big yet, and there were a lot of ranches to cover. She might suggest that they move on to another ranch that night instead of going back to the Chandlers'.

If the rustlers did know what they were up to, they'd change up the way they chose ranches and head over to the east side of town. At least, that's what she'd do if she was a cattle rustler. With everyone focused on the west, the east should be easy pickin's.

Luke took her out for their regular morning ride, and she told him her thoughts on the topic.

"I agree," he said. "Do you want to head over to the sheriff's office this afternoon and talk to him?"

If the sheriff agreed with her assessment, where would they look? There were at least another dozen ranches and farms on the other side of town that could be chosen.

"Yeah, I think it's worth mentioning. I don't know what to do about it, but it might be smart to at least have someone out patrolling the entire area. What do you think?"

Luke considered her ideas for a moment and nodded. "I agree. It makes the most sense for them to know what's going on and move their targets to where we aren't looking at all."

They took their time checking the fence lines on the outer perimeter, as well as those inside some of the larger fields where they had their cattle and bulls. Once they were done, they took their time heading back in, enjoying the clean air and beautiful vistas in Big Sky Country.

When they got inside, the mail had come, and she had a nice-sized package waiting for her.

"Oh, I bet I know what it is." Callie opened up the overnight box with gusto and pulled out a white ladies' bulletproof vest.

Luke and Matthew both eyed the item, and Luke's left brow rose.

"It's from my dad. He wanted me to have a little extra protection." She shrugged and took the vest back to her room to try on.

When she came back out into the living room with the vest between her tank top and button-up cowgirl shirt, she smiled at those in the room. "Well, how do I look?"

Mrs. Manning stood up and walked around her. "I can barely tell you've got it on. Is it comfortable? Won't you get too hot in that thing?"

She shook her head. "Nope. It has a cooling technology built in to help keep out heat. I'm actually surprised it came so fast. My dad must have called in a favor to get it shipped so quickly."

The men in the room—Matthew, Mr. Manning, Luke, and Mark—all tried not to stare too much at her torso.

Luke was the only one courageous enough to say anything. However, he did have a tinge of pink on his cheeks. "I think you look great. And I'm glad your dad sent that. It'll keep you safer tonight when we go out on patrol again."

Mr. Manning rubbed his chin. "Maybe we should get ourselves one, too? What do you think, Callie? Are they worth it?"

Her wry laugh belied the seriousness of the topic. "Um, yeah. If you get shot, this could be what saves your life. I mean"—she waved a hand—"unless you all are Superman, or some other superhero who can stop bullets?"

Matthew straightened his shoulders and puffed out his chest. "I've been compared to a few super-heroes before."

"Don't you mean super-klutzes?" his dad quipped.

The room was full of laughter, and Callie realized that for the first time in several days everyone seemed less stressed and happier, like when she first arrived. The cattle rustler had put the entire ranch on high alert, and it had affected everyone's mood.

After lunch, Luke took Callie into town to see the sheriff. She told him her suspicions, and he eyed her carefully.

"I see you're wearing a vest. Did you bring one with you?" Sheriff Roscoe leaned back in his chair and tried to look relaxed, but Callie saw the tension surrounding his eyes.

"No, my father knows someone and had them overnight it to me." Callie wondered if he was starting to suspect her somehow.

It was a crazy thought; she didn't even get to town until after all the issues had started. Plus, how could she have known her SUV would break down here? Although, looking at it from his perspective, she might think the same thing. It did seem a bit convenient that she had to stay in town so long.

Had she just bought her SUV, she would have suspected herself as well. But she'd had it for many years now.

"Must be nice." He still sounded a bit leery of her. "Alright. How 'bout your team patrols the highways and streets on the east side of town tonight? If you hear or see anything suspicious, call me right away."

"What about the Chandler ranch?" Luke asked. "Don't they still need a team out there?"

"I'll call in another team and have them patrol both the Chandler and Monahan ranches. I think you might be right about them seeing through our patrols." The sheriff stood, signaling their meeting was over.

Unease ran through Callie as she got up. If the sheriff hadn't been lifelong friends with Mr. Manning, she might suspect he was involved somehow. Something seemed off, but she couldn't put her finger on it, not yet. She would make sure she kept an eagle eye out tonight as they made their way around the east side.

It wasn't that it all seemed too easy—it was that the sheriff was looking at her so strangely, like he was worried she had caught on to his plan. Callie didn't want to think the sheriff might be dirty, but she got a niggling feeling that wouldn't leave her alone. It was probably just nerves because they'd be over on the other side of town basically on their own.

If they needed help, it would most likely take at least twenty, maybe even thirty minutes before help arrived. And what if she was wrong? She'd look mighty stupid in front of everyone if someone did hit the Chandler ranch during her time slot.

After dinner that night, Mr. Manning called the family, including Callie, together for prayer. They had two teams going out that night for patrol, and the family wanted to make sure everyone was spiritually protected.

Standing at the fireplace, Mr. Manning pulled out his Bible and opened it. "If you have your Bible, or an app, open it with me. Luke chapter 10 verse 19: *Behold, I give unto you power to tread on serpents and scorpions, and over all the power of the enemy: and nothing shall by any means hurt you.*"

Everyone bowed their heads, and Mr. Manning prayed for the family as well as the teams. When he was done, he looked out to his children and guest. "I'm so proud of you all for volunteering to help our neighbors. And I want you to remember that God is with you. He'll give you the strength to combat your enemies when needed. Trust in Him and you will prevail."

Tonight's verse reminded her of a coffee mug she'd kept on her desk at work. Philippians 4:13 was printed on it: *I can do all things through Christ which strengtheneth me.* They could do this. Even if they found a large group, they had God on their side. If He wanted them to prevail, and if they trusted in Him, they would.

Everyone wished Mark well, and he took off to get his gear and horse ready for his shift at the Wilson farm. Mark and his team weren't going to leave the Wilsons'—at least, not yet. The only team who was really going anywhere different that night was hers. Someone was going to be called in to help Mr. Chandler patrol the fence line in their place, but that was the only change so far.

Callie said goodnight to everyone and went to take a nap before her shift. She set her alarm for ten o'clock and lay down. So many things were going through her head, like that night's devotional and her coffee mug. Even though she knew God was on her side, she still had a few nerves.

Their schedule change that night was all on her suggestion. If she was wrong, and the thieves went to the Chandlers', she was going to feel horrible. If they lost cattle, it would be all her fault. She didn't even want to think what might happen if someone got hurt.

She needed sleep, and her mind wouldn't shut off. An idea hit her, and she got out of bed and bent down next to her mattress. "Dear Lord, I'm sorry I keep taking this worry back onto my shoulders. I freely give it to you to take. Please keep everyone safe tonight, and help the town find the rustlers and who's behind it all. Help me to remember that you're in charge, not me or even the sheriff. I ask for a hedge of protection around us all. Not just my own team, but all of us. In Jesus' name I pray, amen."

A feeling of relief washed over her, and she got back in bed. Within minutes, she was asleep.

Chapter 22

"Matthew, slow down. I think I see something ahead and to the right." Callie looked intently out her passenger window.

They had all four of them in Matthew's truck, and he pulled a four-horse trailer behind them for when they needed to get out and patrol fences. For now, they were driving down some of the more remote roads and checking for any signs of cattle rustlers.

"I see it, too." Matthew slowed down and pulled to the side of the road. He turned his headlights off, and in the distance several lights of a cattle hauler sparkled in the field to their right.

"Let's get the horses and check it out." Luke opened his door and headed to the back of the trailer.

Once they were all mounted, Callie asked, "Could it be something as simple as the other night at the

Chandler ranch?" Conflict surged through her veins. She wanted to find the vermin who were terrorizing Beacon Creek, but she also didn't want to be the ones to find them.

"I doubt it would happen twice. That's too much coincidence. But it's always possible." Matthew took the lead, with Logan next to him.

The lowing of the cattle could be heard over the sounds of engines sitting idle. When they got closer they could hear men's voices, but nothing distinctive yet.

Callie touched the butt of her shotgun as well as her Taser, comforting herself that she was prepared. Silence was important, and she didn't want to let the rustlers know they were coming if she didn't have to, so she kept praying to herself for comfort and safety.

Luke patted his pocket to feel for his phone. A niggling deep down in his gut told him this was it. Something didn't look right. Who would load up their cattle in the middle of the night? And out in the middle of a field?

Normally, you ran the cattle home and separated the calves from their mommas. It was the older cattle who were sold at market, not the young. There wasn't any way to separate them here on the side of the road. Luke had driven past this ranch many times and knew they drove their cattle back toward their barns when they took them to market.

As they approached, Callie could see an entire section of fencing had been removed. It was a split-rail fence, like what the Mannings had, as well as most ranches, and they'd pulled the rails out and put them to the side. Instead of running over the fence and destroying it, they were preserving it. Would they put the rails back when they were done so no one knew exactly where they went in? If so, they were getting smarter.

It wasn't fear that Luke felt, but trepidation. He wasn't worried for himself or his brother, but he was worried for Callie. Which was stupid. She had more training than he did when it came to criminals, thanks to her dad. But that didn't stop him from wanting to take care of her and keep her safe.

He looked out of the corner of his eye and saw determination written all over her face. This woman next to him was unbelievable. She had taken to ranch life so easily, and now she was in cop mode and helping him to protect their town. Luke sent up a word of thanks as well as a request for protection from his Heavenly Father.

Matthew and Logan pulled back on their reins, and Luke and Callie both did the same. They all stopped and looked at the truck that didn't have any identifiable features on it, and watched under the light of a partial moon as men ran around and corralled the cattle into the truck. They weren't very good at it, but they were getting the trailer full, if the lowing sounds were any indication.

Matthew turned his head and whispered, "Luke, call the sheriff. Then you and Callie take this side and pull out your guns. Let's try to get them to stand down. Logan and I will go to the other side."

"Isn't there time to wait for the sheriff to come?" Callie asked.

Logan shook his head. "No, I think the trailer's just about full. Once they're done, they'll be leaving. It'll take too long for the sheriff to get here."

Luke pulled his phone out the moment Matthew told him to.

The sheriff picked up on the first ring. "Please don't tell me you found them."

"Sorry, but we did," Luke said. "We're out on the ol' East Ranch Road, about five miles past the Delaney ranch."

The sheriff let loose an expletive, which was rare for the man. "Sorry, is there time for me to get there? I'm about twenty minutes out."

Luke shook his head. "No, they're almost done. We're on horseback and going to try to stall them until you can get here. But there's a lot of them. They have a full-size semi and a trailer full of cattle. And I can make out at least four trucks."

"Alright, let the semi go if you have to, and focus on stopping the trucks. I'll notify the state troopers, and they can stop the truck. What color's the semi?"

"Green."

"Alright, see ya soon. And stay safe, Luke."

"Got it, Sheriff." Luke hung up. He looked to Callie and nodded.

They both headed to their side of the truck, and before they got there, they could hear the yelling of the men on the other side. Matthew and Logan had made it and were trying to corral the men.

The sound of an explosion rocked Callie's ears. Someone had used a shotgun, and it wasn't very far away.

The semi began to move. She and Luke steered their horses to the side so as not to get run over. Then she pulled the shotgun from its holster on her horse and pointed it at the men in front of her. "Halt! On your knees with your hands on your head."

The report of another weapon went off, and Luke screamed before he fell over and clung to the neck of his horse.

"Luke!" Callie screamed.

She looked at him, and he turned his head. "I'm fine. Don't let them get away."

All she could see was red. "Bad move." She shot her gun at the man coming toward her with a cigarette in his mouth. He carried a pistol that was no match for her firepower.

Her shot went off and the shotgun kicked up, but her aim was true, and her buckshot hit the man in his right shoulder. He dropped the gun and fell to the ground.

She yelled out again, "I said drop your weapons. This is your last chance."

They didn't listen, and another man fired at her. He missed when her horse moved to the right, and she shot again, not bothering to hold the reins anymore. She hit the man in his leg. Since she didn't want to seriously hurt anyone, she aimed for appendages in order to stop them. She knew it wasn't right. All cops were trained to shoot to kill, because you never knew when someone who was down might get their gun back and shoot to kill you. But she was more interested in stopping them. There were too many of them, and she had to just start shooting at all moving targets.

Luke pulled the reins and signaled for his horse to move back, out of the firefight. He went behind the tree to check the damage to his right arm. He wasn't going to shoot with any accuracy, if at all. When the shot hit him, he dropped his rifle. All he had left was his handgun. It held nine rounds. But he'd never done more than a few shots with his left hand.

He took out a handkerchief and wrapped his bicep where it was bleeding. Then he left the relative safety of the tree to get back into the fight with Callie. He had to make sure she was alright. He couldn't leave her to fight alone, no matter how much he hurt.

Once the semi was out on the road, the fighting opened up, and Callie saw Matthew and Logan shooting their rifles at men who had guns. The rustlers weren't great shots; other than Luke, the rest of their shots seemed to go wide. It helped that Callie's team was on horseback, and the horses kept moving around. Moving targets weren't easy unless you were experienced at shooting moving targets.

Whisker's ears twitched and she moved again to the left this time, missing another shot. It was almost as though this horse had been trained to assist her rider in a gunfight. It couldn't be the case, but Callie was grateful for the uneasiness she sensed in her mount, and all the movement that seemed to come at just the right time to help her avoid getting shot.

Callie only missed once, when a man ducked as she brought her shotgun to bear. But her next shot got him.

The sounds of the fight were dwindling. Most of what she heard were men screaming in agony with a shot here or there.

Callie heard a horse behind her, and when she turned around, she smiled at Luke. Then she turned back to the field and felt her breath leave her instantly. The pain in her chest was sharp, and her eyes widened. The momentum of the bullet hitting her pushed her off her horse.

When she fell to the ground, she landed behind the horse, that acted as a shield from the rustlers that were still standing.

Callie heard a voice screaming her name, followed by the report of a gunshot. The scream that followed didn't quite register in her ears. She lay back on the grass and looked up at the stars as she tried to breathe.

The pain was awful. There would at the very least be a cracked rib, maybe even a broken one.

Luke ran to her and fell at her side, ignoring the burning pain in his arm. "Callie! Oh Lord, please let her live." He ran his hands down her arms and looked everywhere for the blood. But there wasn't any. "Where are you hit?"

She eked out, "Chest."

Luke's brow furrowed. "There's no blood."

Callie took a few shallow breaths. "Bulletproof vest." It was difficult to get the air in, but she concentrated on her breathing, and soon she was able to get some deep breaths in and out.

Luke leaned down and hugged her. "I thought you were dead."

She smiled. "You can't get rid of me that easily, Luke Manning."

He chuckled. "Does it hurt a lot?"

She coughed. "Yes. I might have a broken rib, but hopefully it's just bruised or cracked. I think the fall hurt more than the bullet."

He ran a hand behind her head, and she winced. "I think you hit your head pretty hard, too. There's already a bump." He pulled his hand back and saw blood on his hands. "You're bleeding, a lot."

"Head wounds always bleed a lot. Don't worry, I'm fine. What's happening? I don't hear any more gunshots. In fact, I hear sirens." She tried to sit up, but it hurt too much and she lay back down.

"Don't move. The ambulance should be here soon."

Another face peered over her, and she smiled. "Matthew, what happened? Are they all down?"

He nodded. "Yes, Logan's got his gun on those not shot. Nice shooting, by the way. What happened to you? Fall off your horse?"

"She was shot," Luke informed his brother.

"What? Where? Is the blood on your head from a gunshot wound?" The horror in Matthew's eyes sent shivers down Callie's spine.

Before she could answer, Luke said, "No, her vest took the hit and she fell off Whiskers and hit her head."

"Who did it? I'll kill him," Matthew ground out.

"Don't worry, I got him." Luke grinned.

"How? Your arm is all messed up, too." Matthew took his hat off and ran a ragged hand through his hair. "Ma's gonna kill me. I should have been with you both."

"Don't worry, we'll both be fine." Luke stood up and looked around. "Wow, what a war zone."

Behind Luke, the sheriff walked up and asked what happened.

Matthew explained that they needed ambulances, lots of them. He didn't think any of the rustlers were in danger of expiring, but he was worried about Callie. She probably had the worst of it with her fall and taking a shot to the chest.

The sheriff's men went around and rounded up everyone they could find. Not a single man was on his last leg, but most needed the hospital. They'd have to be taken to Bozeman General; the Beacon Creek clinic couldn't handle all these gunshot wounds. Not only were most of them shot, but a few took a tumble and were injured from falling on rocks.

Only one man had stopped shooting and got on the ground. Logan told the sheriff what happened, and the sheriff grabbed the rustler and handcuffed him before putting him in the back of his cruiser.

Callie could hear the man getting his rights read to him as they walked to the car. "Really, he waited until all his buddies were injured before he surrendered?"

Luke wasn't sure if the look of disgust on her face was from pain, or if she really did think the gunman was a loser. He sure thought they were all idiots, but anyone who would steal another man's cattle was a loser.

"Seriously? You're worried about that sorry excuse for a human being when you're laying here with a head wound?" Luke put his hand to her forehead. "Nope, you ain't delirious from fever."

She started to laugh, and then winced. "Don't make me laugh, it hurts."

Luke's grin turned to chagrin, and he apologized. "Is there anything I can do to help?"

"Yeah, you can take me to the Beacon Creek Clinic. They have an x-ray machine, right? That's all I need." Callie wanted to take her vest off right then, but she was having a tough time moving, so she didn't even try.

"But Callie, what if you need more than an x-ray? What if you need an MRI? Or a CT, or something else?" Luke's furrowed brow worried Callie.

"Oh, Luke, I'm sorry. What about you? You were shot, too. Do you need more than an x-ray?" She would have hit herself if it wouldn't have hurt so much.

"No, it was through and through. I'll need it disinfected and maybe some stitches, but that's it." Luke figured he'd be on antibiotics for the next two weeks as well, but that didn't matter. All he wanted right then was some Tylenol to help dull the pain. He couldn't imagine how Callie felt.

"Do you want me to call your dad now, or wait until morning?" Matthew stood behind Luke, wringing his hands.

Callie winced. "I'd rather you waited. He'll be asleep now anyways, and there's nothing he can do now. You might want to make sure that the sheriff has guards on the man who shot me. I doubt my dad will be happy that the shooter is still kicking."

Matthew chuckled. "I bet my pa and yours will get along great. Your parents will be welcome to stay with us, if they come out."

"Thanks, I appreciate that." Callie moaned and turned her head back up to the stars. It hurt less if she stared straight ahead.

"Oh, darlin', I'm so sorry. But I'm going to be forever grateful your dad sent you that vest. It was a godsend." Luke felt tears prick the backs of his eyes. Not from his own pain, which he felt, but from the fear of almost losing Callie right in front of his eyes.

"I agree," the sheriff boomed from Whiskers' other side. "I hope your dad does come to visit you. I'd like to meet the man who taught you how to outsmart these criminals. If it weren't for your suggestion, they would have gotten away with a truck full of cattle, and we wouldn't have known in time to get roadblocks up."

Logan blew out a breath of relief. "Did they get the truck already?"

"I just heard they're in the process of stopping it now. They didn't get far, thanks to you calling me so quickly." Sheriff Roscoe tipped his hat to Luke.

When Callie heard the roar of the sirens coming, she breathed deeply and smiled before closing her eyes.

Chapter 23

"**D**ad, I'm fine, honestly." Callie rolled her eyes as she spoke to her father over the cell phone from her hospital bed the next morning.

She had been taken to the Bozeman hospital. The medics in the ambulance said that the Beacon Creek clinic was closed, and they had no choice but to head into Bozeman. They took Luke with them at the same time.

The criminals had to wait for more ambulances to arrive before they were carted into Bozeman with the sheriff and his deputies escorting them. Only Deputy Chris Deacon stayed behind to wait for the state troopers to come and take the scene over.

One of the ranchers who had been deputized earlier in the week took the lone man who surrendered and locked him up in the Beacon Creek jail. He also stayed there with two other special deputies until the sheriff came back to relieve them.

It seemed cattle rustling was a pretty big offense, and the local sheriff's office wasn't equipped to handle the investigation. And given the fact that the state troopers were the ones who caught the truck full of cattle, they took jurisdiction. Sheriff Roscoe didn't argue the point; he was already down one full-time deputy, and there would be a large mess to clean up and people to talk down off ledges.

If he wasn't careful, there'd be a lynch mob heading to his jail cell, or the Bozeman hospital. Sometimes being a sheriff or police officer wasn't just about catching the bad guys, it was about making sure normal, law-abiding citizens didn't go crazy.

Bozeman only had one hospital, and the moment they arrived, the hospital administrator told Callie and Luke both that they would be treated in a different area from the cattle rustlers, and they had nothing to worry about.

Callie hadn't worried about them; she knew none of them would get near her. Not with the Manning family around.

Matthew must have called his parents, because they were already at the hospital waiting for her when she arrived. It warmed Callie's heart to know they were just as worried about her as they were about Luke.

Two nurses helped Callie get out of her vest before taking her to x-ray.

Luke had been right; the doctor wanted an MRI of her head, and he considered ordering a CT of her chest to make sure her heart didn't suffer any damage from the shot. However, once the radiologist read her x-ray, they saw she only had a hairline fracture in one rib, and it wasn't near anything vital.

"Honey, your mom and I will be on the next plane to Beacon Creek. Is the hotel in town still booked solid?" Paul Houston's tone would brook no argument. He was going to see his little girl who got shot stopping real-life cattle rustlers.

"It has rooms, but the Mannings offered you a room at their ranch. It's where I'm staying. There's plenty of room. The place is huge." Callie smiled up at Mrs. Manning, who was in her room and sitting next to Luke.

Luke hadn't left her side since the moment the doctor discharged him. The hospital wasn't too happy he hadn't gone home to rest, but he told them in no uncertain terms he wasn't leaving his woman alone in the hospital.

Two young nurses practically swooned, but they were shushed by the charge nurse.

"Tell them we'll be honored to accept their kind offer." Paul handed the phone to his wife.

"Honey, are you sure you're alright? Do you want to come home and have our doctors look you over?" Crystal had only just gotten herself under control before her husband handed her the phone. She wiped the last of the tears off her cheeks as she spoke to her daughter.

"Mom, honestly, I'm going to be fine. I'll be laid up for a little while, but I guess it doesn't matter, since my car won't be ready for another few days anyways." Callie really wasn't sure when her car would be ready, but she'd worry about that later.

"Alright. If you can leave soon, maybe we'll drive you home and then fly back to Louisiana from St. Paul."

"Thanks, Mom. We can discuss plans when you get here. I'll see you later today." Callie hung up and sighed.

"I'm looking forward to meeting your parents. They sound really nice." Luke's right arm was in a sling, and his eyes were a bit glossy. The doctor had given him some pain medication before they stitched him up, and he was still a bit groggy.

"So am I." Mrs. Manning had stayed the night with them both, while Mr. Manning left to head back to the ranch and check on things. He was going to come back when Callie was released and pick them all up.

"I'm going to apologize now for my parents. They're a handful. Especially when one of their daughters is injured." Callie wasn't looking forward to her dad looking for the sheriff and sticking his nose into the investigation. Maybe it was a good thing the state troopers were taking over.

The pain in Callie's head had lessened, but her chest still hurt like someone had hit her with a sledgehammer. She'd never done well with pain meds, so she refused the morphine they offered her. Instead, she was taking a non-opioid anti-inflammatory and pain reliever. She figured the extra pain was better than barfing up everything they put in her stomach.

When the nurse came in to take her vitals again, the doctor showed up with a big smile. "How's our superhero doing?"

"I'm ready to head home, if you're done with the testing?" She gave the doctor two thumbs up, hoping he would say she could go.

Dr. Raine looked at her chart, asked her a few questions, and did a quick exam. "I think you can go—on one condition."

"What's that?"

"You get plenty of rest. That means no more stake-outs for at least a month. No driving until you see your primary care, and no horse riding for a month. You need to let your body heal, and the jarring motion on a horse will only make things worse for you."

Callie nodded.

Mrs. Manning stood up to shake the doctor's hand. "Of course, Doctor. I'll make sure she stays down and gets plenty of rest."

Once he'd left, Luke called Matthew and told him to get to the hospital. They were going home.

As she got out of the truck, Callie winced. "I'm telling you, the doctor was right about not traveling or riding a horse for a while."

Her pain level had increased at least two points by the time she got back to the ranch and made it to her bedroom. She gritted her teeth as Mrs. Manning and Elizabeth helped her change into her jammies and get into bed.

"Do you want anything to eat or drink?" Elizabeth offered.

"Just water. I'd like to get some sleep if I can. Then maybe when I wake up, I can get some more of those chocolate chip pancakes?" Callie loved the pancakes at the ranch. She'd never thought to put chocolate chips in them, and would be happy to have them every day.

Mrs. Manning chuckled. "Of course, dear. Whatever you want. Just text me when you wake up. We'll leave you be to rest." She and Elizabeth left the room and closed the door behind them.

"Thank you, Lord, for protecting us all. Thank you that no one was seriously injured, either." Callie was very grateful for the hedge of protection the Lord had put around them all.

Even though she was injured, she didn't die. Neither did Luke. He'd be back up and riding before she was. Now she needed to sleep and rest up before her parents arrived. Before falling asleep, she sent another prayer asking for the Lord to keep her dad under control, and away from the rustlers.

The next thing Callie knew, she was being awoken by her mother. "Mom? How'd you get here so soon?"

Crystal Houston's auburn hair swayed as she chuckled. "Dear, you've slept the day away. It's already dinnertime."

"What?" Callie's eyes bulged, and she sat up too quickly. "Ohhh." She leaned back down on the bed. "I feel like I've been shot and run over by a semi." Her entire body ached. She didn't think there was a single muscle that didn't hurt.

Her mother's brows furrowed, and she ran a hand down the side of her head. "Shh, don't worry. You're going to feel this poorly for a few days. How about after dinner I run you an Epsom salt bath? That will help your muscles."

With a huge sigh, Callie relaxed. "Yes, please." She was grateful her mother was there to help take care of her. Then she thought about her dad. "Where's Dad? Please tell me he hasn't gone looking for the rustlers."

Crystal smiled. "No, dear. He's here talking to Mr. Manning and his sons, getting the entire story from them."

"Oh good. Can you help me get up and get dressed? I want to see him and make sure he doesn't go ballistic." With her dad here at the ranch, Callie would be able to manage him a little bit better, but she couldn't do it from her bed. She would have to get up to ensure her dad didn't go all Detective Houston on anyone.

When Callie entered the living room, her father stood up and came to her. "Oh, sweetheart, it's so good to see you among the living. Can I hug you?" He put his arms out for a hug, and she entered his warm embrace.

Callie hadn't seen her parents since Christmas, and she missed them. "Thank you, Dad, for sending that vest so quickly. I never would have made it without it." A stinging sensation pricked the backs of her eyes, and she blinked quickly to keep the tears at bay.

Someone behind her sniffled, and Callie thought it was probably her mom.

"I'm so grateful to Steve. I owe him big time for ensuring you got it in time." Her dad's hug was careful, but she still ached.

Her ribs were killing her, and her breaths came in slow, ragged gasps. She tried to pull out of her dad's hug, but he held her a beat too long. "Ah." She couldn't keep the sound of pain from her voice.

"Oh, darling, I'm so sorry." Her father stepped back, and his face fell when he saw the look of pain across his daughter's face.

She put her hand up as she took in a few breaths. "It's fine. My ribs."

Paul Houston nodded and gave his wife a knowing look. "I've been there before. It'll take a few days before you can breathe properly again. But it does get better. In fact, I bet tomorrow you'll feel more like yourself."

"The Epsom salt bath will help," her mother added.

"Yes, we have a big bag of it. Ranchers use it regularly." Mrs. Manning laughed and motioned for everyone to sit.

Callie held her arms across her chest and sat back on the sofa next to her mother. Then she looked to Luke, who sat in the recliner across from her. "So, what has my dad been telling you all?" It could have been anything. Her dad could have gone off on them for letting her get hurt, or he could have been telling them all about her childhood and how proud he was of her. It was a toss-up as to which tack her dad would take.

"I didn't know you were a girl scout." Luke's eyes glistened, and his lips curved up.

"Only for about five seconds. When I realized they didn't do the same stuff the boy scouts did, I dropped out. I wasn't interested in earning patches for sewing and selling cookies." She held her hands up. "Not that there's anything wrong with those things. I had several friends who were girl scouts, and I respect the organization. It's just I wasn't interested in girly things." She shrugged and realized her mistake. A pain shot through her chest and she winced.

Her mother leaned over with worried eyes. "Oh sweetie, is there anything I can do? Do you need more medicine?"

Callie started to shake her head, then stopped when a pain shot behind her eyes. "Maybe Ibuprofen?" She slept everything off that day. If she wanted to get ahead of the pain, she'd have to remember to take the over the counter stuff as often as the label said.

Mrs. Houston reached into her purse and took out a small bottle and handed her daughter two bluish-green capsules with a glass of water.

Callie took the offered medicine and thanked her mother.

Mrs. Manning stood up, and Elizabeth followed her. "I need to get dinner out of the oven and onto the table. We're having pot roast tonight. Then tomorrow we're having a big barbecue to celebrate our kids catching the cattle thieves."

"Mom and Dad, wait until you taste their beef. It's the best I've ever had. I had no idea meat had so much flavor until I came here." Callie smiled appreciatively at Mrs. Manning as she left the room. "And their barbecue! I thought St. Louis had the best barbecue in the world." She shook her head. "Nope, they've got nothing on the Triple J Ranch." A smaller pain shot through her head and she remembered she couldn't shake her head, not today at least.

Just the thought of their famous barbecue made Callie's mouth water. She didn't think she'd ever get tired of their beef, no matter how they cooked it.

Mrs. Houston raised her brows and stood up. "I think I'll see if Judith needs any help with dinner."

Paul Houston rubbed his hands together. "What's your barbecue setup? Is it a smoker, or a grill?"

The Manning men all laughed. Mr. Manning offered to show Paul their equipment. In fact, all the Manning men got up except for Luke. When the other men left the room, Luke came over and sat on the couch next to Callie.

"I'm so glad to see you up. I was gettin' worried about ya. But Ma said to let you sleep." When his eyes glided over her body, she blushed. He took her hand in his. "You look like you might be feeling a bit better. When you first walked in the room, you were a little white."

After taking a deep breath, Callie said, "Yeah, it was a bit painful at first. But my muscles are warming up. The Ibuprofen is helping." She turned her head and looked him up and down. "How are you doing? How's the arm?"

"Boy, we make a good couple, don't we?" Luke chuckled. "But I doubt I'm in as much pain as you are. I took a short nap after you did, and I'm feeling better myself."

"So, does that mean you're going riding after dinner?" She smirked. There was no way he was feeling good. He'd been shot less than twenty-four hours ago. He had to be in a lot of pain, even if the bullet just went through the fat and muscle in his arm.

"Ah, no." He chortled. "I think I'm going to wait for you to get back on a horse. Plus, with my right hand in a sling, it would be a little difficult to mount and dismount." He lifted up his right arm in the sling and winced.

Luke never expected a gunshot through the arm would be so painful after the stitches. "At least you didn't have to get stitches. Did you know I can't take a regular shower until they come out?" He scoffed. "I have to take a bath!"

When Callie lightly laughed, the sound sent warmth through his soul.

"I think I'd take stitches over a cracked rib any day." She lightly rubbed her ribs and winced. "Laughing hurts, so please don't make me do it again. At least not until I'm healed."

"Deal." He wanted to put his right hand out to shake, but then realized it was in a sling. How many things would his body try to do instinctively, only to be denied when the sling kept him from moving this way or that?

Instead, he scooted closer and put his left arm around her shoulders. "Does that hurt?"

His husky voice sent shivers of pleasure down Callie's body. "Not at all." The huskiness in her voice shocked her, and she cleared her throat.

"Good. I think I want to stay here next to you the rest of the night." He leaned over and kissed the top of her head.

It wasn't a real kiss, just a show of endearment, but it meant the world to Callie. She hoped that when they were both feeling better, he'd give her a real kiss. One that she knew would curl her toes.

They stayed like that for who knew how long, not talking, just enjoying the feel of being close to one another. When Callie saw Luke get shot the night before, she'd thought she was going to lose him before she had a chance to tell him how she really felt. Now wasn't the time, but she would tell him. Even if they couldn't be together, her soul screamed for Luke to know the truth.

She must have closed her eyes at some point.

When someone cleared their throat, she startled.

"Sorry, I don't mean to interrupt, but dinner's ready." Mark's smirk caused Callie's cheeks to burn.

She lowered her gaze and hoped he hadn't been there watching them for too long. Callie had never had a chance to talk to Mark, but it seemed like he had lost interest in her about the time she realized she only cared for him as a friend. Maybe she wouldn't have to say anything at all.

Luke cleared his throat. "We'll be right in. Thanks."

Mark turned around and headed back into the dining room.

"Do you need any help gettin' up?" Luke looked into her eyes, and her heart skipped more than a few beats.

She shook her head, and then reconsidered when she tightened her stomach muscles before standing. The pain shot through her abdomen and chest, and she had to lean back and take a few shallow breaths. "Yeah, maybe I do. But give me a sec." She closed her eyes and waited for the pain to pass.

Luke walked over to the side of the sofa and used his left arm to help her up once she opened her eyes again. "Ready?"

Callie took a deep breath. "Yes."

He lifted her under her left arm, and she put most of her weight on her legs. Without using her stomach muscles, she was able to stand up.

"Okay, stand still for a moment until you get your bearin's. Then we'll head into the dinin' room." Luke kept his hand on her arm in case she swayed.

When Callie could take a few deep breaths, she took a step forward. Then another one. After few attempts, she was able to walk without Luke's help, but she wasn't about to tell him that. She enjoyed the feel of his hand on her arm.

"Here they are. Our heroes!" Mr. Manning led both families in a rousing round of clapping.

Matthew began hootin' and hollerin'. His brothers joined in, and by the time Callie was seated in the chair next to Luke, everyone was smiling and laughing.

"Hey, Matthew and Logan helped us take them down. Luke and I couldn't have done it without them." The credit had to go to all four of them. Callie wouldn't take all the glory. And she was confident Luke wouldn't, either.

Matthew waved his hand. "Yeah, yeah. But we didn't get shot."

"I think that means you did a better job than we did," Luke said wryly.

Once everyone was seated, Mr. Manning stood. "I'd like to say grace and thank the good Lord for protecting our family."

Dinner went well; Callie had an easier time of eating than poor Luke. Since Luke was right-handed, and he couldn't use his right hand at all to cut meat, he had a tough time of it. Callie offered to cut up his meat for him after he made few failed attempts on his own.

Everyone enjoyed the meal and the company. But when dessert was done, Callie was waning. Even though she wanted to stay up and talk to everyone, her eyes were drooping, and she still needed to bathe before going to bed.

When her mother noticed her eyes closing, she said it was time for bed. "I'll help you get into the tub for a good soak. I'll bet after a long night of sleep, you'll be feeling ready to go tomorrow." She chuckled.

Callie wasn't one to sit around, and the Houstons had discussed how well their daughter would listen to the doctor's orders and rest. Crystal said it would last two days, and her father said maybe three. It would all depend on that cracked rib.

Luke stood up and helped her get out of her chair.

Crystal noticed the way Luke and Callie looked at each other, and she smiled.

Once her daughter was settled in the tub of hot water and Epsom salt, she sat on the commode and asked about Luke.

"Mom. I hardly know him. We just went through something pretty stressful together." There was no way Callie wanted to discuss Luke with her mom. At least, not yet.

There wasn't anything to tell her mom other than how she felt. But she wasn't sure if Luke returned her feelings. The cowboy was attracted to her—she was pretty sure about that. But like she said, they'd gone through a pretty traumatic experience together, so it would naturally bring them closer. The only question was, would that closeness bond them romantically, or as friends?

Chapter 24

Two days later, both Callie and Luke were feeling much better. Luke was still complaining about taking baths instead of showers due to the need to keep his stitches dry, but his biggest complaint was not being able to work the ranch.

His parents and brothers told him until he was cleared by the doctor, he was not allowed on his horse, nor was he allowed to do a lick of work.

Callie wasn't much better. No one would let her do anything either, but since too much exertion made it difficult to breathe, she wasn't too upset. Yet.

Instead, the two of them spent most of their time talking, playing games, and watching some TV. Neither of them were big TV watchers, but it turned out they liked similar movies and got caught up on a few blockbusters they had missed.

Although, there was a rom-com Callie had missed and wanted to watch, but Luke wasn't interested. So she watched it with the other ladies in the house while the men watched sports in the other room.

When their movie was over, Crystal decided it was time to begin her matchmaking. She had patiently watched as Callie and Luke sat next to each other, laughed, and just generally enjoyed their time together. However, she hadn't seen them holding hands or kissing yet, and she worried they may not know how they felt about each other.

"Callie, please tell me what's going on with you and that handsome cowboy."

"Mom, please." Callie was mortified. She couldn't believe her mom had asked her about Luke in front of his mother and sister.

Elizabeth continued to stay at the ranch. Until the leaders of the gang were all captured, everyone thought it best she stay there. And with the visitors, Elizabeth was needed to help in the kitchen.

The ladies laughed, and Mrs. Manning added, "Yes, please tell us. Has Luke told you yet how he feels?"

Callie moaned and put her head in her hands.

"Come on, Mom. Leave Callie alone. This is all so new. Give them time to figure it all out before you grill them." Elizabeth giggled and winked at Callie.

Callie knew she had a friend and compatriot in Elizabeth.

"Elizabeth, why don't you tell us about your wedding plans? The last I heard, Logan was having a conniption and was worried the plans were all falling apart." Changing the subject to a wedding would always get women's focus elsewhere. And at the moment, Callie wanted them looking anywhere but at her.

The bride-to-be shook her head and sighed. "I swear, Logan's more of a drama queen than a high school cheerleader."

Everyone laughed and agreed men were so full of drama.

"The wedding planner has had her hands full, but she's helping us get everything together." Elizabeth went into detail about her wedding, and how the plans had to change a little bit. But she was very happy with where they were going now. The fall wedding was on track, finally.

In the other room, the men were all watching a baseball game, but Paul had been keeping an eye on Luke. He noticed that his daughter and this boy had eyes for each other, but no one had said anything to him yet. He thought it was time to grill the cowboy and see what his intentions were for his baby girl.

Paul had been on his best behavior so far, and only went to the sheriff's office once to find out what was happening with the investigation. Since the sheriff wasn't involved, there wasn't much to learn. So now he would use his investigative skills to find out if this boy had his sights set on his daughter, or if he was someone to warn his daughter about.

Itching to do something besides sit around, he got up and went over to where Luke was sitting. Paul had learned that during an interrogation, it was always good to have the high ground. So he stood next to the cowboy instead of taking a seat.

Paul crossed his arms over his chest. "Luke, tell me about my daughter's time here before the shooting."

The cowboy in question looked up into the stern face of Callie's dad and gulped. For a moment, Luke thought he was in trouble. But he hadn't done anything wrong, had he? He took a moment to scan his memories for anything untoward, and there was nothing he could think of.

Maybe the fighting with Mark in front of her wasn't gentlemanly, but it wasn't too far out of line, was it? Did a city girl think those types of antics too much? Would her father? He didn't want to get off on the wrong foot with Callie's dad, so he stood up and put his hands in his back pockets. Standing next to the man, he could look him straight in the eyes, like a man with nothing to hide.

"Sir, we went horseback riding every day. She's a natural, by the way. We picnicked, and she attended church services with us every Sunday." Luke thought about some of the other things they did, but he didn't want to tell her father that he had held her hand or kissed her on the top of her head.

Of course, Mr. Houston knew about the stakeouts and the final fight. But other than that, there wasn't anything much to tell. He and Callie didn't spend much time alone, unless you counted their daily rides, but those were out in the open.

There were too many people on this ranch for him and Callie to be alone for very long. Certainly there wouldn't have been enough alone time to get into any kind of trouble. Besides, the cowboy code wouldn't allow him to be anything other than a gentleman. His folks raised him proper. He might not be perfect, but he was a God-fearing gentleman cowboy, and he would never take advantage of a lady.

"Ah-huh. And have there been any promises yet?" Paul arched a brow and flexed his overly-large biceps. For an older man, the cop definitely stayed in shape.

Not quite certain what Callie's father meant, Luke furrowed his brows and waited for an explanation. When nothing else came, he had to ask, "What do you mean?"

"I mean, young man, have you made any promises about the future to my little girl?"

Luke's Adam's apple bobbed up and down, and his mouth went dry. It was way too soon for that. No matter what he felt for Callie, he wasn't ready to promise a future. Was he? "No, sir. That wouldn't be appropriate."

Paul leaned forward with a menacing growl. "And why is that?"

Luke understood how Mr. Houston could get perps to talk. If he treated them anything like what was happening now, all those guilty would spill their beans. Even though he wasn't guilty of a thing, he wanted to confess. If for no other reason than to get away from the intimidating man.

"We don't even live in the same state, and we hardly know each other." There were other reason, but Luke didn't think Mr. Houston wanted to hear about his insecurities.

If he was being grilled this hard, did that mean Callie really liked him? He could tell she was attracted to him and enjoyed spending time with him, but did she return his strong feelings? They hadn't even discussed anything of the sort yet.

"And what are you doing to rectify this situation?" Paul uncrossed his arms and fisted them at his sides.

Was it getting hotter in the room, or was Luke imagining it? His throat was tightening up, and he had to lick his lips to get some moisture on them. If he wasn't at home, he would have thought they were in the Sahara Desert with as hot and dry as his body felt at that moment.

The next thing he knew, Mr. Houston was asking him his credit score and for a copy of his credit report.

Mr. Manning chuckled, and Matthew busted up laughing.

"Oh man, I'm so glad I didn't leave the room. This is priceless," Mark said between chuckles.

Roman leaned next to his brother. "Aren't you glad you realized there wasn't any chemistry with you and Callie?"

The fiery gaze in Paul's eyes when he turned toward Mark made his laughter die in his throat.

Mark lifted his hands. "Whoa now. We're just friends, nothing more."

John took the opportunity to twist the knife. "But you did take Callie out on a few dates. Don't lie."

Mark backhanded his brother and scowled at him.

"Ow!" John rubbed his shoulder and backed away from Mark and his stinging backhand.

"So who all is dating my little girl?" Paul reached to put his hand where his gun usually rode on his belt, but it wasn't there. His arm lowered back down to his side, and then he crossed both arms over his chest.

"Okay, this has been fun, but boy howdy am I glad we only had two girls, and one is already engaged." Mr. Manning stood up and walked to Paul. "My sons both spent some time with Callie, but early on it was obvious that Mark and your daughter were only going to be friends, and nothing more."

"Uh-huh. And what about with Luke?" Paul was actually having a great time scaring some sense into Luke, as he called it. This was how he had treated all suitors for his daughters. He was about to dial it back when the doorbell rang.

Everyone looked to Mr. Manning, who said he'd get it.

While waiting for the patriarch of the family to return, Paul eyed Luke and pursed his lips. It was the only way to keep from laughing. He couldn't wait to tell Crystal how this all went down.

"It seems we have a guest." Mr. Manning led Sheriff Roscoe into the room.

"Sheriff, it's nice to see you again. Do you have more news on the cattle rustlers?" Paul had been meaning to get back to the sheriff's office and hang out to see if he could glean any more information on the case. But he knew that in order to get anything worthwhile, he had to wait until they had enough time to gather some information.

"Actually, I came to visit your daughter, Mr. Houston."

"Please, call me Paul." He walked over to shake the lawman's hand. "Do you have some follow-up questions about the crime scene?"

"No sir. I had a favor to ask of your girl."

Mrs. Manning entered the living room with the other women on her heels. Visitors to the Triple J wasn't common, so everyone was curious as to who it was.

"Sheriff Roscoe, so good to see you again." Mrs. Manning shook his hand. "Can I get you an iced tea?"

"That'd be mighty nice. Thank you, Judith." He took his hat off and nodded to the women. "Miss Callie, might I have a word?"

Callie pointed to herself and raised her eyebrows. "Me? Is everything alright?"

The sheriff chuckled. "Of course. Nothing's wrong. I just wanted to ask you a favor."

Callie shrugged and led the man to the dining room table.

Mrs. Manning prepared iced tea for everyone while Callie and the sheriff got settled.

"So, what can I do for you, Sheriff?" She wasn't sure what he wanted. Unless it had to do with the case.

"How're ya healin' up?" He gave her a cursory glance, but nothing seemed amiss. In fact, unless you knew what happened, you'd never know Callie Houston was injured. Except for when she moved the wrong way and winced, which she did just then.

"Mostly fine. The headaches are gone, as are the sore muscles. Just waiting for my ribs to fully heal."

"When do you see the doc again?"

That was a mighty personal question. Then again, most people in Beacon Creek were all up into each other's business, anyway. She wondered what the Diner Divas were saying about her now.

She furrowed her brow and realized she needed to get into town with her parents and make sure the rumors didn't tell of her early demise. "I'll be going to the Beacon Creek Clinic in a couple days." She didn't have a local doctor, so she figured she'd go with Luke when he went in for his follow-up and see the same doctor.

The sheriff nodded. "Good, good."

"What's this all about, Sheriff?"

Mrs. Manning set a pitcher of sweet tea on the table in front of them with glasses full of ice. Then she left the room to take a tray in to her family and the Houstons.

Once the sheriff took a drink, he set the glass down. "That's some mighty fine tea. I bet you don't want to leave it any time soon, do you?"

Callie's lips parted, and she blinked a few times, not really sure what he was getting at. "You're right, it is pretty good." She took another drink and waited for the sheriff.

He cleared his throat. "It's come to my attention that you don't have a job at the moment."

She nodded.

"Well, it just so happens we have an opening for a deputy. With all the rich folks from California who've moved here, and the recent spate of crimes, our budget was increased for another deputy. I've just not gotten around to hiring one." He looked at her out of the corner of his eye.

"I doubt my dad would want to move here. He's close to retirement with the New Orleans PD." She wondered why he was telling her this and not her father.

"I'm not looking to hire your pa. I was hoping you'd apply for the job."

She held a hand up. "Wait a minute. I'm not a cop. I'm a buyer and contracts negotiator."

The sheriff disagreed. "I'd say you were born to be a cop. Your previous job just gave you some more skills you can use on the job. Negotiating is a large part of being a sheriff's deputy. With your understanding of the criminal mind, you could work your way up to sheriff by the time I'm ready to retire."

She giggled. "I doubt the good folks of Beacon Creek would want me as their sheriff."

"Actually, I had several ranchers come in this week and ask if you were going to join the department." He looked her squarely in the eye. "We could use someone with your skillset. What do you say?"

"But I've never been to an academy."

"That's the great thing about Montana—you don't have to. With your education, all you have to do is apply. There'll be courses you have to take in your free time during the first year, but we can work around any schedule you need." He took another drink from the tea and waited for her response.

She opened and closed her mouth a few times, not really sure what to say.

<h1 style="text-align:center;">Chapter 25</h1>

When the sheriff left, Callie pulled her dad aside and told him what the sheriff wanted.

"Honey, that's great. You know I've always wanted you to be a cop. While I'd prefer it if you worked with me, I'd be very proud to see you on the force here." Her dad beamed and squeezed her shoulder lightly.

Callie still didn't want to be hugged; it hurt too much. But a touch on her shoulder felt almost like her dad was hugging her.

She had taken daily Epsom salt baths for five days and her muscle aches were mostly gone, except for the muscles around her cracked rib. Those would take time. Her head was doing much better as well. She only ended up with a small lump at the base of her skull. While she still wasn't up for the bumping and jostling of riding a horse, she was looking forward to getting back on Whiskers soon.

"Do you really think this is for me? You know I've never wanted to be a cop." Callie leaned against the edge of the chair in the front room. None of the ladies were in there; they were all still in the living room with the rest of the group.

"But being a country sheriff is very different. You'll mostly just have to give parking tickets and take calls about cats up trees." Paul laughed. It was more complicated than that, but it definitely wasn't anything like a city cop, especially one in New Orleans.

"True, there won't be any crazy people spouting off about vampires and witches out here." Callie remembered one case where her father had to track down a drug dealer who had laced marijuana with PCP, and people were seeing the craziest things right out of horror movies. Then there was the zombie drug going around a few years ago. She shivered. Cases like those were what made her leave Louisiana in the first place.

"Honey, I think you've seen the worst of things here in Beacon Creek and survived it. Just always do me a favor?" He looked at her with love and warmth radiating from his eyes.

"Of course, Daddy. What?"

"Never forget your bulletproof vest." He laughed.

She started to laugh, then winced. "No laughing, Daddy. Not yet." She lightly rubbed her offending rib. "I think I'll have a couple of them on hand so I'll never forget to wear one."

"Does that mean you'll apply?" Hope shone in her father's eyes, and a little bit of pride, if she wasn't mistaken. Only Paul Houston would want his daughter who just got shot in the chest while stopping crime less than a week ago to apply to be a sheriff's deputy.

"Just because I apply doesn't mean they'll take me. Keep that in mind."

"I think you've got an in with the sheriff. I wouldn't worry." He chuckled.

Taking a deep breath, she said, "We'll see."

When she went back into the room, she announced she'd be applying for the position of Beacon Creek Sheriff's Deputy.

The room was louder than the rodeo with everyone hooting and hollering. People were talking over each other, and some were asking her questions but not giving her a chance to answer.

Callie put her hands in the air and yelled, "Hold up. Let me answer a few questions before you move on." Even though it was nuts, she was happy and could feel the love and excitement of everyone in the room. "The sheriff came by to ask me to apply for his open position. I'm going to apply, but keep in mind that doesn't mean I'll make it."

"How long do you have to wait before you can apply?" Matthew asked. His eyes went back and forth between Luke and Callie.

"I'll have to ask the doctor when I see him in two days. But I imagine since one of the first steps after filling out the application is a physical exam, I'll have to wait until my rib is fully healed and I've been given the green light by the doc." Callie wasn't sure how long that would be, but it couldn't be longer than a month away, could it?

"You should move in here. We can help you pack up your stuff in St. Paul and get it all here before you even apply." Luke took one of her hands in his, and the entire room went quiet.

"Um, while I love having Callie here, I think it might be best if she lived in town. You know, closer to the station?" Mrs. Manning gave her son a pointed look.

"I'll not have my daughter shacking up with the man she's dating." Paul pointed his finger at Luke and gave him his scariest cop stare.

"Oh, no!" Luke waved his hands in the air. "You've got it all wrong. I don't want her moving in with me. Callie could stay in the guest room where she is now. It would all be above board."

Wincing, Callie raised her hand and squeaked. "Excuse me." She could feel the heat in her cheeks rising. "I think I would prefer living in town. It would be easier to be close to the station whenever I need to be there. I love the ranch and would want to visit as much as possible, but getting my own place really would be best."

She could feel the tension in the room ease as everyone realized that Luke was just over-excited and hadn't though through what he said.

Elizabeth jumped up. "I've got a great idea. How about you move in with me for a few months? That would give you plenty of time to find a place in town." She and Logan weren't getting married until October, so there was room for Callie until then.

"Are you sure you want me living with you? With the wedding coming up, won't you be really busy and need the extra space for everything?" Callie liked the idea of living with Elizabeth until she found the right place, but at the same time, she didn't want to get in her way.

With a wave of her hand, Elizabeth put a stop to that line of thinking. "I would love to have you stay with me." The corners of her lips turned up. "Just be sure you move out before my wedding."

With both hands holding her chest in place, Callie was able to laugh without too much pain. "Totally. I don't want to be there when Logan moves in."

"Perfect. When your parents leave, you can move in with me then. I'll even see if I can get a few days off to go help you pack when the time comes. Until then, I have a spare room with everything you'll need."

"Elizabeth, this is so wonderful. I can't thank you enough." The only thing Callie needed now was her car. Well, that and Luke to ask her out on a real date. Not one with his family around.

After dinner that night, Luke finally got Callie to himself. "How about we take a walk outside? There's a full moon and lots of stars." He put his hand out, and she took it.

"What a crazy week, right? Did you ever think you'd get shot trying to stop cattle rustlers?" Callie giggled and shook her head. It was never a scenario she had pictured herself in.

"Actually, I had thought about it before." He walked her to the side of the house so they wouldn't have an audience.

She stopped in her tracks. "What? I thought cattle rustlers were rare?"

He chuckled. "They are. But when you're a ten-year-old boy, sometimes you like to play cattle rustler instead of cowboys and Indians." Luke shrugged. "It's a thang."

"I see I have a lot to learn." A sound in the distance caught her attention, and she turned to listen again. When a horse whinnied, she relaxed. "I haven't seen Whiskers in a few days. What do you say we go visit the horses?"

"Sounds like a good plan." Luke led the way to the barn.

Halfway there, he slowed his pace and looked down to the ground before looking back up at Callie. "Would you like to go out to lunch with me after our doctor's appointment? I was thinking we could head into Bozeman for a nice meal at my favorite steak house." There, he'd asked her out for a real date. Not one that his brothers could hone in on, or rustlers could interrupt.

Finally! she wanted to scream. It was about time. Callie had wondered if he'd lost interest in her after her Dad's interrogation. Her mom told her about it, and she was thoroughly embarrassed. The only good thing was that she doubted the Diner Divas would hear about it.

"I'd like that." She was fairly certain her voice didn't break when she spoke. Her heart was beating so hard, and the rushing sound flowing through her ears kept her from hearing too well.

They entered the barn, and Callie took in a deep breath. The scent of hay, horses, and wood wafted through her entire being. It was her second-favorite scent. Her first being Luke. His leather, horse, and ginger scent always sent a chill of excitement up her spine when she was close to him.

These scents now enveloping her were home. She had never had a scent that made her feel safe and secure like this. Spending the rest of her life here in Beacon Creek felt like a dream come true. She prayed that she'd get the deputy job, and everything would work out as planned. Especially now that Luke had asked her out on an official date.

Chapter 26

Two days later when Callie came out for breakfast, Luke was sitting at the table with his head in his one good hand.

She took the seat next to him and put a comforting hand on his back. "What's wrong? Did something happen?"

"Good morning, Callie." He leaned in and kissed her temple. He had done that several times over the past two days, and noticed that it was something Callie enjoyed as much as he did. Her scent of lemon, vanilla, and horse enveloped his senses and worked to calm him down, just like it did every time he got close to her.

When she first arrived, Callie only smelled of lemon and vanilla. Luke loved that she now smelled as though she belonged on the ranch. Add in the womanly fragrance of lemon and vanilla, and he thought her scent should be bottled and put into one of those smelly candles. Although, this is one he would happily light every day.

"Good morning. Is everything alright? You look sad."

He nodded. "Yes, and no. Since I won't be getting my stitches out yet, Pa said I can't drive. So we won't be able to go to Bozeman today."

"I can drive. I don't have to worry about stitches." She hadn't gotten her SUV back yet, but Mikey had called to say that the part was in the US and on its way yesterday. So, she should have her SUV all good as new within a few days. But surely they would let her drive one of their trucks, right?

Her parents had a rental car, but they would be leaving right after her doctor's appointment and heading to the airport to go home. Her dad's leave of absence was up, and he had to get back to work.

"Actually, you can't." A new voice had entered the room, and Callie turned as she remembered it.

"Harper. It's good to see you again." Callie got up to give her new friend a light hug. Hugging was still something she was leery of, as it could hurt depending on where someone put their hands and squeezed.

"Hiya, Callie. I came to pick you and Luke up for your doctor's appointments. The doc said neither of you were to drive yet." Harper sat down, and Mrs. Manning put a cup of coffee in front of her.

Callie took a sip of her coffee. "My parents could have taken us into town. You didn't have to come out here."

"I wanted to come and see if I could beg a plate of those outstanding chocolate chip pancakes." Her cheeky grin caused Mrs. Manning to laugh.

"Of course you can, dear. You know you're always welcome here." Mrs. Manning went to the stove and put on pancakes for both Callie and Harper.

Since the incident, Callie had been sleeping in, so it was already past eight in the morning when she came in for breakfast. The rest of the house had eaten. The Houstons were packing up the last of their bags while their daughter ate breakfast.

"I don't understand why I can't drive. It's been over a week since I was shot. The hospital said I could drive after a week. So what's the problem?" Callie was certain she had been released to drive already, hadn't she?

"The doctor here is worried about your ribs. If you have to stop quickly, then the seatbelt is going to kill you with pain. You could easily lose control. It's just not safe yet. Plus, you could end up with a full break on your rib." The sad look in Harper's eyes caused everyone to stop and think about Callie's injury.

Callie rolled her eyes. "Fine, I'll talk to the doctor about driving again. I'm sure he'll let me drive to-day." He better; she had a date she needed to be on that afternoon.

It was hard to accept that she had remembered the instructions wrong. The hospital said to speak with her primary care about when she could drive, and since she had to follow up within a week, she must have figured that would be when she could drive again. How else did they expect her to get to a doctor? Especially since they didn't have Uber here.

Her parents came into the kitchen to say their goodbyes. "Oh, darling. I'm so proud of you for what you've done here. But," her mother leveled a finger in her direction. "You had better always wear a vest. Just because you won't see much action here, doesn't mean someone won't get the drop on you. You've seen what has happened to your Dad over the years."

Callie's heart warmed with the love she had for her parents. "Yes, Mom. After what happened, I will most definitely wear a vest every day." She hugged her mom and then turned to her dad.

"I've already reached out to my friend and he's put an order in for you. Since you'll be down for a few weeks, I told him not to worry about overnighting it. But I second what your mother said. A broken rib isn't anything to laugh over, but it's a heck of a lot better than dying." Paul Houston hugged his daughter lightly in an effort to keep from hurting her sore ribs.

"Thanks, Daddy. I really do appreciate it." And she did. After getting shot by the rustlers, she had learned how important it was to wear a bullet proof vest when chasing down criminals. She wasn't about to put on a uniform without first slipping on her new vest.

Callie wasn't worried about where she'd go after she died, but she still had things to here on Earth.

Chapter 27

After her parents left, Harper drove Callie and Luke into town to see the doc.

Luke was sitting in the waiting room after seeing the doctor. He had been first, and knew what the doctor was going to say to Callie. While he waited for Callie's turn, he called Elizabeth.

"I have an idea, but I don't know how you'll feel about it," Luke said before he even greeted his sister.

"Well, hello to you too, little brother. You really need to learn how to make small talk when you call someone, or at least greet them properly." She chuckled into the phone.

"Yeah, yeah. Sorry. I don't have much time. Callie's in with the doctor, and she's going to be told she can't drive for six weeks. We had our first date planned for today, but with both of us unable to drive, I wondered if you and Logan might want to double date with us and head out to Bozeman for a nice lunch. It's on me."

She considered his offer, but her work schedule wouldn't allow for her to take a long lunch that day. "How about dinner? I know I can't get away today, but I'll get off before five tonight. Logan opened the store, so he'll be off before me. We can come and pick you both up at the ranch and head into Bozeman. Would that work?"

"That would be fantastic. Thanks, Elizabeth. Call me when you're on your way. I'll see you later." He hung up and waited impatiently for Callie.

She wasn't too happy when she came out of the doctor's office. The sadness on Callie's face hit his heart hard. He started to bring his right hand up to rub at the pain in his chest, but remembered he couldn't. Instead, he sighed. He knew this was going to hurt her. She was an independent woman who hated relying on someone else. Without being able to drive, she'd be stuck at the mercy of others.

When he told her his new plans, the smile that lit up her face was enough to make his heart beat so hard in his chest, he thought it might runaway.

"I think that's a great idea. Your sister has quickly become one of my best friends. I guess living through what we have the past week bonded us quickly." Or maybe it was all the time they spent together since Elizabeth was first attacked? Callie didn't know what it was, but there was most certainly a bond between her and Luke's older sister.

While she did want the date to be just the two of them, she had resigned herself to knowing that she wouldn't be getting any alone time with Luke in the near future. Until Luke got the all clear to drive, it would be double dates with other couples Luke knew. Or just spending time together in town at the diner.

Not having come from a small town, Callie wasn't quite sure what to make of the Diner Diva's. She really didn't want them gossiping about her and Luke, maybe they could find out when those ladies were off doing something else, and then head to the diner?

One thing was for certain, she was not in Minnesota anymore.

Luke didn't know how long it would be before she could apply for the deputy position, but he hoped this healing period wouldn't set her back too much.

Luke would be happy to help her with bills if she needed money. But he also knew she would never take his money. The car wasn't going to cost her anything. The only costs he could see were the ones associated with her move. He knew Elizabeth wouldn't charge her rent, and her car was paid for, but he didn't know about any other costs or how much she had in her savings account.

They'd have the next day at the ranch, and then on Saturday she was moving to Elizabeth's place. He hoped they would have time to talk about her near-future plans.

"Then how are we getting back to the ranch now?" Callie hadn't heard what those plans were. And she wasn't in any mood to hang out in town. The only good part of the day was going to be when they double-dated for dinner, and she needed to get back and clean up for a dinner date. What she was wearing was fine for a lunch date, but dinner required something a bit nicer. Maybe even a dress.

"Roman's on his way into town now to get us. He should be here shortly." Luke sat next to Callie and put his arm around her shoulder. "I'm sorry we aren't goin' to get to have a date with just us for a little while. But at least we do get to go out tonight."

"True. I'm sorry I'm being a downer right now. I really thought I was going to be able to drive after this appointment." She didn't know how she was going to pack up her apartment in St. Paul and get it all back here. She couldn't afford a mover, and her dad had just taken a week off for her. He wouldn't be able to take another week off.

"Don't worry. I completely understand. We'll figure this all out. It's goin' t'be fine. You'll see." With God in control, how could it not? Luke was confident everything would work out fine in the end, as long as they believed in Him and followed his lead.

Dinner that night was exactly what Callie had hoped it would be. And she was very glad she decided to wear a dress. The steak house in Bozeman was nicer than she expected. It was all dark wood paneled walls, the nice kind. Not fake stuff on the walls. Either the restaurant was seriously old, or they used reclaimed wood on the walls. It was beautiful with the various colors running through the wood and the uneven texture across it all. She felt more like she was in an upscale barn that was decorated for dinner. The tables and booths were lighter in color, to offset the dark walls. It was perfection.

Their table had a red and white checked tablecloth and the chairs were a light wood, maybe a pine? Callie wasn't a wood expert, but however they did it, the restaurant managed to create a warm and inviting feeling. In the center of their table was a candle with a fake flickering wick. She had to do a double take to figure out it was fake. The decoration looked so real. However, she was glad it was fake. With all the wood in the place, it wouldn't be a great place for real candles.

Luke held her chair out for her and smiled up at him when she sat down, and he helped her to scoot in...with one arm. He was always such a gentleman. Callie couldn't remember a man whom she had dated that had ever had such manners. "Thank you."

"You're welcome." Luke's warm smile sent her heartbeat into overtime.

The evening went very well. Everyone had plenty to discuss, besides the cattle rustlers. It seemed no one wanted to discuss anything that had to do with criminals.

Callie looked over to Luke's plate and noticed he was having trouble again trying to cut his steak. "Here, let me help."

Luke tried to stop her, but she wasn't going to let him do his stupid macho act and not let her cut the steak for him. The man only had one working arm at the moment. He had been shot for Pete's sake.

"Luke, you might as well get used to it. She's going to be your partner. When you can't do something, she will. And when she can't do something, you'll do it for her." Logan's matter of fact tone ruffled Luke's feathers.

"But I'm not a little boy. I can cut my own steak." He knew he sounded like a little boy being thwarted.

Callie stopped and set his knife and fork down. "I know you can cut your own food. But you don't want to do anything to cause your arm to be worse, do you? Those muscles need time to heal."

She understood what he was feeling, she had felt the same way earlier that day when she was told she couldn't be in the front seat of a car for another six weeks. Something about the seatbelt crossing her chest and causing more injury should she be in an accident, or even come to a very sudden stop.

Just wearing her bra had hurt, so she could somewhat understand the restrictions, but it still didn't make it any easier to accept.

Luke reluctantly sat back against his chair. "Fine, just don't get used to babyin' me."

The entire table laughed, probably a bit too loudly for their neighbors looked at them.

Callie sucked her lips in her teeth to try and stop her laughter. "I'm sorry. But I don't think I'll ever be allowed to baby a cowboy. Especially one who got shot only to get right back up and get back into the fight." She gave him a pointed look.

The sheepish look on his face told Callie he still didn't think he had done enough. "I never should have got shot to begin with."

Elizabeth looked at her little brother. "I'm just glad you both walked away from that night." She took Logan's hand in hers and squeezed a bit too tightly. "We were very blessed with the outcome. I give God thanks each and every day that no one died or was seriously injured."

"Same here." Callie took Luke's knife and fork in her hands and finished cutting up his steak.

That was the last they said of the incident the rest of the night. When dinner and dessert were done, each of them took a small doggie bag with their leftovers. One of the best things about that steakhouse was the portion sizes. Even cowboys who worked hard would sometimes have leftovers, especially if they wanted to leave room for dessert.

Logan and Elizabeth lead the way out of the restaurant. Luke put his only good hand on the small of Callie's back and she went out the door before Luke. He used his broad shoulders to hold the door open for them.

A woman who looked as though she hadn't eaten in days sat to the side of the entrance looking at something in her purse. When Callie moved toward her, Luke followed.

"Hi, my name is Callie. Would you like my left-overs?" She put her doggie bag in front of her and smiled at the dirty woman sitting on the ground. She wasn't sure, but she thought she might have recognized her from the other day when they had handed out lunches to the homeless.

The woman smiled up at Callie and Luke. "Thank you. That's mighty kind of you."

Luke added his bag to the offering. When he turned at the sound of boots behind him, he noticed his sister and Logan also offering their leftovers to the woman.

"Hi, Grace. I haven't seen you around for a while. How ya been?" Elizabeth walked closer to the woman and kneeled.

"Oh, you know how it goes." She shrugged and took all four little bags. "Thank you." She looked inside Elizabeth's bag and smiled. "I haven't had steak in ages."

"If you came home with us, you could have it almost every day." Elizabeth had wanted to get Grace off the streets for some time now, but the woman always said no.

Grace snorted. "Right, and have Big Bart come after me? No thanks."

Elizabeth stood up. "Well, if you change your mind, you know how to reach me. We would be happy to come and get you." She looked to Logan and back at the woman. "And we can protect you from Bart. There's no need to worry about him."

With a mouth full of steak, Grace replied, "Yeah, okay."

Everyone said goodnight and went to their truck.

The group was quiet until Elizabeth spoke up. "I would like to get another group together to visit our friends on the street. I think some of the ladies might be getting ready to leave." She turned to Logan who was driving. "What do you think?"

It was Luke who spoke up first. "Just give me another week and then I'll be happy to join you all."

"I'd like to go, too." Callie wasn't about to let an opportunity to help those women get past her.

"Alright. I'll see when we can get another group together. Probably the weekend after we get you moved in will work." Elizabeth turned in her seat to look at the couple in the back. "Do you think you'll both be up to it?"

Luke and Callie both nodded and smiled. She knew she was right where God wanted her. With a little time, she was going to heal, as was Luke. They were now officially dating, and she couldn't be happier, even if they had to have chaperones.

It was probably a good thing they couldn't be alone anyways. With another couple around, they wouldn't have to worry about letting anything get too far, or out of control. Everything was going to work out, she just knew it.

When they got home that night, Luke walked Callie to the side of the house. "I hope you don't mind, but I wanted a few minutes alone without anyone watching us."

"I know what you mean. Sometimes it feels like we're in a cage and everyone is looking at us like were cute little hamsters running on a wheel, or something." Callie laughed, not really knowing how to act. She hoped he was going to kiss her, but at the same time, she was nervous.

Luke interlaced his good hand with hers. "Yeah, I know exactly whatcha mean." He cleared his throat. "Don't be mad, but I'm kinda glad your dad left earlier today."

She furrowed her brow. "Why?"

"He asked me for my credit report the other day and said he was gonna run a background check on me. If he was here after our first official date, I've no doubt he'd be sittin' inside at the kitchen table cleanin' his guns while he waited to grill me when we got back." He shook his head and chortled.

Laughter shone in her eyes as well.

Callie's laugh sent a thrill through Luke. The soft sound she made would never get old for him. He knew that her laugh would always put a smile on his face, no matter the situation.

"Yeah, he's got the act perfected. But don't worry. I think he approves of you. And I know he's not going to run a background check on you." She had spoken to her dad about this very thing before he left.

His brows raised and he waited for her to continue.

"I told him that no matter what, you were the man I wanted to be with. I knew you better than any background check could. Plus, you got back into the gunfight after you were shot. That says more about your character than anything a piece of paper could offer." The moment she saw him get back into the fight, she knew he was the man for her. It took more than physical strength to get back up from his injury and come help her. That was only something someone with a strong moral compass would do.

Luke stopped when they were on the side of the house and he was sure no one was watching them.

Callie leaned against the side of the house and Luke stood directly in front of her. He was staring into her eyes and she noticed how black his were. Her mind was clouding up and she tried not to look at his lips, but that was all she wanted to do.

A quick glance at his lips had her licking her own. When he smiled, she knew he could read every emotion flowing through her. Callie's heartbeat was going so fast, she feared she might drop dead if he didn't kiss her soon.

No words were being exchanged, only stares of desire and heat. Even though it was a cool evening, she felt as though a fire was licking along her skin.

Luke's only good hand slowly raised up, and she felt a tingling sensation over every part of her arm that he touched. When his hand cupped her jaw she leaned in to his touch and closed her eyes. His rough, calloused hands were soft against her skin and her toes tingled with anticipation.

With her eyes closed, she didn't see him lean in, but she felt his breath mingling with hers. When his lips lightly touched hers, her body exploded, and her toes curled. In her mind she saw fireworks light the sky around them. She returned his light kisses until he deepened the kiss. Then her toes curled as she knew they would and she accepted his offering of himself. Her arms wrapped around his neck and she pulled him closer, not wanting to let go of him.

After what felt like a lifetime of love, but was probably only a few minutes, he pulled back and stared deeply into her eyes of molten lava. "Wow." Luke couldn't think at all. He could only feel the connection between them both.

Words couldn't form on her tongue. All she could do was take deep breaths and get much needed oxygen into her brain. With her arms still around him, she leaned up and gave his lips another small kiss before letting her hands fall to her sides.

"I think it's a very good thing we won't have much alone time together for a while." Luke chuckled and took two steps back. He pulled his cowboy hat off with his good hand moved it to his right hand still in the sling. When he ran a shaky hand through his hair, he looked into Callie's eyes. He wanted to pull her to him again and kiss her forever. But he knew that wouldn't be a good idea.

With her body still zinging from the adrenaline and pheromones coursing through her system, Callie stayed right where she was, leaning against the wall. She didn't think she could stand on her own two feet yet. She had kissed a few men in her time, but nothing felt as wonderful and right as that kiss had. "I agree."

At first, when she agreed to move in with Elizabeth, she wasn't sure if she would like to live away from the ranch. But after that kiss, she knew moving into town would be the best thing for them both. All she wanted to do was kiss him again...and again...and again. His lips were like chocolate, so smooth, and delicious. Her body wanted more, but her head told her more wasn't good for her.

"Come on. I think we should head inside." He put his hat back on his head and then reached for her hand.

Callie held his hand tight and walked as close to his side as she could get.

When they stepped across the threshold, she felt her cheeks warm and she let his hand go. "Thank you for a wonderful evening."

He leaned in and kissed her cheek. "Thank you for agreein' to the double date. I'm glad we did this, and I hope we can do it again, very soon."

"Me, too. Goodnight, Luke." Her voice cracked and she cleared her throat.

Neither moved to head to their rooms on opposite sides of the house. They stood there staring at each other.

Someone cleared their voice and Callie jumped.

"I take it you two had a nice night?" It was Mrs. Manning who stood just inside the hallway to the boys' wing.

They had been caught standing there staring into each other's eyes. Callie knew her cheeks were turning red so she looked down at her feet.

"Hi, Ma. We did." Luke kissed his mother's cheek and winked at Callie before turning down the hallway to his room.

Feeling as though she had been caught with her hand in the cookie jar, Callie walked toward her room.

No one said anything the next day about Luke and Callie, but everyone smiled knowingly at them. Her move into town couldn't come fast enough. Now that she and Luke were officially dating, she was ready to move out of the ranch. Although, she'd miss her daily rides with her cowboy, but she knew that what was on their horizon was much better than horse rides through the ranch.

When the day came to move Callie into town, Luke was sad but also hopeful. He too, was going to miss their daily rides. However, since the shooting they hadn't been able to ride, and it would still be a few more weeks before she could get back on a horse.

Instead, he looked forward to going into town as much as possible and meeting up with Callie for lunch or coffee while they both recovered. Luke knew it would all work out for the best for them both. His future with Callie was looking very bright, and they were both healing up quite nicely from their ordeal.

<h1 style="text-align:center">Epilogue</h1>

Four months later

Everything did turn out, just like Luke had believed. While Callie couldn't do much physically, he could once he got his stitches out. Luke, two of his brothers, Harper, Elizabeth, Logan, and a small U-Haul truck later, they had Callie all moved out of her St. Paul apartment and back in Beacon Creek only two weeks after Luke's stitches came out.

While Callie did have to wait three months before she could apply to be a sheriff's deputy, the crooks they caught had a reward out for their arrest. Logan, Matthew, Luke, and Callie all split fifteen thousand dollars.

Callie's portion didn't last long, since she had to pay for moving expenses, but it got her through until her first paycheck as a deputy came in.

Luke and Callie were having a picnic dinner on the side of Beacon Creek while the sun was setting. The sky was full of oranges, reds, and streaks of fluffy white clouds.

"I still can't believe I live here. This is the most beautiful place I've ever been." She leaned her head against Luke's shoulder.

"And I can't believe you're my girlfriend. I think I should send a thank-you note to the cattle rustlers."

She sat up straight. "What? Are you crazy?"

He kissed her temple. "Think about it. If they hadn't targeted our little town, you and I wouldn't be here right now on the side of the creek enjoyin' dinner. And you certainly wouldn't be my girlfriend."

"Oh, I don't know. I think if God wanted us together, He would have found a way for us to get together. I just wish it didn't involve us getting shot." She cringed thinking about the pain she'd had to deal with for weeks while her ribs healed.

"Agreed. However, it would have happened, I'm just glad you're in my life."

"And I'm glad I'm in your life as well." Callie smiled up into his shining hazel eyes.

Luke leaned down and feathered a kiss across Callie's lips. A tingle began in her bottom lip and made its way down her entire body until her toes curled.

The End

What's Next?

Keep reading for my author's notes and some exciting news!

But first, are you interested in knowing what the next book in this series is? Then check out Runaway Cowgirl Bride!

A woman unsure why she's in white. A man who offers the comfort she needs.

Will a traumatic beginning bless them with a happily-ever-after?

The only thing Claire Brown feels is confusion. After waking up on the side of the road with no memory, she's stunned that she's wearing a wedding dress. Praying for deliverance, she's overjoyed when a handsome cowboy pulls over and offers his assistance.

Matthew Manning is a perfect gentleman. So when he stumbles upon a bride suffering from amnesia, he doesn't hesitate to offer shelter at his family's ranch until she can recall her identity. But with no ring on her finger and no one searching for her, he can't help but want to be the man she deserves.

As an undeniable attraction forms between Claire and the rugged rancher, she begins to believe God placed this kind soul in her life for a reason. And the more Matthew's interest in her grows, the more he fears a groom suddenly arriving to claim the woman he's come to cherish.

Will a forgotten marriage stop true hearts from beating together?

Newsletter Sign-up

Did you enjoy Second Chance Ranch? Want to know more about Mimi and Hank? Then check out Finding Love in Montana today!

By signing up for my newsletter, you will get a free copy of the prequel to the Triple J Ranch series, Finding Love in Montana. As well as another free book from J.L. Hendricks.

If you want to make sure you hear about the latest and greatest, sign up for my newsletter at: -https://jennahendricks.com/newsletter/. I will only send out a few e-mails a month. I'll do cover reveals, snippets of new books, and giveaways or promos in the newsletter, some of which will only be available to newsletter subscribers.

Author's Notes

I hope you've enjoyed reading about the brothers of the Triple J Ranch! The rest of the series will focus on them. We will see Elizabeth and Logan again, as they are an integral part of the Triple J Ranch, as well as Luke and Callie. But each book will be about a different Manning brother.

But, up next will be Christmas books! I've heard a lot of questions about Chloe, Elizabeth's twin sister. She left at the end of book 1, Second Chance Ranch, and went a few hours away to Frenchtown. She's going to start out the brand new, exciting Christmas Series, Big Sky Christmas!

This new series is really making me take a look at myself, and my belief in God. It's helping me to grow closer to Him, and I hope it's helping you as well. I started this series for several reasons. One of which was that I wanted to help provide more options for those who want a clean romance with Christian values. If this is you, then I hope you'll keep an eye out for the next book in this series. But the most important reason was that I felt God leading me down this path.

Thank you to all of those who have left reviews of my books! I read them all and I can't tell you how much I've loved what everyone has said! If you enjoyed this book, or even if you didn't, I hope you'll take the time to leave a review so others will know what you thought of my story, in addition to me. Again, thank you so much for your thoughts and words of encouragement!

May God Bless you all in everything you do!

Jenna Hendricks

Her Montana Christmas Cowboy

Chloe Manning's first Christmas in Frenchtown was heartbreaking. Will Santa give her her heart's desire during her second?

Brandon Beck left behind a woman for the benefit of his family ranch last Christmas. Now that he's back after a year, why can't he get her out of his heart and mind?

When Santa plays matchmaker, will Chloe and Brandon fall under his Christmas Magic? Or will past hurts keep them apart?

Don't miss out on the first Christmas story of the heart-warming Christmas Cowboy romance series, Big Sky Christmas. Where the romance is clean, and Christmas takes center stage!

Her Montana Christmas Cowboy https://books2read.com/u/m2Zx0r

Contact Me

For those of you who love social media, here are the various ways to follow or contact me:

BookBub: https://www.bookbub.com/authors/jenna-hendricks
TikTok: https://www.tiktok.com/@jennacleanauthor
Instagram: https://www.instagram.com/j.l.hendricks/
Twitter: https://twitter.com/TinkFan25
Facebook: https://www.facebook.com/JLHendricksAuthor
Website: https://jennahendricks.com

9 781952 634321